PRAISE FOR FOUR FANTASTIC "LADIES OF THE NIGHT"

New York Times and *USA Today* bestselling author
SUSAN SIZEMORE

". . . enraptures readers."
—*Romantic Times*

". . . passion, betrayal, and fast-paced action."
—*Library Journal*

New York Times and *USA Today* bestselling author
MAGGIE SHAYNE

". . . [is] rich, sensual, and bewitching."
—*Publishers Weekly*

". . . is better than chocolate.
She satisfies every wicked craving."
—Suzanne Forster

USA Today bestselling author
LORI HANDELAND

". . . is an exciting voice in paranormal suspense."
—Sherrilyn Kenyon

CARIDAD PIÑEIRO

". . . provides an enthralling supernatural romance."
—*Affaire de Coeur*

". . . unique paranormal elements . . .
[and] intense in-depth characters."
—*Romantic Times*

MOON FEVER

SUSAN SIZEMORE

MAGGIE SHAYNE

LORI HANDELAND

CARIDAD PIÑEIRO

Pocket Books
New York   London   Toronto   Sydney

Pocket Books
A Division of Simon & Schuster, Inc.
1230 Avenue of the Americas
New York, NY 10020

Tempting Fate copyright © 2007 by Susan Sizemore
The Darkness Within copyright © 2007 by Margaret Benson
Cobwebs Over the Moon copyright © 2007 by Lori Handeland
Crazy for the Cat copyright © 2007 by Caridad Piñeiro Scordato

First Pocket Books paperback edition October 2007

POCKET and colophon are registered trademarks of Simon & Schuster, Inc.

For information about special discounts for bulk purchases, please contact Simon & Schuster Special Sales at 1-800-456-6798 or business@simonandschuster.com

Cover art by Omar Davis; cover design by Min Choi

Manufactured in the United States of America

10 9 8 7 6 5 4 3 2 1

ISBN-13: 978-1-4165-1490-9
ISBN-10:   1-4165-1490-2

TEMPTING FATE

Susan Sizemore

CHAPTER 1

September, ten years from now

*D*esiree Gill didn't recall how she'd gotten there, seated in a dark corner, across a small round table from one of the most famous men in the world. She had vague memories of sitting in the back of a limo and talking for hours and hours. Of lips brushing sensually across her wrist, sending an arc of desire through her. A moment later, the slightest pinprick of pain sent her soaring with fiery pleasure. Her responses had been so intense she'd finally blacked out from sheer bliss.

She knew exactly where they were now: under the green-and-white–striped outdoor awning of her favorite café on the edge of the French Quarter. A sign on the shop proclaimed that it closed only for Christmas and some hurricanes. It had closed briefly for one a few years back but had quickly reopened. The Quarter had refused to bend to the will of Katrina, even if the rest of the city was still a little ragged around the edges a full decade later.

"*You were here then,*" he said.

It was not a question. And something in his voice took her back to struggling through waist-high water on a street full of the stench of harsh chemicals and garbage, where an abandoned dog barked inside a ruined building and something darker than the night followed close behind her. But she didn't want those memories right now. All she wanted was to be in this moment forever.

"All right," he said. "We'll let it go."

The aromas of warm grease and sugar filled the air; powdered sugar dusted the tabletop, spilled off a tall pile of beignets on the paper plates between them. A few fat, sleepy pigeons wandered across the floor, trolling for crumbs. Rain poured down in an almost solid curtain beyond the shelter of the canopy. Despite the late hour, there was still plenty of traffic moving slowly, almost swimming through the water in the street. It was a September night in New Orleans, and she had no idea how she'd ended up there after the concert, seated across from the singer she'd had a crush on since she was fourteen. A big fan of the dinosaur stadium rock band Coyote, she cherished the CDs her mom had collected as a teenager as much as she did her downloads of the band's recent work. One of the things she liked best about Coyote was that they were always relevant. They were survivors.

Also, Jon Coyote was the most gorgeous man she'd ever seen, and the most confident. She loved the way he could walk out onto a stage in a sold-out stadium, announce to the screaming audience, "For the next two hours, you belong to me," and completely make good on that boast. In another age, he would have given Alexander the Great a run for his money as a charismatic world conqueror. In this day and age, he took all that god-king charisma on the road. There was something heroic about him.

Jon Coyote looked into her eyes and said, "Welcome to my world."

"This isn't your world," she said. "You're from New Jersey."

"I've got family here." He gestured toward a shadowed far corner. "There's a bunch of my cousins sitting right over there."

She looked and saw several pairs of eyes staring at her out of the darkness. Those eyes were glowing, red, gold, and green.

"Don't pay any attention," Coyote said. "They're just showing off."

Desi didn't know what to say. She didn't know what to do. All she could figure was that she was dreaming. Dreaming of being with Jonathan Coyote was the best fantasy she could imagine, so she relaxed and went along with the whole thing.

"What are they?" she asked. "Werewolves?"

"Nah." He took a sip of chicory-laced coffee. "We're vampires."

"Oh." She looked at the bite mark on her wrist. "That explains it."

So, she was dreaming that Jon Coyote was a vampire. Seeing that this was New Orleans, that almost made sense. Except that it seemed more like the sort of thing a tourist would dream about happening in her dark and mysterious city, rather than a native like her. She might be embarrassed about what her subconscious was pulling up if she was awake.

He took her hand and stroked a finger, slowly, suggestively, across her bruised wrist. The touch sent hot shivers through her. "I'll give you a diamond bracelet to cover this, if you'd like."

She had no use for diamonds, even in a dream. She shook her head.

"What would you like?" His voice was silken, with a dark edge that hinted at danger and ecstasy.

She held up her other hand, the wrist turned toward him. "More of the same, please."

He smiled his famous knowing grin; his sapphire eyes took on a blue-neon glow. "Oh, honey. I'm gonna give you better than that."

He carried her into a bedroom more luxurious than anyplace she'd ever dreamed of. The city glittered below the wide windows, brighter than the diamonds he'd promised her. He set her down on a deep carpet of indigo blue patterned with stars. A domed ceiling arched overhead, painted with the night sky. The huge bed was framed with twisting, gilded pillars and hung with blue velvet. She wondered if she could tone down all this lavishness but didn't have the faintest idea how to manipulate a dream.

"Just relax and enjoy the ride," Jon advised. His hands slipped under the hem of her shirt and pulled it over her head. "Actually, I have no intention of letting you relax."

"I'm happy to hear it," she said, and did the same with his shirt. His chest was sculpted and nicely fuzzy. She pressed her cheek against it and breathed in his scent, losing herself in the slow, slow, steady thrum of his heartbeat. It seemed too slow. She glanced up at him worriedly. "You don't have any condition I need to worry about, do you?"

He laughed and ran his fingers through her short, curly hair. "I may be older than I look, but I'm healthy enough for what we have in mind." He picked her up again and carried her to the bed. "As for my condition . . ." He sat down with her on his lap and nuzzled and licked her cleavage. "You'll find the symptoms very pleasurable."

Desi barely paid attention to his words. His touch burned her, and she liked it. She arched her back to offer easier access to her breast. "More, please."

"Gladly."

His mouth came down on her hot skin once again. This time, his lips covered an already hard nipple, and his tongue swirled wickedly around the peak while he gently suckled. She felt the nip of sharp teeth when he moved on to her other nipple. Pleasure burst through her.

Jon's sexy laugh sent deep shivers through her, but the sound also brought her back from the edge of pleasure. She grabbed his head and brought it up for a kiss. The feel and taste of him were incredibly, deliciously male, and he very much liked being in control. His tongue delved into her mouth. His hands slid over her skin. Each touch sent all her nerve endings into overload.

She very nearly melted into the bed from all the pleasure he was giving her. Then it occurred to her that she wasn't holding up her end of this mutual pleasure fest. This was her dream, and there was an unending number of things she wanted to do with Jon Coyote, so there was no time like this unreal present to check a few erotic things off her list.

It took her a while to get his attention. In fact, he seemed to like it when she resorted to burying her nails in his shoulders. She soon got the hang of scratching and biting, and for a while they engaged in the sort of rough play she had never imagined could be fun.

"Up for a bit of bondage?" he asked when he had her pinned beneath him, her hands held over her head. His bright eyes twinkled with mischief. "I could pull down the curtain cords and—"

"I don't think so," she blurted out. She giggled. "Maybe next time."

"I'll hold you to that."

"You're holding me right now."

"So I am."

He easily held her wrists immobile with one hand and caressed her with the other. His fingers traced and teased from the side of her throat all the way to the curve of her hip. Then they glided slowly across her thigh and moved to the damp heat between her legs.

She moaned when a fingertip pressed against her swollen clitoris. She grew feverish and frantic as he stroked and caressed her inside and out. The pleasure coiled and grew until a white-hot bolt of release shot through all her senses.

His mouth covered hers as she came, and their souls met in that moment. His kiss was a completion, yet it wasn't enough. She arched against the hard length of his body, needing more, needing all of him.

He came inside her in one swift thrust. He filled her; she surrounded him. For one long, perfect, silent moment, they were one. Their gazes met, sharing fire.

Then Jonathan Coyote laughed, threw back his head, and howled like a mad, happy version of his namesake, and his hips began to thrust while she rose to meet him. For the longest time after that, she belonged to him.

CHAPTER 2

Desi woke up to find her body sticky with sweat and the residue of sex. Great sex. Only she didn't remember whom she'd had sex with—and that was just wrong. She was in her own bed. That bed was in a tiny apartment in a rickety old courtyard building in the Quarter. The place had a squeaky, termite-eaten staircase that she remembered climbing alone. She'd come in late, and she remembered that there'd been rain.

And there'd been great sex. But she couldn't remember where or with whom.

Well, she thought it was with Jon Coyote, but that was just wishful thinking.

And music. Such beautiful, rousing, hot music. The night had been filled with music. And rain. Sweet, warm beignets with white sugar that melted on the tongue. And there'd been kisses, hot and strong as the black coffee that had gone down so smooth and rich. And hands on her, all over her, big, strong hands with a gentle, knowing touch. Hard thighs and wicked hips that had ground against her. And a wide, strong back she'd scratched and bit and held onto while each thrust took her higher and higher, over the edge and up again to yet another erotic peak.

Damn!

Desi sat up and looked at the alarm clock on the beat-up old table next to the narrow bed. She saw the time and blinked.

And remembered where she'd been last night. In the second row at the Coyote concert. She'd laughed and danced and sang along with all the songs—the old standards and the new ones—and Jon Coyote had smiled his dazzling smile at her and reached down and touched her hand for a brief, electric moment—

And the world had gone white-hot bright, and he'd called to her, and her soul had answered, and—

And he'd moved on to the next fan reaching up toward the stage, and the next song. It had been a wonderful show. The best Coyote concert she'd ever attended, and she'd been to every performance in New Orleans since she was fifteen.

And then she'd come home—and had a hell of a wet dream.

She blushed, a little embarrassed at her erotic fantasies. Then she smiled and laughed, because if she was going to have sex in a dream with anyone, Jonathan Coyote would always be her first choice.

Her body felt as if the lovemaking had been real, which meant it had been way too long since she'd had real sex. She shrugged off the stiff muscles as evidence that she'd stood for hours on a hard concrete floor holding her own to get a good view in the huge, shoving, pushing, happy crowd. Her ears still rang from the cranked-up amplifiers and the shouting audience. Her body quivered with reaction from the superhot dream.

"Sensory overload," she told herself.

She sang in the shower while she covered herself with thick jasmine-scented lather. She didn't notice what the song was until a cold shiver ran through her: "Tempting Fate." It was her favorite song in the whole world, but sometimes hearing it gave her the oddest feelings. Something niggled and nagged at the back of her mind like the echoing of a fist banging on a far-away door.

She closed her eyes and hummed "Tempting Fate" as the water poured down her body and she tried to capture something lost.

Her sense of smell had overloaded and shut down after the first couple of days, which was a good thing—with the humid heat and all the water in the streets, the stench wasn't likely to go away soon. When the wind shifted, it blew in ash and smoke from the houses still burning in the Garden District and other parts of the city. There were plenty of dead bodies of humans and animals in the houses, and even some floaters in the water. It was the stuff of nightmares. The Ninth Ward was not a safe place to be, but she had promises to keep. So she'd waded into the waist-deep rivers that used to be streets once a day since she'd gotten back from Houston to see what she could find.

The first day, she'd almost gotten caught by some patrolling National Guards. If they'd seen her, they'd have evacuated her for her own good, and she'd have ended up camping out with the rest of her family back at the Astrodome—a place she'd left with her family's permission after their first night there. Okay, not quite permission, but grudging agreement that Desi was the best person for the job during the meeting of friends and neighbors that managed to find each other. She'd left without anybody actually saying she should go. Getting back to and into the city hadn't been all that hard, except for carrying the heavy backpack of supplies. Staying in New Orleans was proving harder.

The Quarter was safe enough. The people who hadn't wanted to leave gathered there and took care of one another. The Quarter was home anyway, the base she came back to after each rescue foray. But outside the Quarter—well, it hadn't been all that safe even before the storm hit, and the cops completely stopped trying. Gangs still roamed, and the echoes of gunshots filled the air much more than usual. She'd never been afraid of the city's dangers, but then, she'd never been alone before. At least, she was always so tired after she made her way home that no distant noise could wake her.

She wished she'd brought one of her brother's Catahoula Leopard dogs with her, but those brutes weren't city dogs. They were safer surviving on their own in the swamps until her brother could get back to them. The animals she rescued were more than enough company, even if they didn't make her feel any safer.

She'd learned that it was best to go out at night, except for the dark and scary part. She had told herself that tonight would be the last night she'd go looking. After all, she had six cats and four dogs under protective custody in the back bedroom. The food she'd brought with her was being supplemented with scraps from the bars and restaurants, because everybody was sharing what they had, and without power everything was going to rot soon, anyway. She had enough rescued critters to look after. She kept to the shadows and tried not to splash as she moved along the walls. She envied the rats that swam easily past her; rats never had any trouble getting around. She promised herself that she'd find Mrs. Marceau's poodle tonight, and that would be that. Of course, that was what she'd told herself last night.

She jumped at every sound. She hadn't been this nervous before, but something about the night just felt wrong. She told herself she was imagining that shadows took on odd shapes, that she saw movement out of the corner of her eye. She was creeped out and ready to turn back.

I have promises to keep, *she thought, and kept going even as every step became harder. What was the use of having more than ordinary senses if she wasn't going to trust them? She sighed.* Promises to keep.

The only comfort she drew out of the night was something she didn't notice at first but which grew slowly inside her. It was a sound that wasn't a sound, a thought that was in her head but wasn't her own. Not a thought but music. It was lovely, and somebody was humming it inside her head.

Weird.

She grew so puzzled that she stood perfectly still for a long time and forgot everything else around her. The water and the stench and the whole world disappeared.

Until a hand landed on her shoulder, and behind her a man said, "What are you doing out here, tempting fate?"

CHAPTER 3

Desi came out of the daydream when the water heater ran out and a cold spray suddenly pummeled her. She quickly stepped out of the shower and wrapped a towel around herself.

As she rubbed the chill out of her skin, she glanced at the bathroom mirror. "Girl, what is the matter with you today?"

Despite what she did for a living, she was not prone to visions and fancies. She read cards and palms and scryed the future in a quartz crystal ball, and she was good at it. But she used her abilities strictly for paying customers. Whenever she tried to tell her own fortune, she was plagued with terrible headaches. She guessed this meant there were things she wasn't meant to know, and she'd left the personal psychic stuff alone when she wasn't on the clock since she was a teenager.

Desi dressed and took herself off to her job at the psychic tea room on Jackson Square. Before reaching it, an impulse made her walk to the edge of the Quarter and look across to where all the shiny, new high-rise luxury hotels loomed above the city. The buildings blocked the sight of the river and looked down over the French Quarter. The tourists got great views from both sides, but Desi resented the intrusiveness, even as she accepted that they needed tourism to survive. New Orleans wasn't the great port city it used to be, but it was still a great place to party. This morning, one of the high glass towers seemed more familiar than it used to. She could almost imagine the view of the river from the top of the hotel. Odd, since she'd never been inside the building. And odd was definitely the word for how she felt this morning. She shook it off and turned her back on the outside world. "Welcome to my world," she murmured as she walked deeper into the Quarter.

When she entered the tearoom Desi asked, "Guess where I was last night?"

"At the Coyote concert," her friend Eliza and her boss, Helene Dupre, answered.

"You've only been talking about it for weeks," Eliza added. She looked Desi over from head to toe. "Did you get laid after the show?"

Desi went hot all over. She gave a shaky laugh. "No," she answered, surprising herself at the lack of conviction in the word.

"I don't know," Eliza drawled. "You look like a cat that got all the cream she wanted. She's got that my-man-satisfied-me glow pouring off her aura, doesn't she, Helene?"

The shop owner glanced up from working on her laptop to give Desi a stern once-over. "That's what it looks like to me," she concurred. "Who was he, girl?"

Why were there no customers in the shop to take the women's attention off her? "That's a watching-Jonathan-Coyote-swivel-his-hips-would-make-any-woman-happy glow, Eliza," she answered.

Her friend laughed, and Desi went to pour herself a cup of tea.

Eliza beckoned her over when Desi came back around the counter, cradling the steaming cup. Eliza was shuffling tarot cards as Desi sat opposite her at one of the shop's three tables. Eliza put the deck down on the center of the shiny black tabletop. "Cut."

Desi shook her head. "I don't want a reading."

"I need the practice."

Eliza was better at dream interpretation than she was with the cards. As Desi sipped her tea, she looked at Eliza, who was still watching her expectantly. "All right, I'll give you some practice. I had this dream last night . . ."

Eliza leaned forward eagerly. "Talk to me, girl."

Desi stared at the shining surface of the table, as though she could conjure images in it. When she spoke, the memories that poured out hit her with all the sensory embellishments of sound and scent, texture and sexual excitement that made it seem like it actually happened. She could feel a hot kiss from sugar-coated lips on her mouth and skilled hands stroking . . .

Only having to answer Eliza's occasional question kept her from falling completely back into the odd reality of the dream. Which hadn't been real, she reminded herself.

She glanced up after she finished and found Helene looking at her strangely. "Maybe I better get to work." She glanced toward the shop door in the hope that a customer was going to wander in from Jackson Square.

"Our first appointments aren't until nine," Helene said. She continued her intense study of Desi.

Eliza fanned a hand in front of her face. "And I'm going to need that ten minutes to cool down from those descriptions of last night, Des."

"It was a dream," Desi reminded Eliza. "You're supposed to interpret it, not get excited about it. Not that I can't figure it out for myself. I haven't slept with anyone for a while, so all that pent-up sexual energy took itself out on a dream version of Jon Coyote. What's the matter, Helene?" she asked nervously as the woman continued to stare.

Helene sighed and finally said, "You watch out for that Coyote boy, *cher*. I know his family, and they're trouble for pretty little girls like you."

A chill went up Desi's spine at the warning. "But it was only a dream,"

"Let's hope so," Helene said.

Before Desi could ask one of the strongest psychics in New Orleans what she meant, a first group of tourists came in. Desi took her customer to one of the rooms to read cards for the woman. Then the day turned very busy, and she put the concert and the dream out of her mind.

Mostly.

She had the feeling she was going to be haunted by Jon Coyote for a long time to come. She also had the feeling that this was nothing new, just more intense.

Weird.

CHAPTER 4

"**D**amn, but last night was fun!"

Jon's vision went red, and he whirled furiously around in his seat to snarl at the other Prime. "What the hell do you mean?"

Since Primes didn't back down, Rico sat forward in his seat, his hands held up to show claws as he snarled back. "What the hell's the matter with you?"

Jon noticed the glint of the thick gold wedding band on Rico's left hand, and it reminded him that the other Prime was a bonded male. There was no threat there. He took a deep, calming breath. Why was he feeling threatened ~~a~~ ~~t~~ possession of a female, anyway? He shook ~~~~ ~~~~t none of the confusion cleared out.

~~~~ ~~~~nean about last night?" he asked.

~~~~ ~~~~m as if he was crazy, but he was

"I was talking about the fight at

~~~~t you off?" Then he threw back

~~~~Oh, you thought I was talking

~~~~ou brought with you."

"I didn't exactly bring her with me."

"You left with her." Rico sat back in his seat, and the private jet began to taxi down the runway.

Jon closed his eyes as an unfamiliar sensation as sharp as physical pain rushed through him. Yeah, he'd left with her, and he'd left her. Not for the first time. It had been a stupid impulse to renew the acquaintance in the first place. But the moment he'd touched her hand, he'd known it was her, and . . .

"I was just going to catch up," he muttered. "See how she was doing."

He'd found out far more than he needed or wanted. She'd certainly grown up into a lush and lovely armful, though there'd already been the promise of beauty around her a decade ago, despite the dirt and the sweat and the heat. "My dung-hill flower," he'd called her back then, and she'd made a horrible face. He didn't blame her. He could write great hooks, but he was no poet. And she was still too young, even if a decade had passed. The differences in their ages hadn't meant a thing to him last night, though.

"You're staring into the distance with a glazed look in your eyes." Rico interrupted his reverie. He glanced at his watch. "You've been somewhere besides here for the last five minutes."

Jon didn't remember the plane leaving the ground, but he saw that they were rushing away from New Orleans when he looked out the window. An ache grew in him with every swift mile. They were heading toward Memphis, where there was a show to do, and another job afterward. Once he was busy, this melancholy would pass. The energy from the audience and a little bloodshed should cheer him right up.

Bloodshed. Damn. She shouldn't have seen what he'd done last night. She was young and sensitive and mort—

"Earth to Coyote," Rico said.

Jon glanced at the watching guitarist. "I was remembering last night."

Rico gave a toothy grin. "The raid on the warehouse? Or the girl you left behind?"

"Will you stop bringing up Desiree Gill? I don't want to talk about her."

Rico arched an eyebrow. "You remember her name the next day? That alone says a lot about last night."

"We met before," Jon said. "You remember when we were down for Katrina?"

Rico scratched his arms. "I'm not likely to forget. If you hadn't come up with the cornstarch solution—"

"It wasn't me," Jon said. "It was—"

The last thing he had expected was the skin rash from the mixture of chemicals in the flood water. How ironic that it wasn't the sunlight that made him want to run for cover. He scratched irritably at his left wrist as he set out on evening patrol.

The people left in this city needed looking after, and he and the rest of Coyote were among the unofficial volunteers giving the place a hand. New Orleans was a dangerous place under the best of circumstances, and these were the worst. The predators were out, which gave people like him a chance to prey on the predators. He smiled as he moved through the sludgy water and wondered if the moonlight caught the gleam of his extended fangs.

Amusement at his own vanity disappeared as he detected not only movement but also a ripple of evil energy from the shadows up ahead. He soon focused on a mortal male who followed a young woman farther up the flooded street. The mortal's intentions were ugly; his body burned with deviant anticipation. The girl was unaware of being stalked, and Jon intended to keep it that way. He moved up silently behind the stalker.

He didn't make a habit of killing. He believed in the rule of law. Besides, the pleasure of bloodhunting could be addictive. There was no reason for a vampire to risk his soul in an age when other sources of nourishment were so plentiful. Tonight, however, Jon had no qualms about what he did. There was no mortal law in this broken city, and he was sworn to protect the helpless. He looked into the man's mind, found the crimes the mortal held as precious memories, and killed the bastard before the man even knew he was there. He left the corpse—one more storm victim—floating in the street. Then he moved on to catch up with the girl.

A song was taking shape in his head, and he concentrated on the music as the girl came to a halt in the shadows in front of him. She tilted her head as if carefully listening, though he knew he'd made no sound. Finally, she began to move again. When she was sufficiently far away from the body that she wouldn't see it if she turned around, he caught up with her.

Jon put a hand on the girl's shoulder. "What are you doing out here, tempting fate?"

She gasped and whirled around to face him. She was a little thing, a teenager. She felt not an instant of fear. She squinted at him in the darkness, studying his face. "Do I know you?" She had a dark, rich voice for someone so young. She made him think of coffee laced with cream.

He had a momentary sensation that they'd known each

other all their lives, followed by wondering if she was about to ask for an autograph. "No," *he said.* "Don't you know it isn't safe out here?"

"Of course, I know that." *She laughed.*

The rich sound sent a shiver through him. Young as she was, he was very aware that she was a woman.

"But there's a poodle that needs rescuing," *she went on.* "And nobody else to do it since FEMA wouldn't let us take pets with us when we left."

"You're risking your life for a poodle?"

"Someone has to," *she said over her shoulder, as she turned around and started on her way once more.*

This girl was as much a protector of the innocent as he was, and he was instantly drawn to her bravery and determination. He decided to take care of her while she took care of her chosen innocents.

"Hey, wait for me!" *he called after her.*

Which was how he had met Desiree Gill. They'd found the stupid dog, which had bitten him when he picked it up. He'd still carried the animal all the way back to the French Quarter for her, since Desi already carried a cat they'd rescued along the way. Jon shook his head and smiled fondly. That little girl had him wrapped around her finger from the first moment.

"You know, I could be a serial killer or worse," *he warned her when she invited him up to her apartment at dawn.*

"You still need a place to sleep." *She went up the courtyard stairs, and he followed. When they reached the top, she said,* "I know you're safe to be with. I'm psychic." *She gave him a look that told him she didn't expect any argument or sarcasm.*

He grinned. "Thanks for letting me crash."

Inside, they were greeted by a herd of cats and dogs. They put the recently rescued animals down among the others. A small fight broke out between the newcomers and the current residents, some fur flew, but everything settled down before human or vampire intervention was necessary.

Once Desi saw that all was well with the critters, she looked him over critically, then pointed toward a doorway. "There's a pile of towels on the kitchen table. Get yourself stripped off and rubbed down. You can't afford to stay wet in this kind of situation."

He went into the kitchen, and she disappeared into another room. She joined him in a few minutes, wearing dry shorts and a T-shirt. He'd stripped down to his underwear, but she didn't take any notice of his seminakedness. When she looked him over carefully, it was the patches of rash covering his skin that she concentrated on.

She went to a cabinet and brought out a yellow box of cornstarch. "This'll help," she said, handing it to him. He took the box while he looked at her curiously. "Last year at camp, I took a course in urban disaster survival." She gave that wonderful laugh of hers. "It sounded interesting in the brochure—who knew it would come in handy?"

"Hey, Jon, quit daydreaming." Rico got out of his seat and waved for Jon to join him in the lounge at the back of the plane. "We've got a group meeting."

"Right," Jon agreed. Besides the show in Memphis, they had a rescue op to plan. He had no time to think about Desiree Gill right now, not for a long time to come.

CHAPTER 5

December, ten years from now

"You okay?" Eliza asked.

Desi sank to her knees on the cool tile floor of the bathroom in the back of the shop. She rested her forehead against the white porcelain sink basin and groaned. She'd just thrown up. Again. She was definitely not okay. She barely managed to shake her head, then threw up again.

"Oh, God," she groaned. "Maybe I ought to go to a doctor."

"So I've said for the last two weeks," Eliza asked.

This awful nausea had been going on for nearly a month now. She was beginning to think it wasn't a nasty flu bug, and suddenly the idea of going to a doctor sounded very smart. Maybe because she was scared it was something other than the flu—

"Here, take this."

Desi turned her head just enough to see that Eliza was holding out a box toward her.

"Wha'sat?" she managed to mumble.

"Madame Helene brought it in this morning. She wants you to take it."

Desi managed to turn around. After a few moments, the dizziness that came with the daily nausea cleared up enough for her to read the label.

"Oh!" She looked up at Eliza with horror. Her friend looked both concerned and embarrassed. "I'm not—"

"I'll wait out here." Eliza stepped back and closed the bathroom door.

Desi was vaguely outraged at Helene interfering in her life like this. The suggestion was appalling, ridiculous. She didn't want to think about it. But her boss had been patient and very kind about her frequently being too sick to work recently, so Desi supposed she at least owed Helene this much. She opened the box, unwrapped the packaging, and followed the instructions.

A few minutes later, Desi opened the bathroom door to find Eliza and Helene waiting in the narrow hallway outside for her. Eliza looked worried. Madame Helene had her arms crossed and a stern look on her face. Desi took a big gulp of air and silently passed the plastic stick to Helene.

"It's pink," Helene said, barely looking at the test results. She didn't sound a bit surprised.

Eliza looked at the pink indicator line, then at Desi. "You're pregnant?"

"No," Desi answered. "It's a mistake. It's not possible." Another wave of nausea hit her, cutting off further protest. After she heaved into the toilet bowl again, Eliza helped her to one of the tables in the tea room, and Helene thrust a steaming cup of herbal tea into her hands. The warmth of the cup felt wonderful, since Desi was cold with dread.

"It's chamomile," Helene said. "Good for what ails *you*."

Desi looked up wretchedly. "I can't be pregnant," she told the grim woman before her. The last thing she wanted for Christmas was to find out she was pregnant—which she *couldn't* be. Immaculate conceptions didn't happen in New Orleans, of all places! "Really, I haven't had sex with anyone for—a long time."

"When was your last period?"

Desi had to think about that, as she'd never been regular. "Four months, maybe three."

"Well, then. That explains why you're having morning sickness."

"I'm not! The closest thing I've had to sex in ages was that erotic dream after the Coyote concert." It was funny how she couldn't get that dream out of her mind. Her skin and blood and bones couldn't seem to forget the dream, either. "I have *not* had sex with a man," she insisted.

Helene stepped back, still looking stern, but Desi knew the anger was *for* her, not *at* her. "No, you haven't had sex with a man. You've had sex with—" Helene thought better of what she'd been going to say and said instead, "A coyote."

"That was a dream!"

"That's what he wanted you to think." Helene shook her head. "There's some folk it's better our kind stayed away from, but there's also some things *their* kind have to take responsibility for. There's no way his aunt's going to let him get away with knocking up a mortal girl in her territory."

Our kind? Mortal girl? Dread ran like ice through Desi's blood. She put down the tea and stood, which made her dizzy again. "What are you talking about?" she demanded.

"You'll find out, girl," Helene answered. "Now, sit down and drink that tea. I have to make a phone call."

CHAPTER 6

"What's the matter with you?" Rico asked Jon, who was slumped in a chair across the dressing room.

The other three members of the band hadn't arrived yet. Rico and Jon had showed up at the club they owned early to work on some songs. They used the club as a rehearsal space, for charity shows, and for trying out new material on live audiences.

So far, Rico had played a bit, but Jon hadn't even taken his acoustic guitar out of its case. He'd been staring at the floor while Rico became increasingly concerned.

Jon Coyote was usually the happiest man in the world. He was at his most up at times like this, just before the annual holiday show for BBD, the charity the band had founded to help get runaways off the streets. Or, like the night before, when they'd pulled a successful raid on a sweatshop that was using kids as slave labor. Those kids were safe now, with their memories psychically altered to minimize the trauma. And the ones who'd kept the children in such horrific circumstances had made excellent snack food for a few hours, before being turned over to some helpful authorities hypnotized into not remembering Coyote's involvement.

Jon loved the chase, the rescue, the capture, the helping the needy. He loved being a rock star as much as he loved being a vampire Prime. He was always confident, always cheerful. He didn't mope. He didn't sulk. He exuded charm and superstar charisma.

But right now, he looked as lively as an overcooked noodle.

"So, what's up?" Rico asked.

Jon finally looked at him. "Holiday blues," he answered. "Christmas sucks."

"Oh, yeah?"

"Being alone on Christmas sucks," Jon added.

Ricardo Shagal considered this the Victorians' fault. Christmas was some sort of mass hallucination, caused by mortal and supernatural folk alike ingesting the words of Charles Dickens in huge gulps back in the day. Dickens had done for Christmas what J. K. Rowling had done for Quidditch: invented it. Well, Rowling had made up the sport out of whole cloth, while Dickens had an existing traditional holiday to work with. But the result was a similar shift in the cultural zeitgeist, and even vampires weren't immune to it. Christmas cards and mistletoe, trees and presents, family and loved ones, and lots of partying. Vampires always liked to party.

"You haven't been partying enough lately," Rico told his friend. "That's your problem. 'Tis is the season to party." And since when was Jon Coyote ever alone?

"I've been playing superhero a lot. Too much."

"That's fun, too."

"Normally, yeah." Jon Coyote sighed.

He sounded so pitiful Rico half expected him to go howl at the moon. Except it was the middle of an overcast December day, and they were vampires, not werewolves. They had were-jackals among their crew; maybe he should send Jon out partying with that bunch of wild men.

Rico finally registered his kinsman's remark about having played hero too much. This was not the way a Clan Prime normally felt. The whole point of a Prime's existence was to protect mortals—and get laid a lot. Come to think of it, he couldn't recall Jon hanging with many women lately. Any, actually.

"When's the last time you had sex?" he asked.

This was normally the sort of question more likely to start a Prime fight than to get an answer. It was a measure of how down Jon was that he said, "There was a girl when we were in New Orleans." Then he sighed.

Rico said incredulously, "That was three months ago!"

"Ninety-two days, to be precise."

Rico put down his guitar in shock. "Ninety-two days without sex? Are you crazy?"

"I'm in love."

"Damn. That's worse."

"I know."

"Love love, or bond love?"

It was perfectly possible for a Prime to fall in love many times in his long life. Having richly satisfying affairs with both vampire and mortal women was one of the perks of being a vampire. But bonding—bonding was serious business. It could happen with a vampire female or with a human woman, and it meant the end of casual sex with multiple partners forever. While this was the ideal relationship all Primes were supposed to hope for, an actual bond played hell with the rock 'n' roll lifestyle. Rico knew: he'd met his bondmate, the lovely Gemma Corax of Clan Corvus, ten years before. Of course, this made him the happiest vampire in the world and all, but . . .

Jon ran his hands through his heavy blond hair and gave a sad shake of his head. "Bond," he said softly as the door opened and their bandmates walked in.

"*James* Bond," Bartholomew Corbett said.

"I should have kept my mouth shut," Jon muttered.

Joffrey Reynard jerked a thumb at Jon and asked Rico, "Has he been telling you about his little Desilu?"

"Desiree," Jon corrected, and gave Jof an angry look. "How do you know about her?"

"She's all you talked about on the plane when we left New Orleans."

"Yeah," Rico recalled. "We could barely get through planning an op, with you going on about the girl from the night before."

"I don't remember discussing her."

Jof shook his head. "You're pitiful. Did you buy her the diamond bracelet?"

"No."

Rico asked, "If she's your bondmate, why haven't you claimed her?"

"When we first met after Katrina, she was just this kid I looked after. She was way too young, and I never laid a fang on her."

"But you wanted to," Jof said.

"In the worst way," Jon conceded. "But that would have made me as bad as the mortals we hunt. When I found her again the last time we were in New Orleans, I discovered that she's a fan. She's not in love with me—she's got it bad for the Jon Coyote rock star image. It wouldn't be fair to her—"

"Oh, please!" Corky Cage broke in with his usual sneer. "You're just using that as an excuse not to settle down. Suck it up, and be a Prime."

Corky's real name was Cordwainer, which Rico figured was reason enough to make anybody bad-tempered. He took out a lot of aggression by playing drums, and kicking bad-guy ass with righteous enthusiasm.

While the rest of the band were all Primes of the vampire Clans, Corky was Prime of one of the vampire Families. The Families were more pragmatic in their attitudes toward mortals than the idealistic Clans, but Corky was a convert to the Clan Code, with all the zealotry of a convert. Sir Galahad had nothing on this guy.

"You don't abandon a bondmate," Corky reminded Jon.

"She's not a bondmate," Jon answered. "Besides, she's still too young."

"She's always going to be younger than you," Rico pointed out. "Get her teenage image out of your head, and remember the woman you bedded."

Jon rose angrily to his feet, reacting with typical Prime jealousy. "She's—" Jon's cell phone rang before he could finish. He fished it out of a tight jeans pocket. "Hello?" After a few moments of shouting issued from the phone, he asked, "Aunt Martine?"

The other Primes strained to listen, and Jon winced as the shouting continued.

"Desi?" he asked when he could get a word in. "Why? *What?*" he shouted, and sat down heavily, his eyes wide with shock. At jagged intervals, he managed to shout back, "That's not possible! Me? Mine? No, you can't do that! I can't. You wouldn't? All right, all right. I'll be there."

When he got off the phone and looked at his staring comrades, the terminally insouciant Jonathan Coyote appeared as if he'd been hit in the head with a hammer. Repeatedly.

"I'm—uh—I have to go to New Orleans," he managed to get out. "I—she—"

"We know," Rico answered. "We heard."

"How do you—"

"We're vampires," Jof reminded him. "We have superpowers."

"And Aunt Martine was shouting loud enough to wake the dead," Rico added. "The whole building probably heard her."

"You knocked her up!" Corky cackled. He came over and slapped Jon on the back. "Congratulations, man!" Then he narrowed his eyes and added, "You're going to take care of her, right?"

Jon glared at him for a moment, his bright blue eyes taking on a feral glow. "Right now, we're going to give a show," he said, voice crackling with authority—the true alpha Prime of this pack. His gaze swept over them, bringing them to attention. "The best damn show we've ever done."

One by one, they nodded.

"Then I'm going to New Orleans," Jon finished.

"*We're* going to New Orleans," Rico added after a moment of defiant silence.

Jon glared, but the others nodded confirmation.

"Aunt Martine throws a hell of a Christmas party," Rico said.

"And we wouldn't miss this shotgun wedding for the world," Corky finished.

CHAPTER 7

Martine Shagal, head of House Martine of Clan Shagal, stood on her front porch with her hands on her hips and looked down her fine, arched nose at Jon. "Did you bring a ring?"

Jonathan Coyote, Prime of House Natalya of Clan Shagal, stood at the bottom of the stairs and said, "Where is she?"

Clan women were used to being answered, respected, and obeyed. Theirs was, after all, a matriarchal culture. But Jon wasn't feeling particularly deferential at the moment. He'd come at Martine's demand, and that was going to have to be enough for her. Whatever happened next was his business.

He'd lived too much of his life in public, in the glare of the media, under the eyes of his fans. He existed in the fishbowl of stages, hotels, and tour buses. A lot of cameras had been turned on him in the last twenty years. A lot of people thought they had a piece of him. It was the life he'd chosen, enjoyed, and lived to the fullest, but it wasn't his real life. It wasn't all his life.

He lived in the darkness, as well. He followed ancient custom. He'd made the vow not all Primes were willing to make in this postmodern age. He hunted out evil, he fought for justice, he took care of mortals, and he'd cleverly managed to keep the secrets of his kind, despite everything else.

He wore the jackal head tattoo of an active Prime of Clan Shagal on the inside of his right wrist. He held his arm up to show Martine the mark now.

It was all he needed to do to remind her that he was not to be treated as a child. She gave a sharp nod and stepped aside. "Welcome to my home, son of my sister. The woman waits for you inside. Under my protection," she added. It was a warning to obey the rules of hospitality.

It annoyed him that he wasn't going to be allowed simply to grab Desi and leave. Martine may have acknowledged that he was Prime, but she'd placed limitations on his rights over the mortal woman in her house.

Fair enough, he supposed. The most important thing right now was to see Desiree. The hardest thing he'd ever done was to walk away from her at her apartment, after walking away from her ten years before.

It was almost as hard to walk into his aunt's Garden District home. There was a party going on, of course. There were a lot of musicians in the family, so the music was live and lively. The sound of it, and laughter, filled every room. There was no Christmas tree, but lights were strung everywhere—around windows, along walls, across mantels, over doorways. Mistletoe hung from every glittering crystal chandelier, as thick as Spanish moss in the bayous. And the Primes and their ladies were putting the mistletoe to good use. The very air in the crowded rooms sizzled with joyful anticipation and impending passion. Every now and then, in the darker corners, he noted a hint of fang grazing willing flesh and the scent of arousal and blood.

He ignored it all, even the hot-eyed come-hither looks and suggestive touches from some truly beautiful vampire women. It was a mortal he wanted, needed.

Jon made his way through the crowd of kissing, cuddling couples to the base of a sweeping staircase at the center of the mansion. He'd known where Desiree was the moment he'd entered the house. He'd been wrestling with the psychic connection between them for months, trying not to think about her, trying not to go to her. And it had done him no good at all to fight his fate. He'd paid for tempting fate with three months of loneliness and anxiety. She was meant to be his, whether she was ready for the bonding or not. Now he was about to find out what *she* had paid for his leaving her, and he was going to have try to make it up to her.

He ran up the stairs, dodging party guests on the stairway. He was aware of the looks turned on him—curiosity, interest from some of the females, and assessment from other males, since Primes were always ready for challenges over claims to the women. No vampire party would be complete without a few fights over mating rights. While no Matri or Householder would let the challenges get out of hand in her home, it would also be impolite not to show the female guests how much their beauty and allure were appreciated. The delicate balance of etiquette didn't matter to Jon right now.

He followed his awareness of Desiree down the hallway at the top of the stairs. An ornate banister flanked one side of the hall, tall doorways the other. He moved swiftly, the polished wood beneath his feet making no sound. All he could think of as he reached the door and turned the crystal knob was how vulnerable Desi was, how fragile.

His concern was so deep that he barely had time to dodge the heavy bronze statue that was hurled at his head as he entered the room.

"You bastard!"

Desiree didn't look pregnant yet, but he could sense the life force within her. It was to this that he responded. Jon held his hands up before him. "Desi, honey, I can explain."

She threw another statue at him.

The woman had good reflexes and pretty good aim, but he was a vampire and moved like one to avoid being hit. The statue left a hefty dent in the door he'd been standing in front of a moment before.

He grasped her wrists before she could destroy any more of Aunt Martine's property. Or put any more holes in the old mansion. Or him.

The moment they touched, he felt the child, and the connection between all of them. He closed his eyes, almost overcome by the bliss.

"Let go of me!" Desi shouted.

She obviously didn't feel it or was too angry to acknowledge it. He felt a sharp pain in his shin as she kicked him.

Fragile? Vulnerable? What had made him think that about this little hellcat? Hadn't he learned that a decade ago, tracking her through the flood waters of a lawless town? But she was *his* hellcat. He'd found her again, and he had to protect her.

Jon drew Desiree into an embrace, holding her gently but firmly. "Hush," he said. "Think of the baby."

She craned her head up to glare at him. "Think about the—!"

"I know, I know. If it wasn't for me . . ." He sighed. Her warmth, the scent of her skin, and the psychic energy that crackled like lightning around her were all very distracting. The solid weight of her in his arms was wonderful. "I missed you. I've always missed you. I'm here now."

"What do you mean, you've always missed me? You don't want to be here. If she hadn't called you and made you come—"

"She didn't make me come. I want to be with you. I know it's been a while, but—ow!"

She'd kicked him again.

She clearly didn't believe his words. Jon couldn't understand why.

"You *don't* want to be with me. Somehow you made me think it was all a dream, just so you could, you could . . . have your way with me."

He could feel how she believed that with all her heart. This belief was her armor against him, and her weapon. "I—" But words weren't enough, so he kissed her.

At first, her lips were hard and set beneath his, denying his touch, denying emotion. But he held her, cradled her against him, gentle but insistent. Her body slowly melted against his, and fire ignited between them.

Remember me, he whispered into her mind.

CHAPTER 8

"What are you doing out here, tempting fate?"

She gasped and whirled around to face the man who'd snuck up on her. He was tall and older than she was, maybe in his twenties. Even in the dark, she could tell that he had blond hair and blue eyes. He looked stern, but there were dimples hiding at the corners of his face. "Do I know you?"

"No," he said. "Don't you know it isn't safe out here?"

"Of course, I know that." She laughed, not at him but at the awful place where they stood. His words were a joke. She appreciated that he was worried about her. She looked into his eyes and knew she could tell this man anything. "But there's a poodle that needs rescuing," she went on. "And nobody else to do it since FEMA wouldn't let us take pets with us when we left."

"You're risking your life for a poodle?"

"Someone has to," she said over her shoulder, as she turned around and started on her way once more.

"Hey, wait for me!" he called after her.

She smiled to herself as he caught up with her. Being with him made her feel safer than she ever had before. She knew he wouldn't leave her alone.

But that was exactly what he'd done.

Desi hated that she couldn't help wanting Jon Coyote's kiss. It wasn't fair or right that her body betrayed her like this. She didn't stop being angry at him as he kissed her, but the anger wanted to morph into passion just because his tongue slid over hers and his hard body fitted so perfectly against hers. The way his hand pressed against the small of her back sent a shiver all the way up her spine. Damn, but the man could kiss!

Which didn't stop her from pulling away from him after a few delicious moments. "That isn't going to work," she told him breathlessly.

The triumphant glint in his blue eyes told her he was certain that it would. Her sizzling nerve endings agreed with him, but Desi forced her hands to push against him.

This time he let her go. "I suppose we should talk first," he agreed reluctantly. "You remember how we met now, don't you?"

Desi put a hand to her forehead. She'd never forgotten the young man who helped her rescue animals during the flood, but this was the first time she realized who he was. Was that why she was a Coyote fan?

"You make me dizzy," she told him.

He gave her that famous dimpled smile. "You're my dizzy Desi, then."

She suddenly wanted him to kiss her all over again, and she put some distance between herself and the object of temptation. Up close, the man was even more devastatingly handsome than on a stage or in a music video. He looked like a slightly fallen archangel standing there with his wavy dark blond hair, blue, blue eyes, and fantastic body. Then there were those tight jeans—

Her memories told her that they'd only shared sex in a dream, but now she also knew her teenage memories of him were real. Yet she also *knew* that this was the first time they'd ever been this close—except for that one touch during the concert three months ago. Her mind believed the night they'd spent together was a dream. But her body remembered his touch, how his kisses could make her drunk with lust. Real lust, not just a fan's fantasy.

He'd made her believe in the dream. Why? How could she forgive him?

She backed up until she came up against the ornately carved mantel where there were still plenty of art objects to throw at him. Not that she'd meant to destroy her hostess's property; she'd just been so darned mad when Jon walked into the room. And speaking of Martine Shagal . . .

"Your family is—" she began.

"Not exactly normal," he finished for her.

"Holding me prisoner," she finished for herself.

Oh, they'd been polite about it, even kind. Martine had given her a tisane that cleared the morning sickness right up, and Desi was certainly grateful for that. Martine had also tried explaining the peculiarities of the Shagal Clan in an oblique way, always coming back to how Jon would have to fill in the details when he got here. But the fact remained that once Madame Helene had delivered her to this Garden Quarter mansion, it had become Desi's prison. She resented the confinement almost as much as being pregnant and not knowing how it had happened.

"You're an honored guest of the Clan," Jon said. "Very special and important to the family. I know our ways seem peculiar—"

"My grandma's a voodoo queen," Desi told him. "My Uncle Ray is now my Aunt Rayelle. My brother lives with a pack of feral Catahoula Leopard dogs, and my sister's a Wall Street stockbroker. I don't mind peculiar. I mind incarceration." She swept a hand around the elegant room. "Even in luxury."

Jon considered what she'd said for a moment, then asked, "Any vampires in your peculiar family?"

"Not that I know of—but Aunt Tess claims she lived with a werewolf for a while."

"Do you believe in werewolves? Or vampires?"

She shrugged. "Well . . ."

CHAPTER 9

Jon was glad that Desi was reacting with such spirit to the situation. He'd built up an image of her as sweet and gentle, and passive in the last three months, as well as convincing himself that she was way too young for him. He didn't know why, considering how brave and resourceful she'd been as a kid.

They'd laughed a lot the one night they'd spent together. He'd been in a talkative mood, and she'd been a good listener. Just being with her soothed his soul. Rico was right that she'd always be younger than him, as any mortal he fell in love with would be. But a mortal bondmate lived as long as her bonded vampire. He recalled that she'd read his palm and been really surprised at the length of his lifeline, and she'd showed him that she had a long lifeline as well. He should have realized what that meant then, but the desire that had been brewing for a decade had gotten in the way. Most of their night together had been spent making love, and she'd been—perfect.

"You told me you're a vampire," she answered. "In the dream." She rubbed her temples, then shot him a furious look. "It was *real*."

"Of course, it was real. Maybe I shouldn't have told you so soon, but—"

"You made me forget!"

"I did not!"

"Do you always hypnotize your groupies? Which I am not," she added firmly. "I didn't go to the concert to meet you. I don't even remember how I met you."

Jon laughed. "I don't do groupies. Well—not for years. That got old fast."

"Then how do you explain . . ." She patted her belly.

She really didn't remember? Why didn't she remember? He'd only made the intensity of their meeting fade—he didn't want her to forget *him*. If she truly didn't remember, he couldn't blame her for being so pissed at him.

"I meant to come back," he told her. "I've been meaning to since we met—again. Maybe I should have taken you with me—but it would have been too dangerous right after we left New Orleans."

"You had a show in Memphis," she told him. "How is a concert in Memphis *too dangerous*?"

"I don't just play in a band. I'm a vampire." He showed her the black jackal's head tattoo on his right wrist. "This is the Egyptian god Anubis, my Clan's totem. Our patron Anubis was a guardian, and that's what I am."

"I thought you said you're a vampire."

"I am."

"Right." She patted her abdomen again. "Dead people don't get women knocked up. Or run around in the daylight. I've got the DVD of the concert you did in Barcelona—two hours in the midday sun."

"An awesome show." He nodded fondly at the memory of that particular gig. "I take drugs."

"You're a musician," she countered. "Of course you do. I read that you'd been through rehab."

"I've never done those kinds of drugs. I take sort of allergy drugs," he corrected. "For the vampirism."

"Vampirism's an allergy?"

"No!"

"A lifestyle choice, then?"

"No. We're born, not made. If we want to live in the daylight, we take certain drugs to protect ourselves. We don't need to take the drugs if we don't want to. I find it convenient to live in the light, so I take them. We do need to drink blood as part of our nourishment, but we don't need to kill, or drain our partners like in the movies. Sharing blood with our lovers is emotionally satisfying for both parties. Our sharing blood won't turn you into a vampire, but it will—"

"Is my baby going to be a vampire?"

"Our baby. I don't think so."

"You're not *sure*?"

He sighed. "It's complicated."

Desi folded her hands in front of her stomach. "I'm a prisoner here. I have plenty of time for explanations."

"And you deserve them. If we have a girl, she might become a vampire, which is a very good thing, since there are so few females of our kind. But far more males are born than females, and males with human mothers can't become vampires."

"Oh." She held her hands over her belly, and concern, hope, and pleasure ran across her expression as she looked into his eyes.

Jon stepped closer. He hated being on the defensive; that was no way to spend your life with someone. "Let's get one thing straight," he said, and moved in front of Desiree faster than she could have blinked. As she gasped at his sudden closeness, he said, "Pay attention."

Then he let his fangs grow.

CHAPTER 10

Desi watched in complete fascination as Jon changed before her eyes. This couldn't be some kind of special effect, and it wasn't anything like the fake fangs worn by the Goth types who favored the vampire tours and clubs of the Quarter. These fangs were the real thing, bright and shiny and sharp. Sexy.

Instead of frightening her, the sight of them pressing against Jon's full lower lip sent a strong shiver of desire through her. Desire even stronger than the first time she'd seen him live onstage when she was sixteen. Which *hadn't* been the first time she'd seen him, even though she'd thought so at the time.

She wasn't sixteen anymore, and he was far more than her rock god fantasy man. He was other, alien. Still the sexiest thing alive. And he was the father of her child—and she couldn't remember how it had happened.

"I am a vampire. And I claim you as my bondmate. You belong to me, Desiree." He spoke as solemnly as if he'd made a vow. Maybe he just had.

"Belong?" Her emotions shot from desire back to fury, and the next thing she knew, she'd raised her hand to slap the very real vampire.

He grabbed her wrist before she could move. Then he brought it to his mouth and kissed it, grazing the sharp edges of his fangs along the tender flesh over her pulse.

"Oh, dear!" Desi gasped, and closed her eyes. Her knees went weak. "This I remember," she said on a sigh. She adored the man—except for the fact that she also hated him. "You shouldn't have made me forget," she told him. "That was wrong. It was evil. Cruel."

Jon stepped back and threw up his hands. "I didn't make you forget anything!" Then he looked thoughtful for a moment. "Maybe a little."

"You made me think the best sex of my life was all a dream."

His confusion returned. "Why would I do that? I would never make a woman forget she had sex with me, that would be like—"

"Rape," Desi put in.

CHAPTER 11

Jon suddenly had to sit down. He stumbled back-ward into the nearest chair, trying to come to terms with what Desiree had said. She had every right to be upset, if he'd done what she believed he had.

He struggled to bring up the exact memories of what they'd done that night, ran a hand through his hair, and looked into Desi's accusing eyes. "I remember telling you I'm a vampire. I shouldn't have done that, so I made you forget it. That's not something that we talk about on first dates. Believe me, I wanted to see you again and probably couldn't have stayed away. But something came up, and—"

"Something?"

He looked up at her and couldn't help but smile. She fought it but couldn't stop a faint answering smile. She was small, bright, beautiful, confused, angry, and very, very curious. Her curiosity charmed him. Every-thing about her charmed him—of course it did; they'd been born to be bondmates. What had ever made him even pretend she could be anything else?

One touch of her hand had been the first clue. One taste of her blood had been addicting. One night of lovemaking had been the best night of his life.

She was also far more psychic than he'd believed her to be on the night they'd met. Hadn't she told him so ten years ago? Underestimating her abilities led to his mistake after the concert, and their current problem.

"I didn't mean for you to think the lovemaking was a dream. I would never lie to you. But I did accidentally screw up your memories. Sweetheart, I am so sorry."

He got up and went to her, putting his fingers gently on her temples. "I did too thorough a job when I got into your head. This is the stuff you were supposed to forget."

"You know about BBD?" he asked as the limo glided along the dark street in a very, very bad part of town.

"Big Black Dog," she answered. *"It's your charity. You've spent years helping runaways, getting homeless kids off the streets. You fund shelters and rehab facilities. I've contributed to BBD."*

"Thank you." He stroked her cheek and kissed her. His touch left tingling heat on her lips and skin. *"But we do a bit more than fund BBD. We're guardians of mortals, following the traditions of our ancestors. Apparently, some Primes of our Clan back in ancient Egypt swore an oath to Anubis—the original Big Black Dog—to serve and protect. I took that same oath when I came of age."*

The limo came to a stop in front of a dark alley between two rundown warehouses. Her awareness was more fo-

*cused on the way he made her feel than on what he'd said,
or where they were. But when he opened the door to get
out, a flash of worry went through her. "Where are you
going?"*

*"Hunting." He smiled, showing long, sharp fangs. "Stay
here." He disappeared into the shadows of the alley.*

*It was a command, telepathic, hypnotic. It took her only
a few moments to break the spell and reach for the door
handle. The limo driver tried to stop her, but she eluded
him. Following Jon was easy, even though he moved
silently in the dark, even with the heavy footsteps of the
driver pelting behind her. It was impossible for her not to
know where he was.*

*She dodged through a broken doorway and found him
deep inside the huge old building. There were adult male
bodies on the floor and teenage girls locked up in cages. And
there was blood on Jon's mouth when he dropped the last
body and turned to look at her. His eyes were glowing.*

"That was what I made you forget," he said, bringing her out of the memory. "I didn't mean for you to
see me rescuing those girls—not like that, giving in
to the blood craving that can make me turn violent. I
shouldn't have taken you with me, but I couldn't stop
myself. I needed to be with you and knew we didn't
have much time. I couldn't take you with me to Memphis, because what happened here was only the beginning of a series of raids to break up a forced prostitution
ring. It was dangerous work and—"

"Shhh." Desi put her hand over his mouth. "Let me
think." After a few minutes, she said, "So, in order to
make me forget that fight in the warehouse, you made
me forget everything?"

"I didn't mean to," he answered. "But you're a stronger psychic than I thought."

The door opened, and Martine Shagal stuck her head in. "You two are missing the party. Come downstairs now."

"But—" Jon said.

"Come and introduce your lady to your bandmates." Martine opened the door wider and gestured them forward.

"They're here?" Jon sighed. Of course they were. Though he'd taken the band's private jet to race to Desi, there was nothing stopping the rest of Coyote from taking commercial flights. He wanted time and privacy, but he was going to get teasing and well-meaning advice instead.

"Might as well get this over with," he grumbled. He put his arm around Desi's waist and guided her toward the door.

CHAPTER 12

The level of conversation fell as they stepped through the door, but Rico was used to making an entrance. He smiled and walked into the living room to greet friends and family. He was a Prime in his prime, with his arm around his bondmate, and all was right in his world. Their joined psychic aura was strong around them, so he could enjoy the party without worrying about a challenge for his mate from any unattached pup.

He did smile at all the ladies he saw, for it would be rude for even the most strongly bonded vampire not to show appreciation for all that female beauty. Being Prime, he of course kept a jealous eye on Gemma to make sure she didn't even look at another male. It was a terrible double standard that vampires lived by.

He felt how amused Gemma was by his behavior and swept her under the nearest bough of mistletoe for a long, deep kiss

When they came up for air, a waiter was holding a

tray of champagne toward them. They took the slender crystal flutes and retreated to an empty spot at the bottom of a curving staircase. Pine branches attached to the curving banister with twisting red and green ribbons scented the air, blending with the warm cinnamon aroma of red candles set in tall gold candelabras.

Gemma looked up the stairs and tilted her head to one side. She looked adorable, a small blond woman in a short black dress. A fortune in diamonds twinkled on her ears and around her long, slender throat.

"Fireworks going off up there," she whispered to him after she concentrated with all her senses for a few moments. She waved a hand in front of her face, her cheeks going pink. "The place is warming up."

Rico registered the electric sensation of sexual tension among the guests as typical background noise for a vampire party. Or a Coyote concert, come to think of it. "Jon must be using all his charm on his human mate." He gave a one-shoulder shrug. "Jon with a mortal—who'd have thought it?"

Actually, only about a third of the Clan Primes ended up with vampire bondmates. There weren't as many vampire females as there were males, and even if the population were more equal, the psychic connection that instigated a bond struck where it would. In Jon's case, with a mortal woman. In his own case, a vampire one.

"After he tried to hook up with Flare Reynard and she treated him so badly, I don't blame him for finding a nice mortal girl," Gemma whispered to him.

Rico couldn't help but smile. "It's Flare's loss that she didn't think Jonathan Coyote was good enough for her. It's not like she broke his heart or anything. He got a couple of good songs out of the end of the affair."

Gemma laughed and shook her head. "That's all you guys care about."

"We are a band." He looked around at the rest of the crowd. "And we're all here."

Bartholomew had his arms around two pretty girls, who were taking turns letting him sip from their wine glasses—and their throats. Jof was talking very seriously to a Prime Elder, and the Elder was laughing at whatever Jof was telling him. Corky was standing very still in the center of the room, looking up the stairs as the party swirled around him.

What's he up to? Rico wondered.

"I wonder if the baby will be one of us," Gemma said.

The question took Rico's attention away from Corky. "Wouldn't that be just like Jon?" He laughed. "Pregnant with a daughter on the first date."

Their kind reproduced slowly, even vampire to vampire. It generally took many years of being fully bonded for a vampire and a mortal to have children.

"Let's hope," Gemma answered. "And maybe she didn't get pregnant on their first date." When he cocked an eyebrow skeptically at her, she went on. "Maybe their psychic connection's been going on for years. She's a big fan of Jon's, right? She just fell in love long distance through his songs."

Rico nodded. "You think our music brought them together?"

"Why not?" she answered. "And he was psychically searching for her. I've always wondered who the songs like 'Courtyard Rose' and 'Dreaming Desire' were about. And—"

Just then, Jon and his lady appeared behind Aunt Martine at the top of the stairs. Like everyone else, Rico craned to get a good look at the woman Jonathan Coyote had come to claim. She was small, with short brown curls, a creamy coffee complexion, and huge, dark brown eyes. She didn't look afraid, as a person facing the scrutiny of a house full of vampires might be expected to be. She did look confused, but Rico was certain that was aimed squarely at Jon. No one else mattered to her.

He liked that about Desiree Gill. A singular concentration on the male you bonded with was a proper quality in a female.

Gemma caught this thought and snorted. "Primes are such pigs."

He didn't deny it but drew her closer in his possessive, protective embrace.

CHAPTER 13

Desi wished that Martine Shagal had left her and Jon alone longer; she hated being thrust out into public view when they still had so much to work out.

But suddenly they were in this crowd. How could she think with all this noise and all these people—and that was Rico and the glamorous Gemma smiling up at her from the bottom of the stairs! Smiling at her? They were famous!

Of course, Jon was famous, too. She'd forgotten about that while they'd been arguing. How odd that she'd forgotten to be awed by his fame. She hadn't even been horrified or frightened knowing that he was a vampire, either. He was just—Jon.

Her Jon? Jonathan Coyote, hers? *The* Jonathan Coyote?

Why did that not seem preposterous?

"My mom's going to be jealous," she murmured. "She was a fan of yours long before I was."

He laughed. "Go ahead, make me feel my age."

They reached the bottom of the stairs before she could answer, and suddenly they were the object of attention.

Gemma Shagal took her hands. "I'm Gemma, this is my Rico, and we're very happy to meet you," the glamorous woman told her. "You look shell-shocked. Why don't we get you some ginger ale and a place to sit down?"

"Hey!" Jon called out as Gemma led Desi away.

Desi didn't take more than three steps before she and Gemma were surrounded by a group of male vampires. They were all taller than she was, and they were all handsome and self-confident. Exuding sexuality seemed to be standard operating procedure among this lot. They also all seemed to be wearing black. They were smiling, some with a bit of fang showing. Desi couldn't help but get the impression that they were looking at her as if she were a tasty party snack.

Beside her, Gemma let out a low chuckle. "Boys," she said.

"Hello, Desiree," one of the crowd said.

Desi focused her attention on the male who'd spoken. He was one of the tallest, with long black hair and green eyes. He had shoulders wide enough to block out the sun and looked vaguely familiar. Oh, great—another lost memory? "Do I know you?"

"You do not," Jon said firmly.

The one who'd spoken to her elbowed the males beside him out of the way. One of them actually growled, but the crowd stepped back to give him room. "I've known you for a long time," he said. "I'm Cesare. You've seen me around the Quarter, when I've wanted you to." He glared over her shoulder at Jon. "I would have claimed her if you hadn't come along."

She glanced back to see Jon glaring at Cesare. He put a hand on her shoulder, the connection sending a shiver through her that was psychic as well as physical.

"Mine," he said.

Cesare gave a nasty laugh. "She's not completely yours yet. I saw her first."

"No, you didn't. And you didn't have her first," Jon said.

Gemma sighed and whispered in Desi's ear, "They're kind of cute when they're puppies, but this stuff grows old after a while."

"What stuff?" Desi whispered back.

"They're working up to fighting over you," Gemma told her. "It's a compliment, really," she added when Desi turned a horrified look on her.

"The lady's a guest here, and a stranger to our ways," another male chimed in. Desi recognized him as Corky Cage, Coyote's drummer. He smiled, spreading his arms out to get everyone's attention. "If there's more than one Prime wanting to claim this lovely mortal woman, she has to be won. Lady Martine, isn't this a time to let the woman chose her champion and reward the victor?" He looked between Jon and the challenger. "Prove your devotion to her, if you want her."

"Indeed," Martine Shagal said, taking control of the situation with just one word. Everyone's attention focused on their hostess. "Cordwainer is correct. Let's turn this into a competition rather than the usual brawl. It'll save wear and tear on my holiday decorations."

Jon wondered if his aunt had put Cesare, her youngest son, up to this challenge to prove a point. "I love her,

Aunt Martine," he told her, and he turned Desi to face him. He put a finger under her chin to make Desiree look him in the eye. "I love you," he told her. "I always have. I always will. Know that I'll always be with you."

"Love isn't at stake here," Corky spoke up. "Honor is."

"Cordwainer is correct," Martine said again. "Don't just proclaim your love, Jon. Do something to impress the girl with your devotion." She gave an imperious wave that sent everyone but himself, Desiree, and Cesare to the edges of the big room. Jon and Cesare stepped away from Desiree, leaving her alone in the center of the room, a prize for all eyes to see. She crossed her arms and frowned.

Martine smiled at them, but there was sternness in her demeanor. She gestured, candlelight glinting off the emerald ring on her hand. "Primes, choose your weapons."

Jon grinned. *Fine. Let's do it.* He turned all his attention on the woman he was determined to win. "Somebody hand me a guitar."

Desi was barely aware of the laughter and applause that broke out around them. Jon Coyote was looking into her eyes, and she had no doubt that he wasn't aware of anyone but her. *All* the memories they shared flooded through her, and every last bit of resentment and anger faded away even as she fought to keep it alive.

He loved her. He'd said so.

She had to turn her back on him to be able to think. All right, so he'd messed up her head and gotten her knocked up and disappeared from her life for the last three months.

After all that, was she going to let him get away with a simple *Sweetheart, I am so sorry?*

The first few bars of "Tempting Fate" sounded in the room and in her head. And her heart. And her soul. And her body. And she turned back to face him. He smiled tenderly, and every note he played was filled with love. When he began to sing, the words were all for her.

His rival never had a chance.

Was she going to let him get away with everything he wanted?

Desi smiled tenderly. Of course she was.

He was Jon Coyote, and she'd loved him all her life.

THE
DARKNESS
WITHIN

Maggie Shayne

CHAPTER 1

Nine p.m., pouring rain outside, corn flakes for dinner, and the phone hadn't rung all day. Brian tended to be a last-minute sort of guy, but normally, if he hadn't called by nine, he wasn't going to. For a while, she would get ready, just in case. She would blow off friends, invitations, everything, just in case he called. She still stayed home in hopes he would come by, but she'd stopped getting dressed and fixing her hair at night, because it was usually a waste of time. He would let weeks go by without a word, then call her and give her twenty minutes' warning before showing up at her door. Sometimes he stayed a whole hour after the sex. Usually, he asked to borrow money before he left.

She was beginning to wonder if she was paying him for his services.

She wasn't a stupid woman. She knew he was using her, but being in a man's arms every once in a while felt good, and the sex wasn't bad. Wasn't great, but it wasn't bad.

Caroline scuffed through the kitchen in her worn-out slippers and flannel robe, admiring the gleaming floor tiles that looked like mother-of-pearl and wondering how the hell she was going to keep from losing the home she'd just bought. Her job as a financial planner at a local bank didn't pay enough to keep her afloat. She'd made a lot more as a partner in a two-person tax and accounting business, but her ex got that in the divorce. He was supposed to buy her out, but he had yet to fork over the money.

It had been two months since the closing on her new home, a year since her divorce, and six months since she'd started dating Brian, if you could call it dating. Mostly, it was a series of booty calls. She'd managed to ruin her life in what had to be a record-breaking period of time.

The telephone shrilled just as she sat down with her bowl of corn flakes at the island with the tiles that matched those on the floor. God, she loved this house. She slid off the stool and padded to the phone, saw the name on the caller ID, and felt like crap. But she picked it up anyway.

"Hello, Shawn."

"Hi, hon." That he still called her "hon" after ditching her for a younger woman, divorcing her, booting her out the door, and stealing her business made her stomach turn over. "I'm just calling to tell you—"

"That the check isn't coming on time?" she asked, even though she already knew the answer.

"I'm sorry, babe. The business is suffering right now."

He said "babe" the way most people would say "bitch."

"Shawn, this is the third month in a row. You got the

house and my half of the business, but you're supposed to be paying me for my share of both."

"I know, and I will. I'll catch up."

"Before or after I lose my home?"

He swore, and she felt him getting angry. Closing her eyes, lowering her head, she sighed. She hated confrontation and knew arguing with him would be like arguing with a stalk of corn. A really *cheap* and stone-deaf stalk of corn. "Look, I need the money. Try your best, will you, Shawn?"

"I will. Promise. Thanks for understanding."

"Oh, I understand, all right."

He hung up then, not a good-bye, not a question about her life or anything else. Probably because he didn't care. Then again, he never had. She hung up the phone and stared at it for a long moment. Then she picked it up again and dialed Brian's number. He didn't answer. The machine picked up, though, and while she waited for the beep, she tried to rehearse the words in her mind. She didn't want to make him mad or insult him, because her experience with men told her they didn't hang around long if you pissed them off. And while Brian was no prince, he was better than no one. But damn, she needed some cash.

"Hi, Brian, it's me. Listen, I'm in some trouble here, and um—well, I really hate to ask, but if you could pay me back some of the money I've loaned you, it would really help me out. I mean, no problem if you can't, but you know, if you can. Even a little . . . well, like I said, it would help. Give me a call, okay?"

She put the phone down, gnawed her lower lip for a second, then sighed and headed back to her stool. But her corn flakes were soggy, and she'd lost her appetite.

Thunder rolled in, marbles over metal, in waves that got louder as they came nearer, until she felt it in her gut. She glanced toward the sliding glass doors that led onto the patio, and watched rivulets of rainwater streaming over the glass. To Caroline Connelly, it felt as if the universe were taking a giant, steaming leak on her pathetic excuse for a life.

Lightning flashed like a strobe light. For just an instant, it showed her an image—a woman stood on the other side of the rain-streaked glass. Caroline clapped a hand to her chest and jumped off the stool so fast it fell over. But she couldn't see anything now. No dripping-wet form, no dark, straggly hair, no eyes staring intently at her.

Her heart was pounding, mouth dry, and she'd inhaled so sharply she thought she might have torn a lung. Shaking—just a little bit—she moved toward the glass doors, even though her feet were itching to run in the opposite direction. With a quick lunge, she reached out, locked the doors, then darted to one side and flipped on the outdoor light.

Illumination spilled over the flagstone patio, the empty brown wicker chairs, and the matching glass-topped table. It spilled across the sloping lawn and touched the edges of the kidney-shaped swimming pool. But it didn't reveal a long-haired woman in a soaked white dress that hung down to her bare feet. There was no one there.

It must have been an illusion, a trick played by that flash of lightning and the shadows around it, or some kind of odd reflection. It must have been . . .

She lowered her head, and her heart stood still. There on the flagstone, just outside the glass doors, were two wet footprints. No sudden gasp or knee-jerk response this time. This time, she just stared at the hard evidence her eyes were showing her, not doubting it, clear on what she saw. Not clear on what it meant but perfectly clear on what she saw. Her feet carried her backward until she was pressed up against the wall by the phone. She took the receiver from the base almost in slow motion. Her hands shook so that she almost dropped the phone, but her eyes never left the patio as she hit the buttons.

When her brother picked up, he sounded as if he'd been laughing about something. "Yeah?"

Calmly—which surprised her—she said, "Peter, there's someone here." And yeah, maybe her voice sounded strained and oddly quiet. But calm.

The laughter in his voice died. "Caroline? What do you mean? Who's there?"

"Hell, Pete, I didn't ask her name, but from the looks of her, she's either a half-drowned crack addict or that chick from *The Ring*. And I'm wishing to hell I'd never let you talk me into seeing that movie, by the way. She was standing outside the doors, staring in at me."

As she spoke, she felt a chill and turned slowly. The woman stood in her living room, just beyond the archway, dripping all over the deep-pile carpet. "Oh, shit." God, she looked like something that had just dragged itself out of a swamp. "Jesus, she's in the house!"

"Get out of there, Caro. Get out now. I'll call the police and be there in two minutes. Get *out*."

Caroline was obeying before he had finished telling her the first time, turning to hang up the phone and running for the glass doors. She did not need to be told to get out of the house. Hell, if she were a cartoon, there would be a Caroline-shaped hole in the nearest wall right now. She started to yank the doors open, but they were locked. As she twisted the lock, she sent a frantic look over her shoulder. The woman was coming closer, entering the dining room now. She lifted a hand, reaching out toward her, moving slowly, her eyes intense, almost angry.

Caroline got the lock to release, slid the doors open, and ran out into the pouring rain. Her slippers slowed her, so she kicked them off and raced around to the front of the house, down the drive, and into the street. She didn't stop running until her brother's car skidded to a stop in front of her, its headlights burning her eyes. And even then, she had to shield them with one arm to make out the shapes emerging from the vehicle. Peter from the driver's door, and from the passenger side . . . someone else. Someone tall, and very male.

The two men came around the car, which put them between her and the headlights, and a second later, the stranger was peeling his hooded sweatshirt off, bending slightly forward to do so. As he tugged it over his head, the shirt he wore underneath went up with it, giving her a glimpse of abs so spectacular that she noticed them, despite the situation.

He straightened and pulled his shirt down. Then, without warning, he put the sweatshirt over her head.

"The intruder still inside, Caro?" Peter asked.

"How would I know? I'm out here." She didn't look at him as she answered, though. Her eyes were fixed on the stranger, as she let him work the sweatshirt's sleeves over her arms, as if she were helpless and in need of dressing. He held her gaze with so much force she couldn't seem to look away. And she felt something primal stirring deep in her gut, which was ridiculous. He was clearly too young. Way too young.

He tugged the bottom of the sweatshirt down over her hips, his knuckles brushing her thighs on the way, and hell yes, she was wearing a flannel bathrobe, but she felt it anyway. Hot.

And then she cursed the fates for letting her wear flannel tonight instead of some sheer, damsel-in-distress peignoir number.

He tugged the hood up over her wet hair, still holding her eyes with his. "Are you okay?"

She nodded, feeling foolish now in the cold reality of the icy rain. "I don't even know why I panicked like that. She looked more like a half-drowned cat than an intruder."

"Hell, the way you sounded on the phone . . ."

"How do you know how I sounded on the phone?"

"The cordless was out of reach, so Pete just hit the speaker button to answer."

"Don't tell me. You were watching a game, and he didn't want to move too far from the TV screen. So who was playing?"

"You sounded scared," he said, ignoring her attempt to change the subject.

"I was. But I'm not anymore." She couldn't look away. She'd tried and failed, had no idea where her brother was right now, though she assumed he was checking the house. But there was something about this man. Something about the way his eyes held hers. Something compelling and vaguely . . . familiar. "Who are you?"

He finally broke eye contact, looking toward the

house, then shifted his gaze away from the place again, his manner odd. As if he didn't like looking at it. "Friend of your brother's."

"You're too young to be a friend of Pete's."

He frowned. "Not true. 'Cause that's what I am."

"Bull. How old are you?"

"Twenty-five. You?"

"Older than that."

He smiled a little, one side of his mouth pulling up, as if he didn't want to let it grow into a full-blown one, or as if he were trying to hide it and failing. "By how much?"

"Excuse me?" Pete said. "You two gonna stand in the middle of the road all night? Not smart in the rain, in the dark."

The stranger was holding her eyes captive again. "You find anything, Pete?"

"No."

Caroline studied the stranger standing there in the middle of the street, in the pouring rain, in the wet glow of headlights, and she thought the entire discussion they'd been having was kind of stupid and pointless. And then she wondered why she'd been enjoying it so much, batting words back and forth with him like tennis balls. She dragged her eyes from his long enough to let them slide down his body. He wore jeans, slightly worn and slightly baggy, a pair of Nike Air something-or-others, a baseball shirt, and a matching cap—Yankees, no less—and both currently getting wet.

Then she heard sirens.

"Do you have a name," she asked, "or should I call you Fop?"

He frowned at her.

"For Friend of Peter," she clarified.

"Ji—James," he said. "James Lipton."

She blinked, because the name was familiar. "Lipton, Lipton." She *knew* him. She was sure she did. There was something about his eyes, the crinkles at the corners when he smiled. Not laugh lines; he was *way* too young for laugh lines. But still—they had a hint of mischief to them, those eyes. You could almost think he was interested—which was, of course, ridiculous. Or should be. But damn, he sure was acting that way. And the wetter that baseball shirt got, the more it clung, and the more she liked looking at him.

"You think you can get the hell outta the road before the cops get here?" Peter asked. "Come on, already. I'm gonna move the car. Get her off the road, Jimmy, and make sure her wet weirdo doesn't get anywhere near her."

Jimmy, she thought, turning it over in her mind, because *that*—not James—really rang a bell. He was putting his hands on her shoulders now, as if to turn her slightly, guide her out of the road, while Peter headed to the driver's door, got in, and backed up the car. Jimmy's hands on her shoulders were slightly more possessive than they needed to be to steer a frightened female politely out of harm's way. They squeezed a little tighter than they had to, stayed a little longer, and he stood a little closer, too. And he wasn't moving, or pushing her to move, or walking her off the road. He was just standing there, in the pouring rain, staring down into her eyes—no, at her lips now—as his hands sort of kneaded her shoulders and gave her chills. She felt herself closing the distance between her body and his, her body sort of swaying toward his in response to some unseen force, like gravity. You know, if it were the kind found on Jupiter, where the pull was so forceful that Paris Hilton would weigh in at about a metric ton.

So, yeah, there she was, swaying forward, closer to this gorgeous, hot, young, and apparently interested—in *her*, if you can imagine that—probably nearsighted, but whatever, hunk. So she was leaning in, and he was looking at her mouth the way a guy looks at a woman he's thinking about kissing. And not ordinary kissing, either, but the steamy, open-mouth-insert-tongue kind of kissing—kissing like she hadn't had in . . . ever. And that's when it hit her. When their faces were about two inches apart. So close she could feel his breath on her lips. So close her mouth was starting to open for him. Just at that moment. It hit her, and she blurted it right out while her eyes tried to bug out of her head. "Jimmy Lipton! *Little* Jimmy Lipton?" As she said it, she jerked backward as if he were about to bite her.

He let his head fall forward, rubbed his nape with one hand. "I was hoping you wouldn't remember that."

"I used to babysit for you!"

"Not for me, for my kid brother, because my parents didn't trust me to watch him myself. And to be honest, I used to pray my parents would go out more." He sent her a half-sheepish, half-adoring look.

She slammed her palms on his chest, not hard enough to hurt him but hard enough to drive him a few steps backward and make him lose his balance. "You pervert! I was twenty-five years old, and you were—you were, what, fourteen?"

"Twelve."

She lowered her head, pinched the bridge of her nose. She was going to hell. She knew it. Damn, damn, damn.

The cops had arrived, and somehow, during the ten seconds since that almost-kiss, Jimmy Lipton had maneuvered her off the road and onto the sidewalk, so the cruiser had room to, well, cruise past them and into her driveway. He had his arm around her waist, and he didn't seem too eager to take it away. She probably should tell him to. She really should.

But she was enjoying it too much and was distracted by the thoughts making themselves heard in her mind. Probably because her libido had been talking over them. Talking, hell. More like screaming. But it quieted down just as he said, "They're not gonna find anything, you know."

She was watching her brother talk to one cop, while the other went snooping around the house, toward the back, with a Maglite held in typical cop style: overhand grip and not in the gun hand. But Jimmy's words drew her eyes right back to his.

"You lived here when you were a kid," she said. "Babysitting for you—"

"For my brother."

"—was when I first fell in love with this place. I was so surprised and overjoyed to find it for sale when Shawn and I split up."

"It was never supposed to be for sale," he said. "But yeah, it's had a few owners since then. I always hoped to buy it back myself one of these days, but you beat me to it."

"Yada, yada," she said, making a "speed it up" motion with her hands. "You wanna get to the point here? That cryptic, all-knowing comment about the cops not finding anything?"

He shrugged. "That girl you saw?"

She nodded, and a chill rippled right up her spine, from the small of her back to between her shoulder blades, just like an icy finger. She shivered, nodded at him to go on.

He held her eyes, steady, serious, sincere, and he said very softly, "I know her. She used to come around when I lived here, too. She'd stand by my bedroom window, soaking wet, that dark hair dripping, those big black eyes all hollow and haunted, and just stare in at me. Like she wanted something."

"How can that be, Jimmy? I mean, the same woman, showing up soaking wet in the dead of night—after thirteen years?"

"Not after thirteen years," he said. "I think she's been coming around the whole time. Probably that's why everyone who buys the old place decides to sell it again and move on in pretty short order."

"But Jimmy—"

"I know. Impossible. And I used to swear there was evidence. Footprints, water on the floor, her wet handprint when she pressed her palm to my bedroom window glass. But there never was. The traces she leaves—the ones you see her leave with your own damn eyes—they vanish almost as fast as she does."

She blinked up at him and wondered how little Jimmy Lipton got to be six-two, whipcord lean, sexier than sin, *and* certifiably insane, all in the space of thirteen years.

"Are you trying to tell me she's some kind of a . . . ghost, Jimmy?" she whispered.

His eyes stabbed into hers, but before he could answer that question, Peter and the two cops were crowding up to her on either side, talking and asking questions and telling her there wasn't a trace of anyone around. Not a footprint. Not any water on the floor in the living room, not even in that thick carpet that would have held it for hours. No handprints on the sliding glass doors.

Nothing.

Just as Jimmy Lipton said.

Caroline shivered hard and knew the eagle-eyed kid-turned-hunk saw it.

CHAPTER 2

Jim had really been hoping Caroline wouldn't remember the past the two of them shared, because when he'd seen her, every fantasy he'd ever had about her had come rushing back—only this time, they were the fantasies of an adult male for an adult female. Not of an adolescent boy for his kid brother's hotter-than-hell babysitter.

She still had it, though, whatever it was that had made her so attractive to him then. He didn't know what it was. He did know that it seemed to be fading a bit. Or hidden, maybe, underneath the concerns of the moment. Her divorce, the apparition she'd discovered lurking in her new home, and so on. Seeing him again probably hadn't helped. She'd been feeling something, he was sure of it. That tug in the groin, that twisting in the belly, that flutter in the chest—*that* something. He'd been feeling it, and he was sure she'd felt it, too. She'd damn near let him kiss her.

And that would have been brilliant, wouldn't it?

Right in front of her brother? He'd kind of lost track of common sense there for a few moments. Lost track of everything except sheer, long-term, fantasy-induced lust.

But then she'd put it all together, realized why she knew him, and, because of that, caught on to his age. It was a goddamned blow to his male ego that she thought he was too young for her. He'd really like the opportunity to prove otherwise. He was as much a man as any forty-year-old—more than most of them, he figured. So what was the issue?

Women. They managed to complicate everything. Sometimes you'd just like to strangle them.

Caroline was heading back to the house, walking barefoot between the cop—who was forty something and not taking his eyes off her—and her brother, who'd become Jim's new best friend about two months ago, when he'd learned that Caroline, his childhood fantasy, was buying his childhood home.

"God," he muttered. "It's like the opening of a letter to *Penthouse*."

Caroline turned sharply, as if she'd forgotten he was still plodding along behind them. "What did you say?" she asked.

"Nothing." Hell, he didn't know why she got to him the way she did. Her hair was dark and kind of wild. Her eyes were huge and green. Olive green, which didn't sound as pretty as emerald or jade eyes might sound, but damn, they were hot. The way the green got gradually darker the closer it got to the center, so that by the time you got anywhere near the pupil, the iris was already so black you couldn't tell where one ended and the other began. She kept herself fit.

Though you'd never know it, because she didn't dress to show it. *Frumpy* was the word that came to mind.

She didn't used to be that way, but life had smacked her down. Hard.

He'd always thought of her as the kind of woman who'd bounce right back again, come up swinging, and never give in. Maybe he'd pegged her wrong. Or maybe she was just taking a breather.

He'd made a point of hanging around ever since she moved in, glimpsing her when he could and hoping for an opportunity to talk, or . . . whatever. He'd been hoping for whatever. What he hadn't been hoping for was to meet her like this.

He'd pretty much convinced himself the "wet lady," as he'd called the bane of his childhood, had been a bad dream, maybe even a slight psychotic break. Okay, so maybe deep down, he'd known better. He knew why she came. And the guilt of past sins was crippling enough without her showing up to remind him. But it had been easy enough to ignore all that—until Caroline had clubbed him right between the eyes with it, that is.

Damn.

"Hey, pal," Peter called. "You coming, or what?"

Peter, Caroline, and the two cops were going through the front door of his house—er, Caroline's house. He gave a shrug, glanced both ways for any sign of *her,* and then headed along the sidewalk a little faster to catch up.

Caroline told her story to the cops, but the entire time, she kept shooting him looks—probing, searching looks. Almost as if she wanted him to confirm or deny or embellish her claims by adding his own. He didn't. Bad enough they all thought she was nuts, he didn't

need to go earning that same rep for himself. Hell, he'd
had his fill of cops suspecting he might be a little bit
insane. Maybe criminally so. He didn't need any more
of that bull.

"You working this case, Lipton?" Officer Borelli
asked.

"Not officially, Mike. Just a friend of the family."

The cop nodded. "You come across anything—"

"I'll let you know and expect you to do the same."

"You got it."

By that time, Caroline was looking a little pissed
at him. Hell, this was not the reunion he'd imagined.
Then again, the reunion he'd imagined involved
tangled sheets, minimal clothing, and the sound of her
moaning his name repeatedly.

"You *know* that cop?" Caroline asked, backing him
into a quiet corner in the kitchen for which he could
have come up with much better uses. "What did he
mean about you working the case?"

"I know the cop," he confirmed quietly. "I'm a PI. I
work with them sometimes."

"Caro?" Pete called.

She gave him a look that told him she had a lot more
to say, then turned to go join her brother and the police.

When the police wrapped up, Caroline walked
them to the door, even though they clearly thought
she'd brought them out there for no reason whatso-
ever. They'd started out asking questions about the
intruder, but toward the end, they'd been asking things
like whether she'd been under any unusual stress lately
and whether she'd had anything to drink or taken any
medication or illegal drugs that day.

Hell.

Peter clapped a hand to Jim's shoulder the second Caroline and the cops were out of earshot. They were standing in the kitchen, near the sliding doors where the wet lady had first appeared. He'd been so deep in thought he jumped a little.

"Easy, pal. You're as nervous as my sister is, aren't you?"

He sent his friend an easy smile. "I was drifting. Sorry."

"I need you to do something for me, Jim."

"Sure, name it."

"Stay with her tonight."

Jim's throat went bone dry, and his mind shouted *"Hell, yes!"* He thought that maybe aloud he should try to sound a little more reserved about the notion. "I . . . I don't know, I—"

"Look, you were gonna stay with me while your apartment's being painted, right? I'd do it myself, but I've got the kids, and Mary's under the weather. I abandon her, she'll never let me hear the end of it. Come on, I'd do it for you."

He heard the front door close, then Caroline's footsteps as she headed back toward the kitchen. "If she's open to it, yeah. I'll stay." *Open to it. Right. Best watch the Freudian slips, moron.*

"Thanks, pal."

"You're welcome."

Caroline stepped into the kitchen, ready to give Jimmy Lipton the dressing down of his life for sitting silently while the cops decided she was just another hysterical female, when he knew better. She opened her mouth to speak, but her brother spoke first, and his words drove her own indignation right out of her mind.

"Jim's gonna stay with you tonight, hon, just in case this lunatic comes back. I'd do it myself, but—"

"I don't need anybody to stay with me." Wanting was a whole different thing, of course, but nothing was more pathetic, in her opinion, than a needy woman.

"You're kidding, right?" Peter asked. "There was a stranger in your house an hour ago, Caro. No way am I gonna leave you here alone."

She rolled her eyes. "The cops think I imagined it." She punctuated the words with a cutting glance toward Jimmy.

"Yeah, well, I don't. I'm your brother, hon. I know you better than that. Someone was here. If you won't let Jimmy stay, you can come back to my house and stay with us. Though I warn you, Mary's in a mood, and the kids are—"

She held up a hand. She loved her nieces and nephews, but honestly, six kids under one roof for an entire night was a little more than she felt up to handling right now. She turned to Jimmy. "I don't want to be a pain in the ass."

"I'm out of my apartment for a week. It's being repainted. I was gonna stay with your brother, but—well, hell, this would be a lot quieter."

"You don't strike me as the peace-and-quiet type."

He lowered his head, shook it slowly. "You think you'll sleep a wink tonight if you're here alone? Be honest. Do you?"

No, but she doubted she'd sleep a wink with him under the same roof, either.

When she didn't answer, the men took it as consent.

Peter said, "I'll run home and grab your bag. But your car—"

"Go with him," Caroline said. "Get your car and your bag, and come back."

"I don't like the idea of you being alone that long," Jimmy said. And he said it with a look in his eyes that seemed to suggest a whole lot more. "Ride with me—uh, us?"

"I think enough people have seen me in my comfort clothes," she muttered, glancing down at the sweatshirt with her ratty flannel robe and bare feet below it, thinking sorrowfully of her fuzzy warm slippers getting soaked in the backyard. But not as much as she was thinking this guy must be nuts to be looking at her as if he wanted to eat her alive, when she was dressed like a homeless person. A wet, bedraggled homeless person.

"So go change. We'll wait," Jimmy said.

She rolled her eyes and wondered why she was letting herself be led by males, something she'd vowed never to do again, ever. But in this case, it was caring, not control, that motivated it. At least, where her brother was concerned. She had no idea what kind of deranged sexual appetite was driving Jimmy Lipton. Maybe he had a fetish for sloppy, wet, older women. Either way, she supposed she could relax and let herself be taken care of, just this once.

"I'll change. Be right back."

She didn't meet either set of probing eyes as she turned and left the kitchen, but she felt them on her. They were wondering if she was too scared to go upstairs alone. And in fact, she was. But she wasn't scared enough to admit that, so she forced herself to march up the stairs and closed her bedroom door behind her, despite the goose bumps rising on her arms. But maybe fear wasn't the cause of the goose bumps. Maybe she had them because she was cold and wet.

As the apparition had been.

Hell. She peeled off Jimmy's hoodie and her flannel bathrobe and draped both of them over a chair. She pulled on a pair of jeans, then tugged her nightgown off over her head and added it to the pile of wet things. She opened her dresser and reached for a bra and one of her standard-issue oversize T-shirts. She had a drawer full of them. But she paused with her hand in midair, bit her lower lip, and wondered if she was losing her mind to be thinking about Jimmy Lipton the way she was. Oh, she didn't intend to *do* anything with him. He was way too young for that. Wasn't he? But she couldn't deny that his interest—if it was for real—felt good. And for some perverse reason, she wanted to feel more of that.

She pushed that drawer closed, opened another, and dug deep until she pulled out a tiny T-shirt. The kind she hadn't worn since the divorce but hadn't quite had the willpower to throw away. She pulled it on, grimacing at the snug fit and wondering just how bad it would look, then turned to the full-length mirror. Her eyebrows arched, and she muttered, "Wow," and turned to one side.

She'd lost weight since the divorce. Exercise helped with the stress and filled the loneliness, and with no one to cook for, she often forgot to eat. Not a healthy habit, but the results didn't look half bad. The baby T looked better on her than it ever had.

She headed to the bathroom off her bedroom and

ran a pick through her wet hair, which was already curling crazily, and scrunched in a palmful of mousse to keep it from frizzing when it dried. Just as an afterthought, she dabbed on some of the fragrance she'd bought on a whim weeks ago: vanilla.

She looked good. Maybe ghostly visitations agreed with her. Certainly got her blood flowing. Or maybe that was Jimmy. And with the primping, she'd forgotten to be afraid for a little while.

She went back downstairs, where the men waited in the living room, and they both stared at her body from head to toe as she descended. Jimmy was quiet, just looking, but his expression was purely transparent. He liked what he saw.

Peter not so much. "You've lost more weight, haven't you?"

She shrugged. "Maybe a little. I don't really keep track."

"I thought all women were obsessed with their scales," Jimmy said.

"What did you eat today? You been skipping meals again?"

"Well, I was having corn flakes when the drippy chick showed up. Sort of."

"Uh-huh. Cornflakes for dinner. You need a keeper."

"Had one. Unfortunately, I wasn't the only one he kept."

"Must be a freaking idiot," Jimmy muttered.

Peter swung his head around and speared him with his eyes.

"What? I'm just saying . . ." He stopped there, clearly embarrassed.

Secretly, Caroline warmed to the blatant compliment as she handed Jimmy his wet hoodie. His fingers stroked the back of her hand when he took it from her, and she was sure it hadn't been an accident.

Peter looked at her again, and she hurried to school her expression to one of bland disinterest but feared she'd been too slow. Frowning, Peter said, "Let's go. Caroline, you ride shotgun."

She grabbed a jacket of her own on her way to the front door. Peter reached it first and went out ahead of her. Jimmy caught the screen door as it swung in, then held it for her. She caught his eyes on the way past and wondered why she was torturing the poor guy with the tight little T-shirt and vanilla perfume. It wasn't as if this was going anywhere.

Ever.

CHAPTER 3

The kids were in bed, and Mary was nursing a glass of cola that, Caroline suspected, had more than cola in it, a box of Midol on the end table beside her. Her eyes looked puffy, and her blond hair was reminiscent of Albert Einstein's. She got up when Caroline came in to give her a hug.

"Honey, are you okay?"

"Yeah. Just had a little scare. I'm fine now. Sorry to drag your better half away in the middle of the night."

"Don't be silly. He was just watching baseball, anyway." She looked past Caroline to Peter. "So, did you find anything?"

"No, and neither did the cops. Jimmy's gonna spend the night over there, just in case the nut comes back."

"Oh." Mary looked at Jimmy and then at Caroline, and Caroline saw her noticing the T-shirt and wished she had zipped up her jacket. "Oh."

"I'll just grab my stuff and my keys," Jimmy said. "Be right back."

Caroline nodded and tried not to watch him walk away. She failed, but at least she tried.

"Are you sure you wouldn't rather stay here, hon?" Mary asked. "The kids are already in bed, and Jimmy's here, but you could take the guest room. I'm sure he'd take the sofa."

Caroline snapped her gaze back to Mary, since Jimmy's tight backside had rounded a corner out of sight anyway. "Yeah, I'm sure. I'm not letting some ghost drive me out of my house."

"Ghost?" Mary blinked, looking from Caroline to Peter, a question in her eyes.

Caroline pasted a smile on her face. "I'm being sarcastic, Mare. She was there, and then she wasn't, and there was no trace of her anyplace, that's all."

Mary was still staring at her, probing, questioning, maybe getting a little worried about her mental state.

"It seems everything is conspiring to make me give up that house," Caroline said, seeking to change the subject. "Shawn hasn't given me a nickel in three months, and it's getting tight."

"And your boyfriend has just about depleted your savings," Peter put in with a grimace. "Your taste in men is seriously deranged, little sister. Can't you find even one who's not a total loser?"

She averted her eyes, ashamed of the mess she'd made of her life. "Not so far. Anyway, if I can find the money to keep up the payments, I'm keeping that house. No wet woman peeking in the windows at me is going to make me give it up."

"Good for you," Mary said.

"You should let me get your money out of those two leeches," Peter said.

She pursed her lips. "I don't want it to get nasty, Peter."

"You're gonna lose your house, hon. It's *already* nasty."

Jimmy came back into the living room in time to hear that last bit, but he didn't comment on it, just held up his keys. He had a backpack slung over his shoulder. "Ready?"

"Yeah." She looked at her brother. "Stay out of it, Peter. I love you for caring, but I don't want to stir up trouble or hard feelings. Okay?"

He rolled his eyes but nodded.

"Thanks. 'Bye, Mary." She gave her sister-in-law another hug, then turned toward the door and headed out, not up to any further lecturing or advice. She was several feet ahead of Jimmy, heading for the car that had to be his, a cute forest green Jeep Wrangler, when she heard her brother say, "Watch out for her, Jim. Make sure she's safe."

"I guarantee it."

She rode back in the passenger seat of Jimmy Lipton's Wrangler, not sure what to say. She was alternating between being pissed at him for not backing up her story with the cops and tingling all over with sexual attraction.

"You were wishing I'd tell the cops I'd seen her, too, I'll bet."

His voice drew her eyes to his face, something she'd been deliberately avoiding. "Wouldn't you have been?"

"They would have just thought we were both nuts."

"At least I wouldn't have been the only one, then."

"Wouldn't have made a difference."

"Would to me."

He bit his lip, and it was sexy. Damn him.

"I'm sorry, okay? Cops don't investigate ghosts. I just didn't see what good it would have done."

"You could have at least told Peter."

"Peter believes you."

She sighed and lowered her gaze to her hands, folded in her lap.

"You look great, Caroline."

"Oh, right. Insincere flattery will fix it."

"It's not insincere. It's just a fact."

She pursed her lips. "Thanks."

"What, no reciprocation?" His tone was light, teasing.

"You know damn well you look great. You're supposed to look great, you're twenty-freaking-five."

"Still, it's nice to hear you say it out loud."

She rolled her eyes and turned to gaze out the window. "You're missing our turn."

"Yeah, well, we're not going straight back."

"We're not?"

"No." He kept going straight, then took the right that would lead them into the little town of Lakeside, Michigan.

"Well, do you mind telling me where we are going, then?"

"To Vincenzo's. You need to eat, and I could use a bedtime snack myself."

"Vincenzo's? I'm not dressed for Vincenzo's."

"They do takeout. You don't want to eat there, we'll just order a meal and take it back to Spook Central."

She would have argued, but she was damn hungry, and Vincenzo's was a local legend for everything from its Italian cuisine to its steaks. Besides, she got a shiver at the thought of returning to her house, and not just because of the apparition.

"And by the way," he added, "there's absolutely nothing wrong with the way you're dressed, except that it might distract the waiters."

She met his eyes again. Big mistake. The attraction was crackling between the two of them, and she was worried as hell about her ability to say no and mean it, should he try anything tonight. And she had a feeling he might. And then she wondered what woman in her right mind would be so worried about saying no to a hunk like this one, anyway.

"Let's eat there," she said. "Screw my attire."

"Atta girl."

Vincenzo's was a bad idea. She'd forgotten about the candlelit tables and soft, sexy music and the dark wood and red velvet, making the place seem intimate and erotic. Jimmy sat across from her, with the candle flame painting his face in light and shadow, its reflection dancing in his eyes, and she found herself pretending this was a real date, with a man who actually gave a damn about her.

Wouldn't that be a novel experience?

She'd ordered pork loin basted in strawberry sauce with a touch of curry that made it almost too succulent to bear. He had prime rib—his idea of a bedtime snack, apparently. And he insisted on tasting hers and on her tasting his. She didn't want dessert, so he ordered one, anyway, to share. He certainly made it easy for her to pretend this was a real date.

What the hell was he after? God knew it had to be something. Her experience with the male species had taught her that much, if nothing else. Men didn't ever do anything without an ulterior motive. Not for her, anyway. Maybe for some women but not for her.

She had three glasses of wine with her meal, trying to take the edge off her nerves and secretly wishing for whatever Mary had been drinking instead. Maybe he was only after some easy sex. Maybe that was it. If he was after money, he was going to be sadly disappointed.

"You seem awfully distracted," he said, breaking into her thoughts.

She glanced at him across the candlelit table, realizing he'd paid the check and there was nothing keeping them at the restaurant any longer. She'd zoned out on him. "Sorry. I was thinking."

"About?"

She pursed her lips. "Stuff."

"Ah, a woman of mystery. I like that."

Yeah, right now he liked everything about her. He was coming off a little too good to believe. Fortunately, she didn't. If he wanted a woman he could play—for whatever reason—he should have picked a younger one. The turnip truck she fell off, she thought, was currently rusting in a junkyard somewhere.

His hand slid over hers, where it rested on the table. "You don't have to be afraid to go back to the house, Caroline. I'm not gonna let anything happen to you."

Her heart went soft and mushy. Stupid heart. She tried to harden it back up again but was having trouble getting it past the stage of well-set Jell-O. He was that good.

"Thanks," she muttered. "That's really sweet of you to say. But I'm not scared."

"Then why are we still sitting here?"

She took her hand out from under his and used it to take the napkin out of her lap and toss it on the table. "Let's just get this out of the way, all right? I'm not going to have sex with you tonight."

"Okay." He put his napkin on the table, too. "So, you ready to go, then?"

Caroline sort of gaped at him, then clamped her jaw. That was it? That was his entire reaction? Okay? She filled her wineglass for the fourth time, emptying the bottle.

He got up and came around to hold her chair. She took her wineglass with her. Given the size of the tip Jimmy had left, she didn't think the waiter would call her on it. Jimmy held a hand very lightly at the small of her back as they wound their way around tables to the exit. He opened the Jeep's door for her. Good God, he was pouring it on. No male had manners this good.

She got in, buckled up, and sipped the wine, knowing damn good and well that she was breaking the open container law by drinking in the car, even though he was the one doing the driving. But damn, she needed bolstering.

Jimmy slid a CD into the slot, some hard-core band taking a shot at a ballad. It wasn't half bad. She sipped more wine.

By the time they arrived back at her house, she was pleasantly full, much closer to mellow, and just slightly light headed. Okay, maybe more than slightly. She kept feeling the urge to giggle and squelching it. Women her age did not giggle.

He took her arm when they walked toward the front door, and she leaned a little closer, acting on pure instinct accompanied by the knowledge that she wasn't very steady on her feet right then. Damn wine. He slid his arm around her waist. He didn't take it away when she turned to insert the key and pushed the door open.

He kept that arm around her as they moved inside, and with the door still open, he turned her to face him and kissed her. Just like that. No leading up to it, no asking permission. He just did it, and it was so sudden and so hot that she kissed him right back. And then some. Her arms twined, and her hips arched, and her mouth opened. By the time she started to come to her senses, he was using his tongue, holding her hard, flush against him, one arm anchoring her waist, one hand buried in her hair. And damn, it was good.

She willed herself to push him away, but she didn't want to, so that was as far as it got. She willed it, but she didn't actually do it.

I really should, though, she thought. And then she thought, *Why?*

He must have felt her hesitation, though, because he lifted his head, those sexy eyes blazing down into hers. "Don't think, Caroline. Just feel."

"I'm feeling. Believe me." Her words came out as whispers on broken, ragged breaths.

He smiled. "Me, too. I've wanted you for so long."

"But Jimmy, you're only—"

"You're thinking again."

She closed her eyes and wondered why the hell not indulge herself, just this once? They were both adults. She was a woman, a free, responsible, smart, independent woman. A woman who tended to fall from one lousy relationship to the next without much time in between. But this wasn't a relationship. This was just . . . this. So why the hell not?

Working up every nerve in her body, she said, "Then make me stop thinking."

He swore under his breath and kissed her again. Without breaking the kiss, he reached back to close the door. She heard the lock turn, and then he scooped her into his arms and carried her into the house, up the stairs. Carried her. She didn't think any man had ever carried her anywhere.

Oh, God, what was she doing?

Jimmy lowered her onto her bed and pushed her T-shirt up, running his hands over her breasts despite the bra that stood in the way. She tingled all over.

Oh, God, this would be good. *Please, let it be good*, she thought.

He pushed his hands inside the bra, tugged her breasts out the top, and brushed his fingers over her nipples a few times before squeezing and kneading them. And then he lowered his head to attack them with his mouth, one after the other, sliding his hands lower, over her belly, to the button fly of her jeans. He undid them and wandered inside, touched her, rubbed her.

Oh, yeah. It would be good.

He had her closer to orgasm than good old Brian had gotten her in their entire time together, closer than Shawn had in their entire marriage, and he wasn't even inside her yet. Damn, he knew his stuff. She wanted it to be good for him, too. Female pride dictated that. So she reached for his jeans, rubbed the sizable bulge in them, started working on the snap and zipper, but he covered her hand with his and stopped sucking long enough to kiss a path to her ear and whisper, "Not yet, baby. Let me take care of you first. Just relax. Relax and feel."

"Huh?"

He didn't take time to explain himself. Since when did any man want to take care of her first in bed? This just didn't compute.

Jimmy kissed his way back to her nipple and sucked it in. He deepened the thrust of his fingers and added a swirling and pressing of his thumb right where it counted. The sensations that roiled up in her body shut her mind up once and for all. She let go of inhibitions, of doubts, of thought, and moved against his hand, arching and pressing to tell him the way it felt best, and he paid attention, responding exactly the way she needed. She clasped his head with her hands, and he sucked harder, nipped and tugged and flicked his tongue over her nipples, and she heard herself whimper and cry as her body strained. *Let it happen, please let it happen,* she all but prayed. She was so close, so damn close, and so used to disappointment.

"Relax," he whispered around her breast. "I can do this all night, and I'm not stopping until you get there. So just relax. Don't rush."

In response to that assurance, she stopped trying to hurry, stopped straining for the peak, and just let him work her and work her. And when she started to shake, he intensified everything. Harder, deeper, faster. His teeth bit down a little harder, and she clasped his head so hard she thought she would crush his skull.

And then she was exploding, and he still didn't let

up. He kept going all the way to the very edge, pushing her, playing her, only easing back when the spasms started to ebb.

She came back to herself slowly, to find herself trembling and moaning as he curled onto the bed beside her, folded her into his arms, and held her warm and firm against him. He stroked her hair with one hand. "Now sleep."

She was so incredibly relaxed, so sated in every way, that she couldn't help but do exactly as he told her. Between the heavy meal and the wine and the shattering orgasm, her body was completely sated, warm, relaxed. She drifted to sleep right there, in Jimmy Lipton's arms.

And that was where she woke. Right there, snuggled up against him, her head on his chest, his arms wrapped tight around her, warmer and more cozy than she'd ever been in her life.

And mortified beyond belief. God, she'd had her first nonself-induced orgasm with a kid half her age. Okay, more than half, but still. And she hadn't even reciprocated. Oh, yeah, she was going straight to hell.

She lifted her head to find his eyes open and focused on her. He smiled, the sexiest sleepy smile she'd ever seen in her life, and her tummy tightened in pure animal lust. What the hell was happening to her? She'd *never* felt this kind of sexual attraction for a man. Never.

"Good morning, sexy," he said.

She turned her head slightly, sure she had morning breath. "I'm sorry, Jimmy."

"About what?"

Closing her eyes, she rolled onto her back and tugged the sheet up over her. "About last night, obviously."

"Why? Wasn't it good for you?"

"It was incredible." That came out as a whisper as her eyes drifted closed and her body heated all over again. But she popped her eyes open and attempted to speak in a normal tone. "I mean, of course, it was incredible. But I didn't—I mean, *you* didn't—"

"I will next time."

"That's why I'm apologizing. I mean, you should have, because there isn't going to be a next time."

"Don't hate me for saying so, but isn't that what you said about this time?"

He was teasing, smiling in a soft, sexy way while trailing his fingertips over her cheek. "I mean it, Jimmy. This—it can't happen again."

"Oh." He looked so disappointed she had to avert her eyes.

"I mean, it just doesn't make sense. What would people think?"

"I've never been much for living according to what other people think. I didn't think you were, either."

"Of course I am."

"Yeah? I don't know if that's true. You're dating that jerk Brian, and no one seems to think much of that choice."

"That's different."

"How?"

"Dating a man my own age, no matter how big a jerk he is, is socially acceptable. Dating a kid I used to sit for is not. God, I feel like one of those teachers you see on the news."

"I'm not a kid, Caroline."

She looked at him and knew he was right. He wasn't a kid. He was a man, inside and out, and so far, he seemed to be twice the man Brian or Shawn had ever been. *Seemed to be* being the operative phrase, of course.

Because maybe she was just seeing what she wanted to see, or worse, what he wanted her to see. And come to think of it, how the hell did he know about Brian, anyway? Damn her brother and his big fat mouth.

He leaned in and kissed her, and her entire body went into meltdown. Thoughts dissolved. She heated and trembled when he pulled her hips against his and whispered that he was throbbing for her. When he finally lifted his head, her heart spoke before her mind could stop it. "Well . . . maybe . . . just once more."

"*At least* once more." He kissed her again, then rolled out of bed, wearing only his shorts. She didn't remember him undressing. In spite of herself, she couldn't help but lie there and watch him pull his jeans on and wonder how the hell she'd ended up half naked in bed with a guy who looked like he did. Flat belly, hard thighs, ass to die for, and a chest that made her loins ache. Damn, he was hot.

What the hell did he want with her?

"I'm gonna hit the shower," he said. "And, uh, you might want to get dressed. Much as I hate to suggest that."

She frowned. "Why?"

"I think your brother just pulled in."

"Shit!" She dove out of bed, never mind that she was stark naked from the waist up and her jeans were undone and slept in. She started grabbing up her clothes, then panicked at the thought of Peter seeing her in the same things she'd had on last night. But there was no time. She did up her jeans and was struggling to fasten the bra behind her back when she realized Jimmy was still standing there, staring at her. She looked up, saw the look in his eyes. He looked at her as if he *liked* looking at her, and that made her go warm all over, even though she doubted it was for real.

But hell, he was consistent, if nothing else. You'd think he would have slipped by now. Revealed something of the toad behind the prince mask. But so far, he hadn't.

You don't suppose he could be for real, do you?

She frowned as she tried to answer the question her mind had posed.

"Caroline, babe? Your brother?" Jimmy waved a hand before her eyes as if trying to wake a hypnosis victim.

She snapped out of it. "Will you get out of my bedroom, already? You want my brother to go home for his shotgun?"

He grinned at her and walked into the bathroom. When the door closed behind him, she finished fastening her bra and yanked a T-shirt from a drawer, leaving her baby T on the floor but kicking it and Jimmy's discarded shirt under the bed on her way out of the bedroom. She ran down the hall to the spare bedroom, yanked the covers back, and rolled back and forth on the bed a few times to make it look slept in.

Peter was pounding on the door now. Hell. She headed into the hall, glancing back into her bedroom on the way past, just to see if any telltale signs remained. The bed was a mess, but that wasn't really a dead giveaway, was it?

Trotting down the stairs, she spotted Jimmy's back-pack on the floor near the door. She ducked, grabbed it, raced back upstairs and into her room, yanked open the bathroom door to drop it inside, and froze there. He was out of the shower, dripping and naked, and the best thing she'd ever looked at in her entire life.

She actually felt *dizzy,* he looked so good. God damn, the man was a freaking hallucinogenic.

She swore, dropped the bag, and backed out. Then she tried to wipe the lust off her face and hurried back downstairs to open the door for her brother.

Peter looked her up and down and said, "What the hell did Jimmy do to you last night, sis?"

Her jaw dropped, and she stood there searching for words.

"You never sleep this late." He brushed past her, heading for the kitchen. "Got any coffee made yet?"

"Uh, no, I was just about to put on a pot." Relief almost made her limp as she followed him to the kitchen. She passed a mirror and caught a glimpse of herself. Damn. Her hair was all over, her eyes were glassy—almost sparkling—and her cheeks were so damn pink she didn't recognize herself. It showed, dammit. How could Peter not see it? She was practically radiating sexual satisfaction.

She smoothed her hair with her hands and went into the kitchen, busied herself making coffee and keeping her back to her brother while he sat in a chair at the table.

"Where is Jimmy, anyway? He's usually up at the crack of dawn."

"In the shower, I guess." Even as she said it, his footsteps were coming down the stairs, and then he was in the kitchen, and she glanced his way. He met her eyes and smiled, and she wished he wouldn't, because it was the kind of a smile that spoke volumes. It said, *I made you come last night, and I'm going to do it again.* Where did he get off, giving her that kind of smile in front of her brother? And why did it make her knees weak?

" 'Morning, Caroline. 'Morning, Peter."

" 'Morning," Peter said. "Anything interesting happen last night?"

She gaped, but Jimmy had more sense than she did at the moment. "Not another peep from the intruder." Then he glanced at Caroline. "Thanks for the use of the guest room. I made up the bed so nice and neat no one would ever know it had been slept in."

No you didn't, she thought. *I messed up the bed so anyone would know it had been slept in. Please, Peter, don't go upstairs and check, please, please, please.*

"You know, sis, staring at the coffee pot isn't going to make it brew any faster."

She pasted what she hoped was a casual smile on her face and turned to face her brother. "I'm just dying for a cup, that's all. Maybe I'll run upstairs and shower myself, and it'll be ready by the time I come back."

"Okay, kid," Peter said. "I brought my toolbox and some new locks. Jim and I will grab a cup and get to work on installing them while you do whatever it is you women do in the shower that takes so long."

"Cool. Help yourself to some breakfast if you want."

"Right. I imagine you've got a regular feast full of possibilities in your fridge."

She knew he was exaggerating and rolled her eyes. "I've got . . . stuff."

Peter looked at Jim. "Eggs, probably. A couple of yogurts, some soy milk, and a box of microwave popcorn. Bet you five bucks."

"I'll take that bet, as I know for a fact she has corn flakes."

She closed her eyes and left the room, wondering how she could ever be around her brother again without giving it away. But maybe not. Maybe he was dense enough not to see it. He was male, after all.

Mary wasn't, though. She would see it. God, what was she going to do about Mary?

After the locks were installed, the guys said they had some errands to run. She didn't ask what kind, didn't really care, but she did notice that Jimmy left his bag behind. Which suggested he would be returning tonight. Which made her want to die from the mingled apprehension, excitement, nervousness, and heat that invaded her at the very thought.

She didn't have much time to dwell on it, though, because Brian was knocking on her door twenty minutes after Jimmy and Peter had left.

Brian. Her *boyfriend*. The one who never came to her house, because he was "more comfortable on his own turf." She always went to his place. And they never went anywhere else.

Like Vincenzo's, for example.

Whoa girl. Comparing the two was ridiculous. Jimmy was just sex. He couldn't possibly be interested in anything more than that, unless he had some ulterior motive she hadn't figured out yet. Brian was interested in sex and money. Technically, that didn't qualify as a boyfriend, either, did it?

So wait a sec. If she was going to be used, either way . . .

Brian pounded again.

"I'm coming, already." Caroline crossed the room and opened the door. "This is a surprise. What are you doing here?"

"What, I can't pay my girl a visit now and then?"

"Uh, well, up to now you never have."

He sighed, lowered his head. "Yeah, I know. I've just been busy."

"Yeah, it's been a brutal six months for you." She didn't try to hide the sarcasm in her voice. He didn't hear it, though.

He looked past her, around the house, as if he expected to see something, but there was nothing to see. "So, you gonna let me in?"

"Sure. C'mon in." She stepped aside and held the door, watched him as he entered. He was a big guy, his hair a little too long. She couldn't help mentally comparing him to Jimmy as she watched him walk through the house and plop down on the couch. No comparison, though. Jimmy was lean and tight where Brian was bulky and had the beginnings of a beer belly. Jimmy's hair was short and neat, which she liked better than Brian's sloppy, careless look. Jimmy even smelled better.

Her tummy clenched in pure sexual appreciation when she thought about the way Jimmy smelled, and she bit her lip until she tasted blood to get it to stop.

Brian glanced up at her. "What are you smiling about? Just glad to see me?"

Not particularly, she thought. "Did you happen to bring the money you owe me?" she asked.

"Hon, I told you, things are tight right now."

"Things are tight for me, too, Bri. Too tight. I could lose the house." He sighed, and she saw the beginnings of irritation creeping into his eyes, so she decided to change the subject. Getting money out of him would be like trying to bleed a rock, anyway. "So, if not that, then what did bring you by?"

"I wanted to see you. Thought maybe we could go out tonight, do something, you know, make some plans."

She frowned. "We could have done that on the phone."

"Damn, woman, you're downright cold this morning."

"Yeah, well, I have reason to be." He was up to something. No question.

He nodded. "I heard the cops were out here last night."

She raised her brows and wondered what else he'd heard. Maybe that a stranger's car had been parked in her driveway all night long? Sure he had. He was best buds with the biker at the end of the block. Hell, she was surprised he hadn't shown up sooner. And she wasn't stupid. He wasn't as concerned about losing her as he was about losing the money train he'd been riding.

Sadly for him, she'd figured out that she could do a hell of a lot better.

"So, what happened?" he asked.

"Had an intruder poking around. No big deal. They took off, and the cops didn't find anything. Peter changed all the locks this morning."

"Oh. You'll have to give me a new key, then."

She frowned at him. Not a hint of concern for her, not even an "Are you okay?" or "Were you scared?" Much less an offer of help. God forbid he put himself out. Just a request—no, a demand—for a key. "I don't have an extra one yet."

"Really? 'Cause every lock I've ever seen comes with two keys."

"Yeah, and I gave the extra ones to Peter."

"Instead of me?"

"When I call my brother, Bri, he answers the phone. Or if he doesn't, he calls me back the minute he gets the message. If I need him, he's here for me. I've never been able to say the same about you."

He didn't look amused. But he digested her words and seemed to decide to ignore them. "So, what about tonight? You wanna go out?"

"You know what? I really don't."

"You don't?" He couldn't seem to process that. She'd never said no to him. About anything.

And that, she thought, *is part of what's wrong with me. God, what did I ever see in this idiot that I would agree to anything he asked just to keep him coming around?* Loneliness, she guessed, and the certainty that she'd never find a man who wouldn't use her. So she'd settled.

But today, she wasn't content to settle. At least Jimmy made an effort.

Not to mention he could get her off.

Damn. She caught herself smiling again, wiped it off her face, and tried to focus on her guest.

Brian got up off the couch slowly and stood there, looking down at her really hard. "This have anything to do with the stranger who spent the night here last night?"

She licked her lips. *Aha! I knew it. That's the only reason he showed up.* After a moment's thought, she said, "I'll tell you what it has to do with. I've come to the realization, Brian, that I can do a whole lot better. I'm getting the feeling that you're just using me for my money, and I don't deserve that."

"How can you say that? I'm not using you!"

"Yeah? Well, if you decide you want to prove it, pay me back, and ask me out again with the understanding that there won't be any more cash exchanging hands here. Not a penny. Not ever."

His eyes narrowed. "You are one tough bitch, you know that?"

She almost smiled. She'd never been called tough before, and she felt rather proud of herself for earning it. "I've got stuff to do, Bri. Call me next week if you find the money to pay me back—all of it—and if you still want to go out after that, you're buying."

He turned on his heel and slammed out of the house so angrily that the windows rattled. He spun his tires when he left, too.

Well, hell. Good riddance.

"What took you so long?" a voice whispered.

She turned around, searching the area behind her, but there was no one there. And yet the voice—a female voice—had been vivid. Real. Audible. Not in her head, in her *ears*. "Mary? Is that you?" Dumb question. It hadn't sounded like Mary, it had sounded like someone much younger.

No one answered. She shivered and went to pick up

the telephone, flipped through the memory to find the number for the real estate agent she'd used to purchase the place, and hit the button. She had questions, and they were big ones.

She still didn't have any answers several hours later, when she and Jimmy drove over to Pete and Mary's for a Sunday night barbecue with the kids. It was something she did nearly every Sunday during the spring and summer and well into the fall. She'd brought Brian once, but that had been disastrous. He'd spent the entire afternoon sitting on his ass, slugging back beer, and scowling at the kids. No wonder her family hated him.

She probably should have taken their advice way sooner. That thought came with a grimace as she sat at an umbrella-shaded table enjoying the warmest day April had yet offered and sipping an iced tea while her nieces and nephews raised hell in the backyard. The grimace was because she was imagining what her family's advice would be where Jimmy was concerned. They'd be scandalized.

And why was she even thinking that way? This was not a relationship. It was one night on third base, and she was making way too much out of it.

Ten-year-old Kevin was tossing a football back and forth with seven-year-old Katie. Kristen, who'd just turned four, was sitting on Jimmy's back with her legs around his waist and her arms around his neck in what looked like a choke-hold, while Jimmy flipped burgers and said something that made the little girl laugh hilariously.

"He's great with the kids, isn't he?" Mary said. Krissie, her two-year-old, was on her lap, a bundle of golden ringlets and chubby cheeks. "They all adore him."

Caroline dragged her eyes off Jimmy, realizing belatedly that they'd been glued to him way too often since they'd arrived. But even as she did, he glanced back at her, as if he could feel her looking, and gave her one of those smiles that made her insides start quivering.

She chose not to respond directly to Mary's comment. "Where are the twins, anyway?"

"Inside, probably on the phone or the Net or both. Or more than likely, fighting over the phone or the Net or both. Kyle and Kenny are like oil and water these days. They'll be out when the food's ready, though."

"Thirteen isn't the most sociable age, I guess," Caroline said.

"No, not really. But they love Jimmy, too. Hell, I don't know why we didn't think to invite him for Sunday dinner sooner. He really fits."

Caroline looked at her sister-in-law. "Why didn't you?"

"Well, I didn't want you think it was a fix-up. You know, didn't want it to be awkward."

"Hell, Mary, I wouldn't have thought that. At his age, I mean—"

Mary waved a hand as if brushing off Jimmy's youth. "Doesn't seem to bother him any."

"What's that supposed to mean?"

Mary just smiled and sipped her tea. "Hey, guys, the womenfolk are starving over here. How close are we to being fed?"

Peter looked back at her. "Five minutes. Can you last that long?"

"Well, there's a slim chance." She got up. "Let's get the salads and set the table. Maybe you can shame the twins into helping. God knows they won't listen to me." As Caroline followed her inside, she kept talking. "I take it Jimmy's staying at your place again tonight?"

"Um . . . I . . ."

"I just noticed he didn't bring his stuff back with him. And I know the apartment won't be ready for him for a few more days, at least."

"Oh."

She opened the fridge, taking out salads, condiments, and hamburger buns and handing them off to Caroline one by one. "Do you mind having him there?"

"No."

"And what about Brian?"

"Brian's . . . um . . . well, I told him I wouldn't see him until he paid me back in full. And we both know that's not going to happen."

Mary turned with a dish in both hands, shoving the fridge door closed with her hip. "You ditched him? And you tell me this now, when my hands are too full to hug you?" Her smile was huge. "I'm so proud of you, Caro!"

"Yeah, well, you shouldn't be. It took me way too long."

"Maybe you just needed the right motivation."

Before she could even begin to guess what Mary meant by that, the door from the backyard opened, and Jimmy poked his head in, saw Caroline with her arms full of supplies for the meal, and made a beeline for her to begin taking items out of her hands. Even as he did, he called, "Boys, get your butts out here and pitch in, or you'll handle cleanup on your own."

The stampede of two pairs of feet down one set of stairs was almost deafening. "Hey, we didn't know you were coming, Jimmy!"

"Yeah, you should have told us sooner." The two gangly teens rapidly relieved Mary and Jimmy of everything they'd been carrying and took the lot of it out to the backyard.

Caroline lifted her brows. "Sure. They never get that excited when their beloved *aunt* comes to visit."

"Ah, they're just complacent. You're here every Sunday," Mary said. "Jimmy's a novelty."

Yeah, in more ways than one, Caroline thought. But she grabbed a dish of coleslaw the boys had missed and went back outside. Jimmy held the door for her and then walked close beside her. He sat next to her at the table. He paid attention to her as no one ever had, making sure she had tried every dish, refilling her iced tea glass when it got low, handing her a napkin just when she'd been needing one.

The guy was amazing.

And her sister-in-law was noticing all over the freaking place, damn her. Peter, of course, was oblivious.

They were driving home later, and she was trying really hard to ignore the female part of her that was practically singing all the way. So, he was great with the kids. So, her brother and sister-in-law adored him. So, he was attentive and polite and helpful and funny and smart and just fun to be with. So what? None of that mattered, because this was just sex, and there was no way in hell a guy like him—if he was for real—could be interested in her for anything . . . more.

"I had a ball today," he said. "You guys do that every Sunday?"

"Pretty much, at least during the warm months."

"What would it take to score a standing invitation, do you think?"

She swung her head toward him. "You'd be willing to do that every Sunday?"

"I'd pay to do that every Sunday."

Caroline frowned, searching his face for signs of a lie but finding none. He looked really blissed-out. "Don't you get the chance to do stuff like that with your family?"

"Tommy lives on the West Coast now. Still at UCLA. Mom's in a nursing home about fifty miles away." There was real regret in his voice and on his face as he went on. "Alzheimer's. I took care of her as long as I could, but it got too bad. She needed someone with her twenty-four seven, and I'd have to work twenty-four seven to afford that kind of care."

"I'm sorry, Jimmy. I didn't know."

"It's a bitch. I don't like her being that far away. There are three homes closer, but this one was the best, and I wanted her to have the best."

"Do you see her often?"

"Twice a week without fail, three times when I can manage it." He sighed. "She's beyond knowing I'm there, or so the staff tell me. But I like to think she knows, somewhere way down deep."

Add another notch to Jimmy's list of pluses. He loved his mother. Good grief, was the man even human?

"What about your dad?" she asked.

"He died two years ago. Cancer."

"God."

He shrugged as if it were of little consequence, and she thought there was more there, something deeper to that part of his story, but she didn't ask. He changed the subject, turning her own questions on her.

"How about your parents?"

"Retired, living in Florida, happy as clams. We visit them in the winter, and they come up here for a few weeks in the summer. It's all good."

"I'm glad to hear that. So we got off the subject, didn't we?"

"What subject was that?"

"Me wrangling a standing invitation to your family's Sunday barbecues."

She smiled at him in spite of herself. "I think all you'd have to do is ask. Everyone adores you."

"Really? Everyone?"

He said it with an intense look, and she had to look away. She didn't answer. She was too busy kicking herself, because she was actually starting to believe he was for real. And believing that was insanely dangerous. No guy was as good as this one seemed. It just didn't happen.

"Hmm. No answer. But that's okay," he said. He reached across the seat to trail his fingers along the side of her neck, and his touch gave her chills right to her toes. "I fully intend to see to it that you adore me, too, before the night is out."

She closed her eyes and tried not to hear her body whispering to her brain, *Hot damn.*

CHAPTER 5

It was late when they returned from Pete and Mary's, and the way Jimmy had been looking at her all the way home had her pulse racing long before they pulled into the driveway.

He got out of the car and came around to her side before she managed to get out herself. He took her by the hand and tugged her to her feet. She closed the car door behind her, and the next thing she knew, his arms were around her, her back pressed to the Jeep, his body pinning her there.

"I've had a hell of a time keeping my hands off you today." His hands proved his words by running up her sides from her hips to her waist and back again.

"I'm glad you managed. I'm not sure what my brother would think."

"We're going to have to find out, eventually." He said it as he was lowering his head to kiss her, but she was shocked enough to turn her head aside.

"What is that supposed to mean?"

He took her chin with one finger and gently turned her head back to face him again. "Come on, Caroline. You didn't think this was just a fling, did you?"

Well, duh, she thought. "Of course I thought it was just a fling."

He blinked as if his feelings were hurt but seemed to cover it quickly. "Is that . . . what you want it to be?"

"Jimmy, that's all it can be."

He lowered his head for a moment, let out all his breath. Then he inhaled and looked her in the eye. "Then it's gonna be the best fling you ever had. And the only one you'll never forget."

Oh, hell, now he was ambitious. And not just the ordinary, I'm-gonna-impress-her-in-bed sort of ambitious, but something above and beyond that. It was more like an I'm-gonna-be-the-best-you-ever-had-or-ever-will variety. And she was feeling pretty selfish, because she couldn't wait to see how close he would come. Or how many times she would. And all without even dropping him a crumb in return. Yeah, she felt mean and cruel, but dammit, she wasn't about to leap into an actual relationship with a guy this much younger than her, one whose motives were still unclear. Not as many times as she'd been hurt.

She had to keep her distance here. She had to keep her head involved and her heart in the clear. Her body was already down for the count, so that didn't even bear debate. He had her there.

"Is that okay with you?" he asked.

She'd lost track of the question. Oh, right. Was it okay with her if he was the fling she would never forget? "It's a pretty big promise."

"You know I'm gonna keep it."

She smiled slowly. "Damn, I hope so."

He kissed her then, right there, up against the Jeep, and it was raw and hungry and urgent. His hands kneaded her backside, and she arched her hips against his. Then he slid his hands down the backs of her thighs and pulled them up around his waist. Holding her that way, still kissing her to within an inch of sanity, he carried her into the house. He made it to the staircase and no further, just lowered her down there on the third step and started undressing her, hurrying so much he was clumsy. If she hadn't known better, she'd have believed he was shaking. And maybe he was.

God, she was. When he pushed her blouse open and down her shoulders, bending to nuzzle between her breasts, she braced her arms on the step behind her, arching her back. He pushed the bra straps down, then the lace cups, baring her breasts, kissing and sucking them until she was shivering with pleasure.

"Jimmy," she whispered. "God, Jimmy."

He slid his hands lower, unfastened her jeans, and pushed them down. She lifted her hips up to help and kicked them off her legs. Her panties followed, and then he was sliding down her body, kissing her all the way; her belly, her thighs, and then in between. And when his tongue went to work on her there, she moaned and threw her head back. Her fingers tangled in his hair, her entire body shuddering with every flick of his tongue. He played her, God, he played her like a master, and she prayed he wouldn't stop. Not until . . . and then he was pushing her over the edge, and she screamed his name over and over as her entire body erupted in spasms of mind-numbing ecstasy.

Gently, he kissed his way back up her body, paying extra attention to the crook of her neck, which made her shiver even harder. She was floating in a state of sensual bliss as he scooped her up in his arms and carried her to the bedroom. He laid her down again there on the bed and quickly undressed to join her there. And the moment he pulled her close and started kissing her, the passion she'd thought was spent began to build anew.

He took his time, appreciating every part of her with his hands, his fingers, his lips. He kissed her earlobes and whispered that she was incredible, and beautiful, and that she drove him wild with wanting her. And then he pulled her on top of him and slid himself inside her, and everything in her seemed to catch fire. She braced her hands on his shoulders and moved with him, over him, taking him deeper each time, moving faster. He clutched her hips and thrust up into her, his pace getting faster, more urgent. Locked together, they moved in unison as the flames built higher, and there was no room in her mind for thought or logic. Only feeling, only sensation, only passion. And when she came this time, he did, too, holding her and driving himself deep and then pulsing there.

She collapsed on his chest, and he wrapped his arms around her and cradled her, kissing her hair.

She had never felt so cherished in her entire life. And if this was a fling, then she was a blushing virgin. It wasn't. She knew it wasn't. And the knowledge terrified her. She tried to chase her fears away and just enjoy the sensation of falling asleep contented and safe in his arms.

• • •

"Now, remember, Pete," Jimmy said in the sternest tone he could come up with. "No matter what, you do not tell Caroline about this." He'd spent the entire morning with Peter, and the whole time, he'd been hoping his feelings for the man's sister were not written all over his face.

But last night had been beyond anything he'd ever known before. Better than he had even imagined. And he'd imagined it a lot.

"I'm not gonna tell her," Peter said. "I gave you my word. I just don't know why. She wouldn't be mad."

"Yes, she would."

Pete rolled his eyes. "Okay, she probably would. But she should be grateful instead."

"Yeah, well, I don't want her gratitude."

Peter stared hard at him. "I've pretty much figured that out."

"Figured what out?"

Peter shrugged and nodded toward the camera with the zoom lens that was currently sitting in the front seat of the Jeep, between him and Jimmy. "You knew her ex was cheating on his new wife. You knew where, and you knew when. Clearly, you've been checking into this for a while."

Jimmy nodded. "Well, I am a PI, after all."

"Don't give me that bullshit, pal."

He sighed. "Okay. I heard you and Mary talking about how far behind he was on the money he owes her for the business and her share of their house, and the fact that he transferred the title of their vacation cottage on the lakeshore to avoid having to pay her anything for that. It burns me. I thought maybe I could help. That's all."

"And being a PI by trade, you knew how to go about it."

"We show good old Shawn these photos and tell him he can pay up or we'll send copies to his wife. He'll pay up. Then we'll give him the negatives and all and forget we ever had them."

"Right. And it's not really illegal," Peter said.

"It's only blackmail if you're extorting money that isn't rightfully yours. All we're doing is pressuring him to pay what he owes."

Peter nodded. "Got all that. But there's more going on here, isn't there?"

"Like what?"

"You like my sister."

"Sure, I like her. What's not to like? She's a nice person."

"No, I mean, you *like* my sister."

Jim bought some time to form an answer by focusing on finding a parking spot at the twenty-minute-photo shop. But when he shut the Jeep's engine off, Peter was still waiting. He drew a breath. "Would that piss you off a hell of a lot, Pete?"

"It would depend. You're a lot younger than her. I guess I'd do the old-fashioned thing and demand to know your intentions. You gonna date her till she starts to show signs of age and then ditch her for a fresher model? You gonna use her and break her worse than she's already been broken? 'Cause I gotta tell you, Jim, she can't handle a lot more of that. And I'd have to kick your ass for it."

Jim sighed and lowered his head. "I can't predict the future, Pete, but I can tell you I'm not playing here. I'm serious about her."

"And how about her? Where's she in all this?"

"Scared shitless, I think."

Peter pursed his lips, then lowered his head and shook it. "Yeah, well, she's been burned. She's smart to be gun-shy. Damn, Mary's gonna have a freaking conniption over this."

Caroline was working on some accounts in the study when her next visitor arrived. She opened the door, and Mary raised a hand in the air, saying, "High five! You go, girl."

Caroline high-fived her sister-in-law but had no idea what she was being congratulated for.

"What's going on, Mare?"

"Oh, come *on*. Don't play coy with me, sis. Everyone in town saw you with Jimmy at Vincenzo's the other night. They said he looked at you like he wanted to eat you alive. And then I get this call from Brian saying there's something wrong with you, and I'd better check in. You ditched his sorry ass! Which I already knew. So clearly, you're messed up. I say it's long overdue. But don't you even *try* to tell me this didn't have something to do with Jimmy Lipton. Don't even!"

"Mary—"

"I mean, I had my doubts until I saw the two of you together at the barbecue yesterday. My God, he's clearly nuts about you. It's written all over his face. So, what's been going on with you two? I want details." Mary took her hand and tugged her out the door.

Oh, hell, Caroline thought. *She knows. She's onto me. I knew damn well I couldn't hide it for long.* "Where the hell are we going?"

"Oh, honey, we're going shopping. You've been on the shelf wearing widow's rags long enough."

"I would hardly call jeans and T-shirts widow's rags."

"Well, I would." She opened the car door, and Caroline got in reluctantly.

Mary closed it and ran around to the driver's side, started the engine, and backed up. "First stop, Victoria's Secret," she said, grinning from ear to ear as she hit the gas.

Caroline lowered her head and groaned. God, how was she ever going to live this down? But then she thought about modeling some ultra-sexy lingerie for Jimmy, and suddenly, she got warm all over. Damn, she had it bad.

By the time her sister-in-law had finished with her, the afternoon was waning, and she was loaded down with pink boxes and bags, Mary's treat. Caroline had managed to get through the trip without admitting to more than a slight and possibly mutual attraction between her and Jimmy but she thought Mary could see right through her. She silently vowed to pay Mary back for the piles of sexy lingerie just as soon as she could. She dumped the stuff on the sofa and moved to the phone, which was ringing off the hook. The caller ID showed Case Realty and the number, and she reached for the phone, relieved. She'd left a detailed message about the wet lady and Jimmy's claim that she'd been showing up there for thirteen years and demanded to know why that little fact hadn't been disclosed before she'd bought the place.

She smiled as she picked up the phone. A couple of nights with a hunk certainly had done wonders for her inner strength, not to mention her self-esteem. She used to hate confrontation. Now she felt like shouting, "Bring it on!"

But she settled for a polite "Hello?"

"Caroline, it's Sharon, your broker. Listen to me, whatever you do, just listen."

"I'm listening. Fill me in, Sharon. Seems there are things about this house you never told me. Including some kind of apparition. Makes me wonder what else there is about this house that you didn't tell me before I bought it."

Sharon took a deep breath. "Just this. That James Lipton has been conniving and conspiring to get that place back ever since his parents sold it."

Caroline blinked twice as the words sank into her brain like shards of ice, chilling her slowly from her head to her heels. "What?"

"Look, a few other owners *have* seen some kind of ghostly-looking woman lurking around. Then they get scared and sell, and he shows up almost immediately, with a low-ball offer to buy the place back. It's him, Caroline. It has to be him. He's probably got some love-sick girl working with him to drive people away so he can get the place back."

"But why the hell would he want to?"

"You'll have to ask him. But I'm telling you, Caroline. Don't trust this guy. He's up to something. I guarantee it."

Caroline hung up the phone and closed her eyes. Pain, her old friend, settled over her like a shroud and relaxed as if it had never been gone. It was familiar, and yet she'd let herself believe she'd got rid of it forever. Fool. She was a stupid, blind fool.

Another man had played her. And she'd let him, believed that a young, gorgeous, incredible lover like Jimmy Lipton could really be interested in her. She was kind of pathetic, wasn't she? She looked over at the boxes and bags on the sofa and thought she'd be able to pay her sister-in-law back sooner than she'd planned. Tomorrow, right after she returned every last bit of it.

CHAPTER 6

Jim stood at Caroline's door, wondering if he'd somehow stepped into an alternate dimension. She was pale, and he thought her eyes looked a little red, as if maybe she'd been crying or something. He wondered if she'd been crying over him, then told himself that was stupid. She didn't even *care* about him yet. To her, this was nothing but a fling, and yeah, he hoped to change that, but it was too soon, and she'd been too badly burned.

So, what was wrong with her, and why was she standing in the doorway as if she had no intention of letting him in?

"What's wrong?" he asked, because it was the most applicable of all the questions swirling through his mind. He could feel the tension emanating from her in waves, and not the good kind, either.

"I don't want you here tonight, Jimmy. Go back to my brother's."

Jim thought he took the blow well, though he felt it right to his gut. "You gonna tell me why?"

She lowered her head, saying nothing.

"Caroline, what happened?"

She drew a breath, lifted her head, and met his eyes. "A lot. You made me feel like I was worth more than Shawn or Brian, more than jeans and T-shirts. If someone like you could want me, then—then hell, I felt like I could do anything."

"You can. And you are. And—hell, Caroline, what changed?"

"It's kind of sad, really, that I let my self-esteem get so trampled that I needed validation from a hunk to get it back. But that's what happened. It didn't take much. I don't think it was ever really gone, just dormant." She shrugged and met his eyes, and he ached when he saw unshed tears in hers. "The funny thing is, it didn't go back to sleep on me, even when I found out it was all a lie."

"What was a lie?"

"You. You thought you could use me to get what you wanted. And I deserve better than that, and you know what? I'm done settling for less than I deserve. In a way, I guess I ought to be thanking you. If nothing else, you shook me out of my state of apathy and self-doubt. So thanks. And good-bye."

She closed the door before he could utter another word, and Jim stood there feeling as if he'd just been struck between the eyes with a mallet. What the hell had gotten into her?

And where did she get off accusing him without even telling him what it was she thought he'd done, much less giving him a chance to defend himself?

"Screw this," he muttered, and strode back to his Jeep to drive to Peter's.

Caroline expected the phone call from Mary, asking her what Jimmy was doing back at their place. She'd been trying to come up with an answer that would satisfy her sister-in-law without really telling her anything. *None of your damn business* came to mind, but that would be kind of harsh. She was still struggling for an answer, and Mary was still shooting questions through the telephone line. What she didn't expect was for her brother to jump into the conversation halfway through. She winced when she heard him say, "Give me the phone, Mary. Let me talk to her."

"Mary?" Caroline whispered. "Peter knows about this?"

"Not from me, he doesn't," Mary said. "Here, talk to your brother."

Then, "Caro, what's going on?"

"Pete, hon, I love you, but this isn't any of your business." There. That ought to do it, and it wasn't even all that harshly delivered.

"Is it that loser Brian again? You haven't decided to take him back, have you?"

"No, and I'm not going to." She'd been finished with Brian for several weeks now, she realized. She'd just been too damned lethargic to do anything about it. Half sleepwalking through her own life. Until Jimmy the hunk came along with a sexy wake-up call. Damn, she wished it could have been real.

"What, then?" her brother demanded.

"Look, I've decided I don't need a man to make me

feel worthwhile." And inside, her mind was whispering that she wasn't sure she honestly believed that. Because, damn, she wished Jimmy were there, holding her in those strong arms and making her believe the lie right now. It was dark and lonely, and she craved human contact. The carnal, sweaty, panting kind of human contact she'd only had with him.

"Well, yeah, that goes without saying. You don't need a man. You never did, hon. What you have to get clear on is separating what you need from what you want."

"I only know what I don't want. And I don't want to be used."

"Yeah, so Jim told me. And what is it you think he's using you for?"

"To get this house back. And I'm not saying more than that, only that I have it on good authority he's been trying to get it back for years."

"Well, shit, I knew that. But hon, he never put the moves on any of the former owners to accomplish it."

She blinked, totally taken aback. One simple sentence that did no more than state the obvious, and she was speechless.

"Hasn't it occurred to you that just because he's always wanted the house back doesn't necessarily mean he can't want you, too? Does it have to be one or the other, sis? Could he possibly be genuinely interested in you?"

"I . . . no. God, why would he be?"

"Aha. So all this shit you've been spouting about rediscovering your self-esteem is bull, then."

"What do you mean?"

"You don't think he could want you just for you.

You're so used to being used by the men in your life—present company excepted, of course—that you can't comprehend how any man could genuinely want you. Can you?"

She held the phone away from her ear and blinked down at it for a long moment. Her brother was right. That rotten, insightful, meddling dick was right, damn him. It hadn't even occurred to her that Jimmy's feelings might be genuine. Because she couldn't see what there was about her that could attract a man like him.

Damn. She hadn't experienced a miraculous overnight rebirth at all. She'd only been angry and hurt. What if he did want her? What if he really was for real? A decent, caring, sexy, wonderful man who actually gave a damn about her, and she'd just thrown him out of her life and slammed the door in his face?

Well, she shouldn't be surprised. Her ability to screw up her life was second to none. She should get some kind of freaking award.

Something moved in her peripheral vision, and she glanced up to see the wet lady moving slowly across the back lawn. And that was all she needed right now, just to cap off a glorious day. "Oh, for the love of—I have to go, Pete. Someone's here."

"Give what I said some thought, hon. I know this guy. He's decent, I swear it. Practically asked my permission to pursue a relationship with you, and I think he really cared about my answer."

"Uh-huh." She was distracted now. The wet lady was standing by the pool, pointing at something. "Say, where is Jimmy right now, anyway?"

"He went out. He was sulking, and I think he wanted to be alone."

"Yeah. Okay. I'll talk to you tomorrow, Peter."

"You call if you have any more trouble, sis. I don't like you being there alone."

"Don't worry. I will." She hung up the phone without taking her eyes from the woman, then walked to the patio doors and slid them open, flipped on the outdoor light, and stepped out onto the concrete.

The woman stared at her, wet hair in her face, eyes pathetic and huge.

"Hey, listen up. You can quit with this, okay? I'm not afraid of you."

She stood there, didn't move, just stood there, pointing at the water and waiting, God only knew for what.

"You're gonna regret it if you make me come over there." But there was no response, so Caroline stepped out, barefoot, into the wet grass and strode purposefully across the back lawn toward the pool. "You know, you could get arrested for this. Is he really worth it? I've just recently figured out how dumb and pathetic you have to be to let a man use you. And that's just what you're doing."

The woman didn't move. Caroline was closer now, maybe five feet from her. And she saw there really wasn't much to be afraid of. She was small, maybe five feet tall, and barely over a hundred pounds, if that. She was pale, and the hollow cheeks and dark circles under her eyes said she wasn't in very good health. Though she certainly didn't look old enough to have been coming around for thirteen years.

Then again, she hadn't been. Jimmy probably made

up the stuff about her appearing to him as a child and then used whatever girl was currently infatuated with him to play the part over the years in between. Unless . . .

The girl lifted her hand, pointing again toward the pool.

"What the hell are you pointing at?" Caroline demanded. In about five more seconds, she was going to deck the scrawny wet chick and prove she was no ghost once and for all.

The girl jabbed her finger again toward the pool. Long, torn tendrils of lavender and pink trailed from the draping sleeve of her dripping-wet dress as Caroline's gaze moved down it to her long, slender, almost bony finger, and then on to the water.

There was nothing in the pool. But then she caught it, a reflection in the water of a vehicle parked on the road that ran past her house.

She snapped her head up and turned to look toward the street, and sure enough, there was someone parked there, about a hundred yards down from her house. She could just barely make it out, shaded as it was by trees and ensconced in total darkness. But it was dark-colored, and she thought it was a pickup.

"Brian," she muttered. She turned back to the woman, but there was no one there. Dammit, she'd wanted to grab the bitch by the arm and drag her into the house to hold her while she called the police. *Well, hell.*

"Wherever you are, you need to stop coming around here, okay?" She pursed her lips. "But thanks for the tip. Tell Jimmy a phone call would have done just as well." She glanced at the surface of the water again, wondering how the hell it managed to reflect the pickup on the road at that angle. But now it reflected only the stars overhead.

Well, that was odd. Maybe a cloud had passed over, changing the reflection, or maybe—

"Hi, Caroline."

She spun around to see Brian standing there, way too close for comfort. *Shit.* "What are you doing here, Brian?"

He shrugged. "Who were you talking to?"

"Some chick who keeps showing up unannounced."

"Yeah? And who's Jimmy?"

"A friend of my brother's—and none of your business, by the way. Why are you parked clear down the road? What are you, turning into some kind of stalker?"

He reached out and gripped her upper arm so fast she never saw it coming. "I'm not gonna let you dump me for some other guy, Caroline. So you can forget about it."

"I didn't dump you for some other guy, I dumped you for *me.* And you're hurting me, Bri. Let go of me right now."

He only squeezed harder and jerked her up against him. "You're mine, you got that?"

"Let me go, Brian." She braced her hands on his chest and shoved, but he didn't budge.

"No way in hell." He mashed his mouth down on hers, and she tasted beer on his breath and twisted her head away in revulsion.

God, what had she ever seen in this idiot? "Get the hell *off* me!" She was starting to get scared, and when he grabbed her ass and thrust against her, she knew she was in trouble. She lifted a hand and raked her nails down the side of his face.

He drew back fast, pressing his palm to his cheek and blinking at her in shock and rage, and then he hit her, the back of his hand right across her jaw. Her head snapped back so hard she thought she heard bones snapping, and blobs of light exploded in her head as she hit the ground hard.

And then he was gone, and she didn't know where the hell he went, until she blinked her eyes clear and saw for herself. Brian stood on the lawn, facing Jimmy Lipton, who must have yanked him away from her. Brian's nose was bleeding, and his lip was split, and as she looked, Jimmy landed a blow that knocked him flat onto his back.

Jimmy bent over him and grabbed him by the front of his shirt to tug him up a little. "Get up, you son of a bitch!"

"Jimmy, don't." Caroline struggled to her feet, but she was still unsteady, dizzy, and her jaw hurt like hell. "Just get him the hell out of here."

Jimmy let go, and Brian fell back into the grass again. Then he was at her side, his hands on her waist, helping her, supporting her as he scanned her face. "Are you okay? That bastard hit you. Are you—?"

"I'll be all right." She swayed a little on her feet, though, and thought maybe this was what they meant by the term *punch drunk*. She decided that she far preferred the regular kind of intoxication.

Jimmy scooped her up and carried her across the lawn, through the open patio doors, and into the kitchen, where he lowered her onto a chair. He grabbed the phone, punched in three numbers—911, no doubt—then cradled it between his ear and shoulder as he reached for a dishtowel and filled it with ice. He came to where she sat, knelt in front of her, and gently held the ice-filled towel to her jaw as he told the operator he was calling to report an assault and gave the address.

She heard a vehicle, tires squealing, engine roaring, and turned to look out at the lawn where Brian had been prone only seconds ago. But he was gone.

He'd been angry, furious, jealous. Now he was humiliated to boot and, she thought, maybe even more dangerous than he had been before.

CHAPTER 7

By the time the police took her report and left, there was a big purple bruise forming on Caroline's jaw, and her neck felt stiff every time she moved her head. Jimmy was still hovering, and she couldn't quite bring herself to throw him out.

He came in from the kitchen, carrying two mugs, and handed her one of them. "Tea," he said. "Chamomile. The box says it's supposed to help you sleep."

"I think it's going to take something considerably stronger."

He sat down on the sofa beside her, and she glanced into his cup. "Coffee?" she asked.

"Yeah. I want to stay awake, just in case."

"Ever the protector."

"I'm trying to be."

She pursed her lips, sipped her tea.

"You never told the cops what you were doing out on the back lawn in the middle of the night," he said.

"No, I didn't."

"You want to tell me?"

She set the cup down on the coffee table with a clunk and a slosh of hot liquid. "Why would I tell you something you already know?"

"How would I know, Caroline?"

"Come on, Jim. Cut the baloney. I had another visit from your girlfriend tonight. What was the plan? She scares the hell out of me, and then you show up just in time to offer comfort? Soothe the poor, frightened female's shattered nerves? And then what? I'm so grateful I give you the house?"

He just sat there staring at her, and he looked hurt. "You really think this is all some kind of a trick I'm playing on you? Caroline, that woman you keep seeing is the same one I saw when I was a kid. I never told anyone about that. No one. Not until you."

"No? Not even the previous owners? Or the ones before them, or—"

"No one."

She bit her lip and fought with the gut urge to believe him. It would be too damn easy. But God, she'd never wanted to believe anyone more. "My real-estate agent said you've been trying to get this place back for years, at considerably less than the market value. She said this wet lady thing was just a prank you use to scare people away from here, get them to sell."

He nodded slowly. "So, instead of just asking me about it, you decided to believe it."

He had her there. It was absolutely true. She drew a breath and decided at least one of them had to be honest here. And as was usual, at least in her experience, it would have to be her. "Men have been lying to me for so long that asking for the truth doesn't seem like a very viable option anymore."

"Not me, Caroline. I'm not lying to you. I'm not going to. It's true that every time this house comes on the market, I try to buy it. I actually had enough to offer the full asking price this time, but when I found out you were the other person trying to buy it, I withdrew my offer."

To say the statement shocked her would have been like calling the Mount Saint Helens eruption a hiccup. "You withdrew your offer?"

He nodded. "You can check that with the real-estate agent, if you want. It's on the record."

She stared at him, searching his eyes. "Why did you do that?"

"Because getting this place back was important to me, but the chance to get you back into my life meant a hell of a lot more. Do you have any idea how long I've—scratch that. It's too soon. Damn, I only wanted the place so I could figure out, after all this time, what the woman is, what she wants, why she keeps coming back here."

"Really?"

He averted his eyes, and she felt it right to her gut. He was hiding something.

There was more to this than what he'd said. It was the first thing he'd said to her that felt like a lie.

"It's been driving me crazy for a long time, and I figure the only way to get past it is to solve the mystery. Find the answers. Put it to rest, maybe put *her* to rest, somehow."

She searched his eyes, tried to find the truth behind

the shadows, but they revealed nothing. "This is a lot to swallow, you realize that."

"Yeah. I do. And I'm sorry I didn't warn you about her before you bought the place. I just didn't want your first impression of me after all this time to be that I was certifiably insane." He smiled, but it faded, and he lowered his head. "I guess I should have been more worried you'd think I was a liar and a con artist."

She gnawed her lower lip. His eyes locked in on it for a moment, but then he lowered his head. "Why don't you sleep on it? Check out my story tomorrow, the parts you can verify, at least. And maybe, if you want, we can talk again after."

Drawing a breath, she reclaimed the cup and took a long, warm drink. When she set it down again, it was half empty. "If you're telling the truth, then . . . I owe you an apology. A big one."

"I can wait. Been waiting a long time . . . for you."

"That's even harder for me to swallow than your ghost stories."

"Yeah, well, we'll work on that next. Go on, get some sleep. Brian isn't going to get within a mile of you tonight. I promise."

She nodded, finished her tea, and went to the stairs, then paused and looked back at him. "Thanks for staying tonight."

"Thanks for letting me."

Caroline was frowning when she reached her bedroom. She sank into the chair in front of her dressing table and stared hard at her reflection. He hadn't hit on her. Hadn't touched her. He'd beaten the hell out of Brian for her, even though Brian outweighed him by fifty pounds and maybe could have done him some damage, had he been sober. He didn't even hesitate jumping on the big jerk. He took her accusations without getting angry, and then, to top it all off, he stayed in spite of them.

She looked into her own eyes. "You know what they say," she whispered. "If it sounds too good to be true, it probably is." Then she lowered her head. "Unless it isn't. What if it isn't? What if he's really as great as he seems?"

She was almost afraid to entertain the possibility, because if she did, if she let herself believe it and he turned out to be just like all the rest—damn, she didn't want to be hurt again. She didn't want to go through the heartbreak, not again.

"But what if I miss out on something wonderful, just because I'm afraid?" she asked her reflection. She closed her eyes, lowered her head. "Maybe he's worth the risk."

Jim had to leave in the morning—duty called. He had to keep his PI business running by working the paying cases. She had to leave, too. She'd gotten away with working at home the day before, but a person had to show up now and again if she wanted to collect a paycheck.

Jimmy followed her to the bank and watched as she went inside, just to be sure she was safe before he left her there. He'd programmed his cell number into her phone, so she could call if she needed him, and he promised to keep it turned on all day.

He was either very special and very concerned or the best actor since Dustin Hoffman. She wished she knew for sure which was true.

By lunch hour, she'd confirmed his story with her real-estate agent and bitched at the woman for not telling her the whole story in the first place. He really had offered the full asking price for the house this time, and he really had withdrawn the offer when he learned who else was trying to buy it.

How could the woman have left out important details like those?

She also got the names of the previous owners and contacted them. They confirmed that not only had they never been told any story about a ghost, but they'd never even heard of Jimmy Lipton. One admitted to having "seen something" but refused to elaborate. Some of the others swore they'd never seen anything unusual and had moved for different reasons. Though the nervousness in their voices when she asked about the wet lady gave away the truth. They'd seen her, too.

At noon, Jimmy showed up at her office door, which she'd left open. "Free for lunch?" he asked.

She was, though she almost felt guilty for taking a break at all, when the only work she'd done all morning had been her own personal snooping. She'd delegated everything else, shuffled appointments, and basically spent the day trying to find a reason not to believe the dream man standing in her doorway was for real.

She hadn't found one. Not one. She didn't know whether to be relieved or terrified.

"Sure, why not?" She reached for the mouse to shut down her computer but froze with her hand on it, blinking at the screen.

"What is it?" Jimmy came into the office, around the

desk, and leaned over her to look at the screen, where a photograph had just finished loading, a photograph that bore a striking resemblance to the wet lady.

"I was looking up former owners of the property, clicking on names for related links. I got nothing new, so I broadened the search to items pertaining to Mulberry Street. And this came up."

She read the caption beneath the photo aloud. "Police still have no clues in case of missing girl." Caroline lifted her gaze to meet Jimmy's. "It's her, isn't it?"

He nodded, then covered her hand on the mouse with his own, its warmth taking away a bit of the chill that had suffused her body. He moved the mouse, pressed her forefinger to click on the "full story" link in the local paper's archives. And there they read the tragic story of nineteen-year-old Natalie Bruscheau, who had vanished from her own home in the dead of night with her parents sleeping downstairs and had apparently never been heard from again.

"It happened before my family moved here," Jimmy said. "How the hell is it I never heard about this?"

But there was something off about his voice. Something unsteady, insincere. Or maybe that was her skepticism about men in general rearing its head again.

She told herself to give him the benefit of the doubt for once. "Maybe you did and just didn't make the connection. Or maybe your family kept it from you. I mean, you were a kid. They probably didn't want to scare you."

"But if I'd known—"

"What if you had? What could you have done? Jimmy, whatever happened to her, it had already happened. There's no undoing it."

He nodded, but there was a deep shadow in his eyes.
Time to change the subject. "You're a PI, right?"

"Yeah. So?"

"You have friends in the police department. All PI's
do, don't they?"

"It helps."

"Call whoever it is you know there. See if they ever
found anything further—had any suspects or clues or
anything."

"I don't know that that's going to help, Caroline."

"Please?" She frowned, studying him, wondering
why he would hesitate.

"Are you planning to try to solve this thing on your
own?" he asked.

"Not if you'll agree to help me." She shifted her eyes
back to the photo. It looked like a high school senior
portrait, black and white. Natalie had been a pretty girl
with too much mascara, long dark hair, and an innocent
smile. Caroline thought of the way she'd looked when
she'd shown up on the back lawn. That innocence, long
gone, replaced in her eyes with a look of need, of longing, and of utter despair. Licking her lips, she looked
at Jimmy again. Deep down, she felt that if she started
trying to solve this thing, that would mean she believed it, and that would mean she believed *him*. And
how was she supposed to keep a healthy skepticism in
place if she started believing in him? If she believed
this, then she'd end up believing everything else, and
that might very well lead to heartache.

Then again, she was looking at the face of the girl
she'd seen, or a damn similar one. Which didn't mean
he couldn't have found this story on his own and made
sure the girl he sent to haunt her house bore a strong

resemblance. Still, she felt compelled, and she always trusted her gut.

Her cell phone rang before she got any further in justifying her plans. She answered without looking to see who was calling first, because it saved her from having to think any more about his motives or the reasons for his hesitation.

"Hi. It's Shawn."

She closed her eyes. Great. All she needed today was to hear from her ex. Hell, maybe fire and brimstone would rain from the sky next. It would fit right in. "Look, I don't have time to talk to you today, Shawn. Not unless you're calling to tell me my money is on the way."

"I didn't know you'd stoop this low, Caroline. But you can tell your boyfriend to lay off. The check is in your mailbox."

"My what? What are you talking about?"

"Look, if you're tough enough to play hardball, you ought to be tough enough to own up to it. You got your way, okay? I didn't even waste time to mail it. And it's all there. Half the equity in the house, half the value of the business at the time of our divorce. All of it. I don't want to hear from you—or him—or your brother, either, ever again."

"Him who? Who the hell are you talking about?"

"Good-bye, Caroline."

He hung up without another word, and she was left standing there blinking in confusion—but only for a moment. A second later, she realized what this meant, and she felt a slow smile spreading over her face and a huge weight lifting from her shoulders. "I'm saved," she whispered.

"Come again?"

"I can pay for the house. I don't know what the hell happened, but Shawn says he's paying me, in full. All of it. Today."

"That's great news. Congratulations."

She frowned at him. "He kept saying something about my new boyfriend. You didn't . . . you didn't do anything to him, did you?"

"I didn't know you considered me your new boyfriend. Now, this is progress."

"Jimmy, I'm serious."

"I didn't touch him. I swear."

She searched his face, thought that wasn't a real answer, at least not a whole one, and decided to find out on her own. Because if he was responsible for this—and she had a feeling he was, somehow—well, hell, she owed him.

"You gonna help me dig into this case or not?" she asked.

He met her eyes and nodded. "Yeah, I'll help you, Caroline."

He sounded as if he thought it was a bad idea but seemed to be trying to hide that.

"We need to swing by my place first and grab that check out of the mailbox before Shawn changes his mind and goes over there to take it back. And we need to deposit it. Then we can go see your friend the cop."

"How long is your lunch hour, anyway?" he asked.

"Long enough. I just decided to take the rest of the day off."

She grabbed her purse and headed for the door. He stopped her with a hand on her shoulder. "One thing first."

Caroline turned, and he tugged a small, flat box out of his pocket and handed it to her. "I picked this up for you on my way to work this morning."

Frowning, she took it and removed the cover. A bracelet made of alternating clear and black beads glittered up at her.

"It's quartz and onyx," he said. "It's supposed to be protective."

"Against ghosts?" She took the delicate piece from the box, fingering the cool stones and going soft inside, in spite of herself.

"I don't think our ghost is much of a threat. I was thinking more about Brian." He took the bracelet from her hands and slid it over her wrist, his fingers caressing her skin as he did. She barely suppressed a shiver and knew without a doubt that she still wanted him. Maybe more than ever.

"Caroline, I checked with the cops this morning. When they went to pick him up last night, he wasn't home. They haven't been able to locate him."

Her shiver changed in the blink of an eye, from one of desire to one of fear. She stared at the bracelet that surrounded her wrist, at Jimmy's hands, still there, touching her skin, and then slowly lifted her gaze to his.

"He's going to come after me, isn't he?"

"He might try. But he's not going to get to you. I'm not going to let that happen, Caroline. You have my word on that."

And suddenly, more than anything else in the world, she *wanted* to believe him. *Please, God,* she thought silently, *let Jimmy Lipton be for real.*

CHAPTER 8

They spent the rest of the afternoon at the police department and the library, poring over everything they could find on the case of the missing nineteen-year-old. Jimmy did the searching and printing up of documents and news stories, then divided them into two piles, one for her and one for him. But they didn't find a hell of a lot more than they already knew. Girl disappears from her own bedroom in the dead of night, no clues, never heard from again. Case still unsolved.

It told Caroline nothing, least of all whether her ghost was for real or a fabrication of her young lover.

He was attentive as hell all afternoon—opening doors, doing all the driving, constantly aware of her every expression and mood. He was too damn good to be true. That was what worried her.

In fact, it wouldn't *stop* worrying her. And maybe that was because she still got the feeling he was hiding something from her. Something big.

"You okay?" he asked, once again noting her pensive look as he drove them back to the house that night.

"Yeah. I'm okay. Just deep in thought."

"Anything you want to share?"

She shrugged.

"No pressure. Just do one thing for me?"

"If I can."

He reached across the space between them and trailed a fingertip down her cheek. She shivered right to her toes, and her eyes fell closed in spite of herself. God, she wanted him.

"All this stress and tension. Let it go if you can, just for tonight."

"I'd like to do that. Just . . . it's not going to be easy."

"I can help," he said. And his fingers curled around the nape of her neck, stroking her there until she almost groaned aloud. Her body heated, softened, and she thought maybe she could let go of everything tonight. Everything except him.

"I guarantee you'll feel better after a solid meal," he said.

"Oh?" she breathed. "Are we going out again?"

"Not this time. I'm cooking."

"You sure are." She opened her eyes and met his. She smiled, and he smiled back. And damn if she didn't find herself falling a little harder than before. He was good.

They stopped at a grocery store on the way home to buy everything he needed; then he insisted she soak in a hot bath while he worked his magic in the kitchen. He even ran the water for her. By the time she got out of the tub, the entire house was filled with scents that made her stomach growl. She didn't even bother getting dressed, just tugged on an oversize terry robe, cinched it closed, and headed down the stairs, barefoot, her hair still straggly and wet.

She stepped into the kitchen, eyes closed, inhaling the aromas. "God, what did you make?"

He didn't answer. Instead, she felt his eyes on her and opened hers to find him staring at her as if she were wearing a sexy teddy instead of a baggy robe. His gaze heated, and he licked his lips.

"It smells really good." Her words came out a little breathy. It was something, the way he could get to her with just a look.

He moved closer, bent his head toward her neck, and inhaled deeply. "Mmm. So do you."

"I do?" Stupid reply, but she didn't know what to say.

His breath fanned her neck, and she wanted to purr. Before she could tell herself not to respond, she was tipping her head back and closing her eyes. He answered that unspoken invitation by bending just a breath closer, until his lips touched her skin, and then he kissed a teasing path over her neck, from just at the shoulder all the way up to underneath her ear. Her knees went so weak she had to clutch his shoulders to keep from falling down.

He lifted his head, his eyes dancing from hers to her lips, where they lingered. "I don't want to push . . . but if you don't shove me away in the next second or two . . ."

She tightened her hands on his shoulders, pulled him just a little closer. He groaned, and then he was kissing her, and she found herself kissing him back. Her heart jumped to life and started hammering in her chest. Her breath came faster, just from a kiss. She opened wider to him, and he seemed to catch fire. His arms tightened around her, one hand burying itself in her hair while the other kneaded her backside and arched her tighter to him. She strained to get closer, twisting her arms around his neck to pull her body tighter to his, and even then she couldn't get close enough.

He twisted slightly, never breaking his kiss as he scooped her up into his arms and strode toward the stairs. He didn't stop kissing her, not all the way to the top, and then he did, just long enough to lower her onto the bed, tug loose the robe's sash, and push it open. His gaze moved over her body, and she felt so exposed she wanted to yank the robe closed again, but then he said something that stopped her. He said, "You're more incredible than I imagined, Caroline. And believe me, I imagined you a lot. My God, you're beautiful."

She just stared at him, taking in the words, and the sincerity behind them.

"What, you don't believe me?"

"I . . . no one's ever said that to me before. No man, I mean. Not . . . you know, like this."

He looked into her eyes, and his own showed surprise. "Any man worth a damn would tell you that a hundred times a day, Caroline. And keep telling you until you stopped doubting it, and then keep telling you anyway." As he spoke, he stretched out on the bed beside her, and his hand trailed heat from her chin, down the center of her chest, and over her belly, then slid lower, his touch light, teasing, maddening.

She closed her eyes, her legs parting involuntarily, and that simple movement seemed to give him a jump start. His touch deepened, penetrated her, and his mouth closed on one nipple without warning, sending a jolt of pleasure through her that almost made her cry out loud. He sucked and tugged and probed her. She moaned his name and moved against his hand, clutching his head.

And then she pulled back, just a little, staring into his eyes, panting, and whispered, "Make love to me. Now."

He nodded, the movements jerky and rushed. She reached for his shirt, peeling it off over his head, and he struggled out of his jeans and shorts without getting all the way up, then rolled toward her again and picked up right where he'd left off. By the time he got on top of her, she was panting with need, and when he gripped her ankles and propped them up on his shoulders, she was damn near out of her mind. He slid inside her, and she saw stars.

It was fast, and it was furious. Not gentle, not slow. She didn't want it gentle and slow, and neither did he. It wouldn't last long, she thought, but God, she was already so close it didn't matter. He drove into her, deep and hard, and she arched to receive him over and over, and then she was falling into screaming ecstasy, her entire body trembling with release. He eased back, let her come down slowly, stroked her, and made it even hotter. And then, just when she was coming back to earth and expecting him to collapse beside her, he was rolling onto his back, pulling her with him, so she wound up on top of him. He clutched her ass in his grip and thrust up into her, pulling her down to take every inch, slowly at first, but then building the fire, increasing the pace, sending her on that incredible journey to the peak all over again. Within minutes, she was so into it she'd lost every inhibition she ever had and was bouncing up and down on him, hands braced on his shoulders, head tipped back, eyes closed. God, she was almost there, almost . . .

And then she was, and she exploded even harder than before. This time, he drove into her all the way through it, over and over, making it go on and on, and he was there with her, spilling into her.

As the sensations ebbed, Caroline lowered herself onto his chest, still holding him inside her, sweaty skin against sweaty skin. He wrapped her in his arms and held her there, one hand lazily stroking a path up and down her spine, kissing her head every once in a while. He whispered, "Do you have any idea how long I've been waiting to make love to you? These past few days have been—God, they've been a fantasy come true for me."

"I hope it's been worth the wait," she whispered.

"It has for me. You're amazing."

She smiled, because it was yet another first. No man had ever told her she was good in bed. But then again, she didn't remember ever *being* this good, this enthusiastic, this uninhibited, this turned on.

She slid off him, curling up beside him. And while they lay there snuggling like a couple madly in love with each other, her stomach made a rude growling sound, and Jimmy laughed beneath her head on his chest. "I'm sorry. I intended to feed you first, seduce you later."

She lifted her head and kissed his face. "No reason you can't still do that."

His smile was slow and full of promises she had

every reason to believe he would keep. He kissed her to seal the deal, and they got out of bed. She paused with her robe in her hand. "Hell, I've got all these sexy little numbers from Vicki's Secret in my room. Why am wearing this old thing?"

"You were sexy in that old thing. But if you want to model one of those sexy little numbers for me after dinner, I'm not gonna object."

She smiled slowly and felt deliciously sexy, desirable, wanted. Totally wanted. By a guy so hot it was damn near sinful. This night was just full of firsts.

"What's all this?" she asked later, when she joined him in the kitchen. She'd washed up and put on one of the naughty nighties her sister-in-law had bought her. It was a black corset with matching thong panties and a black satin robe that came to mid-thigh. She wore the robe over the nightie, just to make him wonder what was underneath through the entire meal. And she'd put on high heels, black strappy ones, to complete the torture.

He looked her up and down, closed his eyes as if in some kind of exquisite pain, cleared his throat. "Chicken roasted with rosemary, baby potatoes, glazed carrots, and the best gravy you ever tasted."

"I *haven't* tasted it."

He came closer, until he was standing right in front of her with a spoon. She tasted, and she groaned. "Okay, I admit it. Best I've ever tasted."

"Good. I hope you plan to eat fast, because, uh—" He let his gaze move down to her toes and said, "Because *damn*."

"Nothing to worry about there," she told him. "I'm

starved." She sat at the little tiled kitchen table, which he'd already set, and he took her plate, filled it way too full, and brought it back to her. Then he did the same with his own and sat down across from her. Caroline dug in without another word.

She didn't stop until she was too full to eat another bite. "That was pure heaven. I didn't know you could cook."

"There's a lot you don't know about me." He reached across the table to lay a hand over hers.

She looked at him, and her stomach tightened, not from hunger this time. Whatever she believed or didn't believe about him, he got to her. He got to her on a purely primal level where no one else had ever been able to touch her. She didn't think it was wise or practical or even entirely sane. But there it was.

And she wasn't ready for it.

She took her hand away as she rose from the table, picking up her plate on the way. "You cooked, so I'll clean up. It's your turn to relax for a while."

"If you insist," he said. "I'll take a quick shower. Maybe try some of that cologne I just bought that's supposed to drive women wild."

"You do that just fine all by yourself, mister."

He smiled, stroked her cheek with a fingertip, brushed her lips with his, and left her alone in the kitchen.

It didn't take long to clean up. Apparently, he'd been doing it as he went along while cooking, so there wasn't much. She put away the leftovers, loaded the dishwasher, wiped off the table, and that was all that was needed. She decided to busy herself reviewing what they'd learned today. The two of them had printed up, photocopied, and pored over countless documents, Jimmy taking half and Caroline the other half, filling each other in on what they found.

Since she'd read her half carefully, she reached for the folder that held his and sat down at the table with a cup of freshly brewed coffee.

A few minutes later, she stopped dead, a chill rushing down her spine, when she got to an article that he hadn't mentioned. The headline read, "Twelve-year-old questioned in the disappearance of his babysitter."

She quickly looked up the stairs. The shower was still running.

Then she read the article. The missing girl had been the Lipton's next-door neighbor and favorite babysitter. This had been six months before Caroline's own family had come to town and she'd taken over poor Natalie's former job.

She blinked, stunned to her core. He'd lied to her. He'd said the girl's disappearance had happened before his family even lived in this house.

He'd lied.

And she couldn't think of too many reasons he would. But the ones she could think of scared the hell out of her.

He would be back down soon, Caroline thought. And she needed time, space, and more information. She couldn't think straight when he was near her. She got up and ran to the living room, took her keys off the hook near the door.

"Hey. Where you going, babe?"

She stopped by the door and turned to look at him. He stood on the stairs, a towel anchored around his hips, looking so damn good he made her mouth water.

Too good to be true?

She'd hoped to erase her suspicion from her face and found that her body's need for his touch did that for her. Heat. God, she wanted him. She was sick.

"I don't remember if I locked the car. Just making sure." That said, she pointed the key ring's remote toward the driveway and thumbed the lock button. The car honked an affirmation, and she replaced the key ring on its hook. "There."

"There." He came the rest of the way down the stairs, and she turned and walked toward him, leaving the door, and logic, behind. She couldn't act any differently right now. Not now. She would have time to do more digging. She didn't need to jump to any conclusions. She needed to be practical and sensible, take her time, get all the facts.

Who was she kidding? She was terrified. He'd apparently been suspected of murdering his babysitter. And now he was having sex with her replacement, a woman he claimed to have been obsessed with for years. This was not healthy, and it was not safe.

He stopped, standing close to her but not touching. "You ready to show me what you're wearing underneath that robe?"

She smiled, but it was shaky. She was nervous. What was he hiding from her? Why had he lied? Could a twelve-year-old murder his babysitter and hide it for thirteen years?

He stopped her thought processes by reaching out and tugging on the satin sash that held the robe together, until the knot slid free, and the robe fell open.

"Lord have mercy," he whispered. His hands slipped beneath the robe at her neck and pushed it gently, until it slid down her arms and pooled around her feet. He just stood there, looking at her, drinking her in, not saying a damn thing.

"You're awfully quiet," she whispered.

His gaze rose to meet hers. "I'm not sure I can form a coherent sentence."

"I guess I'll take that as a compliment."

"You're a goddess, Caroline. I should be on my knees."

"I'm not. And you're pouring it on a little thick, Jimmy. I know you've seen better-looking women than me. Younger, firmer—"

"Shut up, Caroline." He snapped his arms around her and kissed her into obedience, and she couldn't help but respond. God, he was only a kid all those years ago. Maybe he just made a mistake about the year his family had moved here. Maybe he really hadn't heard about his murdered babysitter.

Right. None of that was very likely, was it? Even then, he had to have seen the printout. And yet he hadn't told her.

His tongue swept into her mouth and drove every rational thought from her mind, and then he was kissing his way over her chin, her throat, to her chest, where he sucked and tugged on her breasts right through the fabric of the corset. And then to her belly, dropping down to his knees along the way. And then lower. Her pressed his mouth to her panties, kissing her there, blowing hot breath through the satin as his lips made it wet. She had to clutch his shoulders from the power of that sensation.

Then he was pushing the panties down, lifting her feet so she stepped out of them, and returning his mouth to her center, to kiss her there again as she shivered from her head to her toes. But that was nothing compared to when he pressed his thumbs to either side of her, pulled her secret lips apart, and kissed her again, his mouth touching the most sensitive hidden parts of her.

She could barely breathe, barely stand.

He used his tongue, snaking it over her, slowly at first, tasting her, taking his time. It was sheer, excruciating torture. But then he licked faster, hitting all the right places, over and over, as she began to pant and moan. Her knees went weak, but he knew it, felt it. He wrapped one arm around her hips to support her and continued plundering her with his mouth, parting her with his fingers, lapping deep and slow, then fast and ruthless. She felt devoured, possessed by him, worshipped, and on fire. Engulfed in sensation that was too much to bear.

And then she was there, right on the brink, at the edge of oblivion. Her hands closed on his head, and she strained, reached, *felt* with every cell in her body. It was as if he sensed everything she felt, because he caught her clitoris in his lips and sucked it hard, teeth scraping the throbbing nub as he worked it. She screamed when she came. Screamed and clutched his head and shoulders, convulsed deep inside. Then she was pushing his head away, because she couldn't take any more. But he kept licking, kept taking, even then, until she fell to the floor and away from him, quivering and shaking, close to tears as she curled onto one side.

He joined her there, moving her body into the position he wanted. She didn't resist, just lay there like a doll, too awash in sensations to do anything at all. He pressed her onto her back, parted her thighs, and lay on top of her.

God, he couldn't. Not now, not yet, not until the spasms eased.

"Baby, I can't—"

"Yeah, you can. Trust me." And then he drove himself into her, to the hilt, all the way.

He filled her, and the orgasm that gripped her seemed to reset and start over. He thrust deep, as deep as he could, no slow build this time. Harder and faster than he had before, he took her, and in the space of a few heartbeats, she was coming again, and he was, too.

This time, he held her as she came back down, held her while the trembling eased. And she felt warm, safe in his arms. She felt cared for, cherished. But eventually, her heartbeat slowed, and blood started making its way to her brain again. She had to do some digging. She had to know the truth. And she had to get away from him. Soon.

"Why don't we go on upstairs to bed?" she suggested.

"Just as long as you don't think we're finished." He nuzzled her neck, and she laughed a nervous, tight little laugh.

"I can handle it if you can." Bold words from a woman who had experienced more climaxes in the past few days than she usually did in a six-month stretch.

But she could, and she did. She handled it until he was exhausted and snoring softly on the pillow beside her. And then she slid out of bed and tiptoed out of the room, closing the door softly behind her. She headed down the stairs and retrieved the notes she'd been reading, scanning them until she found what she was looking for: the name of the detective who'd been in charge of the case of the missing girl.

She took the cordless phone and stepped out through the patio doors onto the deck in back. As she dialed directory assistance, she prayed the cop was still in the area.

He was. Or at least, a man by the same name was. She dialed the number, looking around nervously as she did. No sign of the wet lady. And no sign of the phenomenal lover she'd left asleep upstairs. She was feeling tense, despite the tingling satisfaction that suffused her body. This was mental tension, and all the great sex in the world wasn't going to ease it until she knew for sure what he was hiding from her and why.

The man answered the phone in a sleepy voice.

"Detective Monroe?"

"Used to be. Who the hell is this? Do you know what time it is?"

"I'm very sorry to bother you at this hour, Detective, but it's important. I promise not to keep you long. Do you remember the case of Natalie Bruscheau, the missing nineteen-year-old?"

There was a long pause. Then, "Of course, I remember. I retired without solving that one, and it's haunted me. What do you know about it?"

"Not a hell of a lot. But I was wondering why it was that the boy she used to babysit for had been questioned."

"The Lipton kid. Yeah. Well, I'll tell you, I say to this day that kid knew something. I was a cop for a long time, I know when someone's lying, and kids are the worst at hiding it. But I didn't have any evidence.

Nothing to back up my gut feeling. Well, almost nothing."

"Are you saying you think a twelve-year-old kid was involved in a murder?"

"I'm saying that I couldn't find evidence. Just one big coincidence and some drawings that could have been done after the fact."

"What coincidence?"

"Kid used to live in Benton, Maine. Same town where another girl went missing, one who lived on the same street. Never nailed down a connection between them, don't know if she babysat for him or not. His family said not, and hers said she babysat for everyone in the neighborhood but couldn't say for sure if she'd ever sat for him. I never believed much in coincidence."

"Did they ever find the other girl, Detective?"

"Never."

She closed her eyes, lifted her head. "Tell me about the drawings."

He grunted, hesitated, and finally spoke. "We found them in the kid's room. Drawings of women, one with a knife in her chest, one with her head smashed in. Graphic. Disgusting. But not proof."

Caroline lifted her head slowly as her heart turned to a chunk of cold granite. She gazed toward the patio doors. The wet lady stood near the pool, watching her. "Thank you for your time, sir." She hung up the phone and stared for a long moment at the apparition. "I'm trying, Natalie," she whispered. "I'm trying, okay?"

The girl didn't respond in any way, just kept staring with those huge, haunted eyes. Caroline sighed and turned to go back into the house. She put the phone on its charger, then stood still and listened for any sign of movement from upstairs.

There wasn't any. Quietly, she moved through the house, took her keys from the rack without jingling them, and made her way outside to her car. She got in, closed the door as softly as she could, put the key into the switch, and turned it enough to let her slide into neutral and roll out of the driveway. Only when she was in the road did she start the motor, flip on the headlights, and drive away.

She hadn't gone very far when she looked up to see a leering grin peering at her from the rearview mirror. She screamed, and he pressed the tip of a blade to her throat, silencing her as fear blocked her airway.

"Keep it on the road, baby. We've got things to do."

She straightened the car and did as he said.

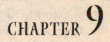

Jimmy woke to find himself alone in the bed. He rolled over and looked around the room. "Caroline?"

She didn't reply. He glanced toward the bathroom, but its door was slightly open, its light off. She hadn't gone in there. "Caroline?"

He flipped on the bedside lamp, flung back the covers, and got up, still naked. He pulled on his shorts and jeans and went through the house, searching. When he got to the kitchen, he saw the files open on the table and rapidly scanned the pages she'd been reading.

Then he closed his eyes and kicked himself. She knew. She knew he'd lied to her about not knowing the missing girl. And if she'd contacted the detective whose name she'd circled on the page, she must know about the other girl as well. And maybe even those damned, morbid drawings the police had found in his room. *Dammit.*

Movement drew his eyes. He looked up through the

patio doors, then sucked in a sharp breath when he saw her there—the ghost, the girl, his former babysitter. Natalie. She stood just beyond the glass, dripping and staring at him. He drew a steadying breath and met the girl's eyes. "Where is she?"

She said nothing, just lifted a hand and pointed toward the front of the house.

Jim turned his back on her, hurrying through the house to the front, flinging open the front door. But Caroline's car wasn't in the driveway. He caught just a brief glimpse of taillights in the distance, wasn't even certain it was her, but he grabbed his keys and cell phone anyway and jumped into his Jeep to follow.

She shouldn't be out in the middle of the night alone, not with her maniac ex-boyfriend still running around and probably still furious with her. He cursed himself as he drove. He should have told her the truth. Not just about knowing the missing young women—but about the real reason he'd wanted the house back.

Now she was putting herself at risk, and he had no one to blame but himself. And dammit, he could not live with yet another woman's blood on his hands.

Trembling—as much with anger as with fear—Caroline drove. "Why are you doing this?"

"Like you don't know."

"I don't. I swear, I don't."

He glared at her, not answering. "Nice nightie you're wearing. Where were you going dressed like that in the middle of the night, anyway?"

"None of your fucking business."

"I don't even care. Turn here. Take the highway to exit seven, then get off."

A terrible fear was taking shape in the pit of her stomach. She knew what was off exit seven. She'd been there before—many times—with him. "Where—where are we going?"

He met her eyes in the mirror. "Can't you guess?"

She didn't know whether to guess or not. Would it give him ideas he didn't already have if her guess was wrong?

"Come on, Caroline. Guess." He pressed the blade's edge harder against her skin, and she swallowed reflexively even as she drew her head back against the seat as far as she could.

"I can't drive if I can't see, you know."

"Then tell me where we're going before we crash."

Crash. Maybe that was the best idea. Just turn the car toward a tree and stomp it. He was still pressing with the blade, though, and she felt something warm trickling from her neck, shocked to realize he'd actually cut her. She was bleeding.

"The lake house?" she asked.

The pressure eased. "Was that so hard?"

She shook her head, reached up, and pulled her seatbelt around her, snapping it, adjusting it. If she could work up the nerve to crash the car, she didn't want them both flying through the windshield. Just him.

"It's been a long time since I've seen the place," she said. Maybe making conversation would help. Or maybe bringing up happy memories would change his mind. "We used to have good times there."

"We're going to have one more. Or one of us is, at least."

She tried to breathe slowly and steadily, but panic was working hard to take hold. Every instinct in her gut, and every word he said, pointed to the same conclusion. He was going to kill her.

"Are you scared, Caroline?"

"Yes." She searched his face in the rearview mirror and wondered, not for the first time, what she had ever seen in him.

"You should be."

Her cell phone played the theme from *Buffy the Vampire Slayer* to let her know she had an incoming call.

"Don't answer it. Just turn it off," he ordered.

She nodded jerkily and reached to the center console, where her phone was still playing.

"Don't even flip it open, Caroline. I'm warning you."

"I hear you." She thumbed the button on the side, which didn't turn the phone off but instead turned off the ringer. Then she held the phone up. "See? All turned off." She flipped it open as if to show him, knowing the action automatically answered the call, and without hesitation shouted, "Kidnapped! Help me!"

"Bitch!" Before she could say another of the key words she'd wanted to get out, like "my car," and "knife" and "lake house," he had yanked the phone out of her hand and snapped it in half. Then he calmly lowered a window and tossed it out.

"You're going to pay for that, Caroline. You just earned yourself a little more pain than was really going to be necessary."

There was no emotion in his eyes when he said it. They were like stones, cold and lifeless and deadly serious.

• • •

Jim heard her cry for help and then a man's voice calling her "bitch." That was all. His entire body went icy cold, and he pressed down harder on the accelerator, even as he hit the buttons to call her brother.

Peter answered, and it didn't even sound as if Jim had interrupted his sleep. "What is it, Jimmy?"

Hell, Jim thought, it sounded as if he'd been expecting the call. And his tone was tense. "Caroline's been abducted. I don't know what happened. She left the house while I was sleeping, and I was driving out to look for her. Just now, I tried her cell, and she picked it up just long enough to say she'd been kidnapped. A man swore at her, and then the call cut off."

"I knew damn well something was wrong. Woke up a half-hour ago with my goddamn heart in my throat. Have you called the police?"

"No. I called you first."

"I'll call them. Head over to that bastard Brian's. He's probably not there, but—"

"I'm already on my way. And if he's not there, I fully intend to sack the place for a clue to where he's heading. I don't give a shit if it's legal or not."

"I'll meet you there."

"No, let's not double up. We can cover more ground separately." He was pulling up outside Brian's apartment building as he spoke. "Besides, by the time you can get here, I'll be done. Get a photo of her for the cops to circulate."

"Right. They'll want to know what she was wearing."

He closed his eyes, remembering the sexy little bit of nothing and the satiny robe she'd worn over it. "The black one," he said.

"The black what?"

"Ask your wife. She'll know." He hung up the phone, pocketed it, and slammed out of the car and into the apartment building. No buzzer to open the main door. Nothing that fancy. He knew the apartment number because he'd been with Caroline when she'd given Brian's address to the police after he'd assaulted her. 2-C. So he stomped up to the second floor, getting angrier and more afraid for her with every step. He didn't knock on the door of 2-C. He pounded on it.

Nothing. He pounded again.

"Jesus, hold on a second," a groggy voice from the other side muttered.

Nice acting, he thought. He took a step back and kicked the door so hard it sprang open, and the wood splintered. It hit the wall and bounced back, but Jim slammed a palm against it, so it hit the wall again.

Brian stood there with his mouth and eyes wide, spluttering, "What the—how the—who the—" He was unshaven and wearing a dingy white T-shirt and a pair of plaid boxers.

Jimmy strode up to him, gripped him by the shirt, and said, "Where is she?"

"I don't know what the fuck you're talking about! Let go of me, you little—"

Jim decked him, uppercut to the chin, so his head snapped back. "I don't want to hear anything from you except an answer. Where is she? What the hell have you done to her?"

Brian jerked free of his grasp and rubbed his chin. "You talking about Caroline? She's missing?"

Jim drew back a fist to hit the bastard again, but Brian held up his hands and backed out of reach.

"Look, I don't know where she is. I haven't seen her. Shit, I've been out of town since that night in the backyard. Dodging cops, thanks to you two. I only came home tonight for some clean clothes and something to eat."

"I don't believe you."

He shrugged, palms up. "Search the place."

He was doing just that even as Brian spoke, moving fast from room to room, checking the closets, under the bed, the fire escape. "My truck's out back. Search that, too. I'm telling you, I haven't seen Caroline."

There was nothing in the apartment, no sign of her. He left the asshole to his own devices and ran back down the stairs, outside, and around to the parking lot in back. The truck was there, but again, no sign of her. And the engine was stone cold. If Brian didn't have her, then who the hell did?

Exit seven loomed ahead. She was deliberately driving slowly, hoping to postpone what she hoped to God wasn't inevitable. She hadn't managed to work up the nerve to crash the car just yet. She'd been thinking her chances might be better at the lake house. After all, she knew the place, and there would be room to maneuver, and woods nearby in which she might manage to lose him. She knew her ex-husband well enough to know he didn't have a gun. Shawn had never owned a gun. Probably wouldn't know what to do with one. So it was just the knife. A lesser weapon.

But a considerably tougher way to die.

She thinned her lips and told herself to stop imagining that blade, which was big and very sharp, plunging into her chest over and over. Or would he just slide it cleanly across her throat and stand over her while she choked on her own blood?

A shudder worked through her, and she changed her mind, tested her seatbelt, took the exit, and picked up speed on the ramp.

"You remember the way, don't you?"

"I sure as hell do." She also remembered the giant maple tree, right on the shore beside the house, just beyond that final hairpin curve in the road. He'd never see it coming. Probably wouldn't believe she had the nerve to do it. Unfortunately for her ex, she'd become a lot tougher since the divorce. Tougher than even she had realized.

She drove a little faster, turning right off the ramp and then left onto the side road that led to the lake. It wasn't more than another ten minutes, and she drove it in silent tension, using the visuals of that blade to keep her nerve.

He wasn't directly behind her now but sitting in the middle of the backseat, leaning forward, the knife in one hand only inches from her neck. She hoped the impact wouldn't end up making her impale herself on the damn thing.

Okay, there was the hairpin curve. She stomped the pedal.

"Slow down. Don't forget that last bend in the— slow down, Caroline!"

"Fuck you, Shawn."

She wrenched the wheel, taking the car halfway around the curve, then straightened it, cutting directly across the lake house's lawn, bounding up over a tiny knoll with a towering tree waiting on the other side.

There were two things she hadn't counted on.

First, that the tiny knoll would act like a ramp, so that the car shot off it like a rocket. They were airborne.

And second, that the giant maple tree would be missing. Someone had cut it down.

She had enough time for those two thoughts and only one more. *We're going into the lake!*

CHAPTER 10

Jimmy was heading back to his Jeep when his cell phone rang. He snapped it up fast, nearly dropping it in his haste. "Caroline?"

"It's Pete, pal. Something just came in over the scanner. A car veered out of control and took a nosedive into the lake."

His brain scrambled to make the connection even as he dove into the Jeep and started the engine. "You think it was Caroline?"

"The location is right on top of the lake house she and Shawn bought when they were still married. The one he screwed her out of in the divorce."

"*Shawn*. Jesus, Shawn's the one who has her?" Jim shifted gears, heading toward the lake. "Address?"

"Twenty-two Lakeshore Road. Take—"

"I know where it is. Meet you there." He shifted again, dropped the phone to the seat of the car, and pressed the accelerator to the floor. But the entire time, he was swamped with nightmare images of Caroline, trapped in her car as it sank slowly to the bottom of Camry Lake. And the only thing that chased those images away was the sudden, blinding realization that this was his fault. He was the one who'd kept the truth from Caroline, made her mistrust him enough to run away when she found out. He was the one who'd blackmailed Shawn into paying Caroline what he owed her. He was the one who'd backed the bastard into a corner, even knowing a cornered animal will usually attack. He'd expected Shawn to come after *him*, not Caroline. Damn, if she didn't survive this—

No. She would. She had to.

Caroline had been wearing her seat belt. Shawn hadn't. Which probably explained why, after the powerful impact with the surface of the lake, as the car began filling with water and sinking, Shawn was leaning forward, his head on the dashboard. She thought there was blood on his face, but it was too dark to be sure. She hoped so. It would serve the bastard right for cutting her. There were probably bloodstains on her brand-new teddy. And he'd trashed her phone, too. And maybe she'd better quit with the damage inventory and start thinking about how the hell she was going to get out of this alive.

She reached for the power button to lower her window, but the water had already shorted it out. It wouldn't budge. She tried pushing the door open, but it wouldn't move at all. There was too much water already pressing against it from the outside. She couldn't get out, wouldn't be able to until the car filled with water, which would probably mean sitting there and battling panic while it sank all the way to the bottom.

Nothing to it, she thought. *I can do this. And I'm only shaking because I'm cold. What kind of a moron takes off in the middle of the night wearing a getup like this, anyway?*

She tried to remember how deep the lake was in this spot, but she wasn't sure she'd ever known that.

Water rose up the side windows, lapped against the windshield. Her heart pounded as she waited. It was coming inside now, leaking from God knew where, chilling her feet and ankles. Damn, it was cold. She released her seatbelt, checked to make sure the door was unlocked. It was.

She glanced at Shawn, but he hadn't moved. She could probably pull him out with her, once the car filled up. He wouldn't be heavy in the water. She couldn't just let him die. Could she?

Maybe he was already dead. Maybe he'd hit his head hard enough . . .

She listened, heard him breathing. He wasn't dead. Bastard. Caroline wondered just how wrong it was to feel disappointed instead of relieved. He'd dropped his knife. It actually crossed her mind to find the thing and drive it into his heart.

Turning away from him, she saw nothing but murky water beyond her window now. The hue was slightly lighter above, darker than pitch below. And she couldn't see very far at all. Just inky black out there.

The water in the car rose higher, creeping up her calves, covering her knees, then her thighs and hips. She was breathing faster than before, trying not to, but this was way scarier than she'd ever imagined when watching those "what to do in an emergency" shows. They made it look so simple. If your car goes in the water, you wait until it fills, open the door and swim merrily to the surface. Of course, those demonstrations were always done in clear blue swimming pools, no more than ten feet deep, with a former Navy SEAL at the helm.

She gasped as the water came in faster, rising up her waist, chilling her right to the bones. When it got to her breasts, she tried opening the car door again. No good. Iciness crept higher, to her collarbone, her neck, her chin. She tipped her head up automatically and, again, tried to push against the door. She thought it gave a little, but it was still so freaking heavy. She pushed, she shoved. The water inched up her face. It covered her mouth now, and she was breathing through her nose, which was pressed up against the ceiling. Even then, the door wouldn't move.

One last breath, a deep one, and no more. She was submerged, and freezing, and wondering just how long she could hold her breath. She twisted in her seat and pressed her feet against the door, bracing her back against her unconscious ex-husband.

The door opened as if in slow motion. *Thank God.* She reached behind her to grip him by the front of his shirt and tugged.

He snapped a hand around her wrist and yanked her toward him. She didn't know what the hell he was doing, trying to keep her there to drown with him or just panicking. She struggled to get free, twisting and pulling, but he wouldn't let go, not until she drove her foot into his belly with everything in her. And it wasn't easy to strike with much force in the water. But it was enough. He released her.

She surged out of the car and headed upward, leaving her ungrateful, murderous ex to fend for himself as she should have done in the first place. How far away was the surface? *God, how far?* Her lungs were scream-ing, her head pounding, every cell in her body begging for a breath. Just one little breath. She kicked her feet, stroked with her arms, pulled herself upward, higher, and still there was only water. Was it slightly lighter now? Hard to tell with the spots clouding her vision. *Dizzy.* God, she was going to pass out. *Kick faster. Pull harder.*

It wasn't going to work. She wasn't going to make it. She . . .

Broke the surface all at once and sucked in huge, greedy gulps of air, damn near hyperventilating on the stuff. She floated there for just a moment, straining her eyes to get her bearings, and then spotted the shore, closer than she had imagined, and began swimming slowly toward it.

Almost there. Her muscles ached with the cold and the struggle. She was freezing and exhausted, but she kept going. And then she heard splashing behind her and turned to look back.

Shawn had made it to the surface and was swim-ming after her, his pace a whole lot faster than hers. Fear snaked through her body like an electric cur-rent, and she swam faster, stroked harder. She didn't look back again, not until he grabbed her ankle just as she reached shallow water. She kicked free and lunged forward, falling face-first into the water and struggling to her feet again, sloshing through the heavy waves, until she finally left them behind and broke into a dead run on the dry ground. She didn't have a clue where to go. Not to the house—it would be locked, and there were never working phones there. Her cell was long gone. He'd destroyed it and hurled it from the car. And Shawn was running, too, now. Chasing her. Why wouldn't he just quit?

She headed for the road, barefoot, nearly numb with cold, and raced down it, debating whether to dodge into the woods and try to hide or keep going, hoping for help to arrive, a car to pass, a house with people inside to come into view.

But she wasn't fast enough. Shawn caught up, tackling her from behind and bringing her down hard. Her chin hit the pavement, her knees scraped its surface, and he was on her, flipping her onto her back, closing his hands around her throat, and squeezing while his wet hair dripped on her face. And she was right back where she'd been moments earlier, struggling for air and not finding any.

She pounded on him, clawed at his hands on her neck, but it did no good. Blackness began to descend. She thought she saw lights, once, bright through her closed eyelids. She thought she heard tires squealing.

Suddenly, the pressure was gone. She couldn't move, just lay there, breathing, waiting for her senses to return. She wasn't even cold anymore.

"Caroline. Caroline, talk to me. Come on. It's Peter. Talk to me." Hands on her face, patting her cheeks, shaking her shoulders. "Come on, Caroline."

She blinked her eyes open. Her brother leaned over her.

"You okay?"

"I don't know." It hurt to talk and sounded as if her voice box had been rubbed with sandpaper.

Peter looked up, then jumped to his feet, and Caroline followed him with her eyes as he lunged a few yards away. Jimmy had Shawn on the ground and was pounding the hell out of him.

"Jim, enough!" Peter gripped his shoulders, but Jim kept on punching. "Jesus, you're gonna kill him. Let up."

"Damn right I'm gonna kill him. This lowlife son of a—"

"Caroline needs you, Jimmy."

He paused with his fist drawn back, turned to look toward where she lay, and dropped Shawn, who landed in a heap on the pavement. Then he was on his feet, rushing toward her. He fell to his knees beside her and gathered her up into his arms, holding her close, warming her right through the chill. She heard sirens then but ignored them. She didn't want to know anything except this, the bliss of being in his arms. She didn't care about his secrets, or his past, or his lies. Not now. Right now, there was only this, and God, she needed it.

"I'm sorry," he whispered as he held her. "This is all my fault. All of it."

"No—"

"Yeah, it is. I pushed Shawn over the edge. I didn't mean to. I got some dirt on him and used it to force him to pay what he owed you."

"That wasn't a bad thing."

"More than that, I lied to you. Made you afraid of me, or you never would have run off by yourself tonight."

"I should have trusted you."

"You can barely talk." He ran his fingertips over her neck, gently, soothing. "Here are the paramedics. We're gonna get you to a hospital, okay? Get you checked out. Make sure you're okay. And then I'm gonna explain everything and beg you to give me another chance."

She tried to smile. "You don't have to beg. I barely gave you a chance to begin with. You saved my life tonight, Jimmy."

"I damn near cost you your life tonight." He lowered his head, and then the medics were easing him away from her, and the police were taking him aside and talking to him. Men in white covered her in blankets, checked her vitals, and bundled her into a waiting ambulance. She wondered if it was okay to sleep on the way, and then she gave up fighting it.

CHAPTER 11

She opened her eyes to seek out the source of the warmth surrounding her hand and found it came from another hand, holding hers. Jimmy's hand. Her gaze slid higher, until she met his eyes, to find them moist and staring into hers.

"The doctors say you're going to be okay. Thank God."

She smiled, tried to speak, but it hurt her throat.

"Here, try some water." He held a glass with a straw to her lips, and she sipped, but it hurt to swallow even more than it hurt to speak. When he took the glass away, he said, "Don't try to talk, okay? Just listen. I've got a lot to say to you."

She met his eyes again as he set the water aside, and she nodded once.

"I blame myself for all of this. If I'd been honest with you from the beginning, none of it would have happened. But I think I was fighting the truth, all along. Hoping that what I suspected couldn't be."

Frowning, she tipped her head to one side.

"I think it was my father, Caroline. I think my father killed that girl in Maine, but he died before I ever worked up the nerve to ask him. I didn't know, not then. I didn't even start to suspect until Natalie disappeared, too, and even then, I was so young. It's been haunting me, though. *She's* been haunting me, begging me to tell the police what I thought, so that they could find her, lay her to rest. But I couldn't. I just couldn't. That's why I wanted the house so bad. So I could find out for myself if it was really true."

She gripped his hand in both of hers, forced words, though they came out hoarse and raspy. "How do you know it is? And how could owning the house prove anything?"

He lowered his head. "We were having a pool built when the first girl went missing, back in Maine. There was just a hole in the ground, no concrete yet. The police checked it and found nothing. I can only assume he hid the body somewhere else until he'd been cleared, then buried her there before the concrete was poured. We moved just a few months later."

She frowned, still not understanding.

"The pool at my house—your house—it was put in right after Natalie disappeared. It's just ... it can't be a coincidence. I remember, Mom didn't even want it, but Dad insisted." He lowered his head, closed his eyes. "It was right after that, when she started showing up, wet and dripping, trying to tell me where to find her, I think."

"God," she whispered. The torment on his face told her just how much he'd agonized over all of this, and for how long. There was no feeling now that he was keeping anything from her. She saw nothing but honesty and pain in his eyes. "But you still don't know, not for sure."

He nodded. "I will. And soon. I told the police what I suspected. They're going to have to rip up the pool, Caroline. In fact, they're doing it now, and the police in Maine are doing the same. I'll pay for having a new one put in."

"I'm not sure I want a new one." She cleared her throat gently. "It's a lot, a huge burden you've been carrying around with you all this time. I guess I . . . I guess I understand why you pretended to be interested in me. It must have seemed worth the effort to get to the answers you've been seeking for so long."

His head came up slowly, and he met her eyes. "Baby, I never pretended anything with you. Not with you. I'll understand if you don't want anything more to do with me after this. The lies, the deception, the fact that I damn near got you killed. But even if you don't, I need you to know this was real. Everything we had together, it was real to me. I'm in love with you, Caroline."

Her heart seemed to melt in her chest, and tears sprang into her eyes. "I'm in love with you, too, Jimmy. No matter what the police find, it won't change that. I didn't think I'd ever find a man like you. I've been waiting so long. I was afraid to believe you could be for real. But I do, now."

A sigh rushed from his lips as he gathered her up from her pillows, into his arms, and held her. "You mean that?"

"I do. I really do."

"I'm gonna make you happy, baby. I swear, I am."

"You already have," she whispered, turning her face up and accepting the kiss her heart had been craving, for what felt like forever.

They stood hand in hand at the cemetery, a good distance from the spot where the service was taking place. Jim didn't want Natalie's family to be further traumatized by seeing the son of her killer at the funeral. His father was long dead. There would be no trial, no punishment, though Caroline liked to think the bastard was getting his just deserts in some other realm. Not only for murdering two innocent young girls but for what he'd put his son through. All these years. It had to have been pure torture. When she thought about the pain in the heart of the little boy who'd drawn those pictures, the nightmares, the haunting, the police suspecting him—it was almost too much to bear.

He had a lot of pain in his past. So did she. But Caroline had the feeling they were healing each other, and they were both going to be okay.

They waited until the service had ended, and all the mourners had gone away, to approach the still-open grave. Jimmy dropped the flowers he'd brought, and they landed atop the casket, which had been lowered into the ground.

They stood there for a moment, silent. And then he whispered, "I'm sorry it took me so long."

Caroline touched his arm. "Jimmy, look."

He lifted his head and looked where she pointed. There in the distance, she knew he saw what she did: a young woman, drifting away among the headstones, translucent, filmy, but there. It was Natalie, no longer wet and haunted but beautiful and smiling. As they stared, stunned, she turned to look directly at them and lifted a ghostly hand to wave. And then, in a shimmer, she was gone.

Jimmy turned to meet Caroline's eyes. No words were needed. They both knew she was at peace, at long last.

And so, Caroline thought, was she.

COBWEBS
OVER THE MOON

Lori Handeland

CHAPTER 1

My first clue that everything was about to change came on the night someone tried to kill me.

Hey, they don't need to hit me over the head with a brick to get my attention. A bullet whizzing past my right ear does the trick just fine.

Roger, my bodyguard, shoved me to the ground behind the limo. Beneath my faux-fur coat, my evening gown tore with a shriek of rending cloth to rival the shrieks of the crowd as they stampeded down Central Park West.

Night had fallen over New York City hours ago. The drifting clouds made it seem as if there were cobwebs over the moon.

I'd been on my way to a charity event—the story of my life. I guess they'd just have to do without me. In truth, there was no one to miss me if I were gone. Not even my father, who'd started hiring men like Roger to protect me as soon as I could walk.

I'd never been able to figure out why J. Thomas

Kelly IV—J.T. to everyone, including me—spent so many of his pretty green dollars protecting a daughter he'd never seemed to care for.

After having my mother committed, divorcing her, then marrying a succession of younger and younger wives who gave him blonder and blonder children, Daddy had no time for his dark-haired, dark-eyed, eldest, rudest child.

I'd learned how to handle the neglect; my mother hadn't. Phoebe killed herself the day the divorce papers arrived.

"Keep your head down," Roger snapped, shoving my nose into the pavement in case I didn't get the concept. Then he dialed 911 on his cell. I assumed the doorman, who'd scurried back into my apartment building at the first sign of trouble, had done the same.

Of course, it was rush hour in Helltown, I mean Manhattan, so it was anyone's guess when the cavalry would arrive.

"Carly." The urgency in Roger's voice made the world narrow to him and me, even as the danger made me hyperaware of every sound around us.

Someone was coming.

"Get behind me." He duck-walked past, his broad bulk blotting out the frosty silver light of a nearly full moon.

Nevertheless, I saw the man who stepped around the limo quite clearly. His eyes went straight to me, and he smiled. I'd never seen another smile like it. Our attacker not only wanted to kill me, he wanted other things, too. Things that would give me nightmares—if I survived them.

Roger fired. Our attacker jerked once, then burst into flames.

I sat back on my rump, hard. The jolt did nothing to dissipate my shock, not only over Roger shooting the man without any kind of warning but . . . since when did bullets cause spontaneous combustion?

Roger stood slowly, keeping his head low as he scanned the street for a second gunman. I didn't bother to get up. I doubted I could.

Several tenants came out of my building and gathered around the flames, staring into them as if they were at a bonfire. I half expected someone to break out the marshmallows.

A slightly hysterical giggle bubbled up at the thought. What was the matter with me?

A thud drew my attention to Roger, who'd keeled over at my feet. The new crisis brought me out of my lethargy as nothing else could. I was queen in a crisis. Give me a hundred members of the Women's League at a Mother's Day luncheon, serve Cabernet with the salmon, and watch me shine.

I crawled across the pavement, ignoring the scrape along my palms and the pain in my knees.

"Roger?" His eyelids fluttered open. "What happened?"

I asked the question as much about him as about the barbecuing assassin.

"I guess that first shot didn't miss after all." Roger touched his chest, and his hand came away covered in blood, which hadn't been immediately visible in the dim light on his black shirt.

"Crap," I muttered.

"I'll be okay," he said, though his eyes drifted shut.

The wail of what sounded like a hundred sirens came closer. "What am I supposed to tell the police?"

"Nothing." His voice was fading.

"People don't explode when you shoot them, Roger."

"I know."

"*What* is going on?"

"You'll have to ask your father about that," he said, and then he passed out.

Daddy. Swell. Just the guy I wanted to avoid.

The paramedics arrived, loaded Roger into the ambulance, and drove away. The police tried to take me in for questioning, but J.T.'s weasel-faced attorney showed up, and that was the end of that. I guess it paid to own the mayor.

Josh Branson hustled me into his limo, leaving the one Roger had hired behind. Half the police were already swarming all over it, while the other half stared at the still-burning corpse on the sidewalk.

"I need to go to the hospital," I said.

Alarm flared in Lawyer Boy's pale gray eyes. "You're hurt?"

"Not a scratch," I said, folding my fingers over my abraded palms and shifting so my dress did not reveal my skinned knees. "I'm worried about Roger."

"Who?"

Branson rarely bothered to learn the names of underlings; he'd no doubt learned that from J.T.

"My bodyguard."

"He'll be fine."

"I'd like to find that out for myself."

"No," he said simply.

I narrowed my eyes, but Branson wasn't scared of me. Despite his fresh face and youthful appearance, he had an ancient soul, forged in the fires of hell. Or maybe just Harvard Law.

"You can call the hospital as soon as I get you to your father," he continued.

"You're taking me to J.T.?"

"Of course. He's worried about you."

I gave an unladylike snort. "If he was that worried, he could have come himself."

"He had a meeting."

Why I found that funny, I'm not quite sure, but I started laughing, and then I couldn't stop. Branson turned toward the window and ignored me.

I'm sure he thought I was a waste of a good penthouse apartment, and he was probably right. If I really hated my father's lifestyle, his choices, his filthy lucre, shouldn't I be living in a rattrap somewhere and waiting tables?

I'd tried it, and you know what? It sucks.

I'd discovered I helped a lot more people by using my father's money and his name to solicit donations for my charitable foundations. Rich people didn't talk to waitresses unless it was to give their order; they did like to impress the eldest daughter of one of the richest men in Manhattan.

And the penthouse apartment? I just liked it.

We reached J.T.'s building on Broad Street, and I got out of the limo with nothing more than a nod for Branson. Before I'd even shut the door completely, the sleek black car pulled away. Guess I'd have to take a taxi home.

A single security guard remained in the foyer. "Miss Carly," Warner greeted as he unlocked the outer door. "You all right?"

"I'm fine."

"Good to hear. Your father said to send you right up."

"Thank you." I headed for the hallway leading to J.T.'s suite.

"You think it's okay if I go?" Warner asked. "Mr. Kelly said I could as soon as you arrived. It's my grand-daughter's birthday."

Warner was retired NYPD. This job was a cupcake compared with that. Still, he took it very seriously, as evidenced by the worry in his eyes.

J.T. always hired men for his security details who were grossly overqualified. Many of our bodyguards were former Special Forces; one had even been a colo-nel in the Israeli army. That guy had scared the crap out of me.

"Go ahead," I answered. "Place is locked up, no one here but us, right?"

Warner nodded. "Mr. Kelly's meeting ended half an hour ago."

"Have a nice time."

The reception area outside my father's office was empty, which struck me as odd. If J.T. was working late, his executive assistant should be as well. Maybe she was inside taking notes, or whatever euphemism they used for it around here.

I'd pegged Julie as the next Mrs. J. Thomas Kelly IV. She had that look, and J.T. hadn't impregnated anyone for a few years. He was due.

I knocked lightly on the door to his inner sanctum, and it swung open at my touch.

"J.T.?"

My foot slid on the ceramic tile, and when I glanced down, I saw a splash of bright red across the Italian marble. My skin prickled, and I wished for the first time in my life that my bodyguard was shadowing me.

J.T.'s bodyguard was at his side, as was Julie. They didn't look any more alive than he did. Then my father groaned; I ran forward and knelt next to him.

A throat wound seemed to be the source of most of the blood. Tiny puncture wounds marred his hands, and the forearms of his usually pristine white dress shirt appeared russet.

"J.T.?" I touched his wrist, which was far too cold. "I'll call nine-one-one."

He grabbed my hand in a surprisingly strong grip, and his blue eyes bored into mine. "Wait."

"I'm here," I said.

If I'd expected any dying declarations of love, I was disappointed, but then I so often was when it came to J.T.

"Go. Now."

"But—"

"Get out." The force of the words made him cough. Pink foam appeared on his lips. That couldn't be good.

"I'll call for help."

"Too late."

"You'll be fine," I insisted.

"Phoebe," he whispered.

My skin prickled again. "Mom's dead, J.T."

"No."

Now I was as cold as the tile floor against my knees. "She isn't dead?"

He closed his eyes, shook his head.

"You bastard," I whispered. "Where is she?"

His breathing became more labored. "Alaska."

That made sense. Phoebe had been adopted as an infant by a wealthy Boston couple. She knew she was Inuit, that she'd been born in Alaska. She'd always wanted to go there. When she'd started seeing and then believing things, J.T. must have granted her wish.

"*Where* in Alaska?" I demanded.

"Secret," he muttered.

"J.T.—"

"Look in the safe. Two. Twenty-five. Eighty."

"The date you made your first million," I murmured. *Figures*.

His lips curved. "Always were smart . . ."

Was that praise?

"Smart ass," he said more clearly.

Nah.

"Trust no one," J.T. continued.

"That shouldn't be a problem." I'd always had trust issues. "Who's after us?"

I could understand people trying to kill J.T.; half the time, I wanted to. But I wasn't *that* big of a bitch.

"Phoebe," J.T. murmured. "You were right."

The silence in the room was so sudden it took me several seconds to register that he'd stopped breathing.

I got to my feet, then stared down at J.T. for several seconds. Interesting that his last words were for a woman he'd abandoned twenty years ago.

Slowly, I lifted my hands; they were covered in blood. The sight cut through the haze that had come over me. Since entering the room, I'd lost a father and gained a mother. I wasn't sure what to think about that.

Better think later. J.T. had been murdered; someone had tried to kill me. I had to get out of there, then get out of town. Convenient, since nothing on heaven and earth was going to stop me from seeing my mother. I just had to be careful. I didn't need to bring whoever was after me down on her.

Sure, I could have notified the police, been taken into protective custody, but hadn't J.T. just said to trust no one?

Not that I'd ever listened to him before. Unless what he'd said suited me, and this did.

Quickly I called the hospital about Roger but no one would give me any information. I was on my own.

I hurried to J.T.'s private bathroom, washed away every speck of blood, then stripped off my formal gown and strappy sandals. I stuffed them and my fur coat—warm but too attention-grabbing—into the linen closet and, familiar with J.T.'s penchant for romantic getaways, easily located a travel bag full of woman's clothes beneath the sink. The name on the tag was Julie's.

"I guess she *was* in line for promotion," I murmured.

Luckily, Julie was almost my size. Her black V-neck top was a little tight, the black jeans a little short, but her boots fit and covered up the high-waters nicely.

I hadn't worn a bra with the evening gown, and there was no way I could shove my C-cups into Julie's almost A's, so the clingy shirt became a bit pornographic, but I'd live. I hoped I would.

My tiny evening bag was pretty, not practical. I'd only had enough room for my ID, tip money, and lipstick.

I was going to need lots more cash to hire a private

plane, which was the best way to leave New York without drawing too much attention. Knowing J.T., there'd be rainy-day money in his safe.

I grabbed Julie's bag and headed into the office, averting my gaze from the bodies. In the bottom right-hand drawer of J.T.'s desk was a dial. I spun the numbers, and the top popped open.

Beneath it lay twenty thousand dollars in cash and a brochure for Lake Delton Psychiatric Clinic in rustic Alaska. The place was located between Fairbanks and the Arctic Circle. *Brrr*.

I stuffed every last dollar into the bag. Straightening, I was unable to keep my gaze from drifting one last time to the bodies.

They were gone.

CHAPTER 2

"What the——?"

I closed my eyes, squeezed hard, and opened them again. Still no J.T., no Julie, no bodyguard. I'd think I'd imagined everything, except the blood was still there. The blood was everywhere.

I had to get out of there, because those bodies hadn't moved on their own, which meant I wasn't alone. And anyone who'd moved them but hadn't mentioned it to me was someone I didn't want to meet.

I wished, not for the first time, that I hadn't sent Warner home. I also wished that I'd thought to relieve the bodyguard of his gun.

I snatched Julie's coat—a nondescript black wool—from her office and headed out the door.

The place was silent, eerily so, and Julie's clunky-heeled boots thunked so loudly the sound bounced off the smooth marble walls, drowning out everything else.

It wasn't until I paused to button the coat that I

heard the faint ticks, like a clock but too staccato—
more like a horse, clip-clopping, faster and faster. *Ta-ta,
ta-ta, ta-ta.*

According to Warner, no one had been in the building but J.T., Julie, the bodyguard, and me. Since I was
the only one left alive, who was hurrying down the cor-
ridor? Must be the murderer.

I glanced back, but whoever it was hadn't reached
the corner yet. As I stared, wide-eyed, a shadow skated
across the gray tile floor, too ghostly to make out, but
something was there. I knew it, even before that something growled.

Giving in to panic, I ran.

Julie's boots made a horrible racket, but bless her,
she'd put some kind of traction patches on the soles, so
I didn't slip and fall.

I raced into the foyer and slammed against the exit;
the impact made my teeth rattle, but the door didn't
move.

"Oh, God," I whispered.

The ta-ta, ta-ta, ta-ta got faster and louder. I lifted a
hand to hammer on the glass, then I saw the latch.

Locked. Duh.

I exploded into the chilly December air. The lock
clicked home behind me as I turned. Nothing was there
but the darkness. I inched closer, then closer still, pressing first my palms, then my body, then my nose to the
glass.

A dark shape shot out of the gloom, smashing into
the door right in front of my face. I jerked backward
with a shriek, catching my heel on a crack and hitting the sidewalk hard. My ass was going to be one big
bruise come tomorrow.

I waited for a second strike, but none came.

Getting to my feet, I tried to reconstruct what I'd seen. Big, black, furry. Ears, tail, teeth.

When had J.T. gotten an attack dog?

"Beast could have killed me," I muttered, then paused.

Had it killed J.T.?

He'd had puncture marks on his hands, which could have been made by teeth, and didn't dogs always go for the throat?

Though the actual killer who'd been after me was ashes, I'd been thinking there was a mastermind to this plan. Why else would J.T. be so concerned that I trust no one and take care of Phoebe, if he wasn't worried a mysterious "someone" was after us all?

But why shoot at me, then sic a dog on everyone else? For that matter, how could a dog kill two grown men, one of them adept with a gun, as well as a grown woman?

I headed toward the subway. I hadn't ridden it in years, but I didn't want to hail a cab and risk being traced to the airport too easily.

I doubted anyone would discover the blood in J.T.'s office until the building opened, if then. No one would have any reason to go into his inner sanctum unless they had an appointment, and J.T. didn't do appointments before ten a.m. By then, I'd be halfway across the country.

Less than twenty-four hours later, I stood on a frozen lake as the bush pilot I'd hired headed back to civilization. The only way to reach this part of the state had been by private aircraft at an astronomical price. Since

I'd pay anything to reach Phoebe, I'd forked over the cash and climbed onto the plane.

I'd been a little creeped out when I'd learned that at this time of year, in the place I was headed, only a few hours of pale light appeared each day, and that was if the sky wasn't cloudy. Any farther north, and the sun wouldn't be visible at all until spring.

A cozy log cabin sat on the shore of the lake. Both matched the photos in the brochure, so I strode to the front door and knocked.

A few minutes later, I knocked again. When no one answered, I got uneasy. Shouldn't they have heard the plane? If I lived out here in the great big nothing, I'd be excited about visitors, no matter who they were. You could be pretty certain you wouldn't open the door to a salesman or a Jehovah's Witness.

I glanced around, which was just foolish, because no one was there to shout, "Stop! Thief!" if I walked right in, so I did. Then I stood staring at virtually the same scene I'd left behind in New York.

Dead woman, dead man, lots of blood.

I couldn't breathe, terrified the woman was Phoebe. Then I realized she was too short, too young, too blond. The man was big, muscular, no neck to speak of—another bodyguard.

Why had Phoebe needed a bodyguard? Everyone thought she was dead.

A better question would be: Where was Phoebe?

"Mom?" I called. "It's Carly. You okay?"

My voice shook. I was getting pretty sick of stumbling into rooms full of dead people. I might be good in a crisis, but this was ridiculous.

I searched every nook and cranny but came up

empty. There was no help for it; I was going to have to call the authorities, regardless of my reluctance to give away my location. I had two more dead bodies and a missing mother. There was no way I could look for her out there.

However, my tour of the premises had not netted a phone. Though I wasn't wild about the idea, I searched the bodies.

They'd been killed by massive throat trauma, same as the last set. The man had puncture wounds on his hands and arms as well.

"No big black dog around here," I muttered as I went through his pockets. Or at least, I hadn't seen one yet.

Neither one of them had a cell phone. I took the guard's gun; he didn't need it anymore.

With no choice, I dug my phone out of my travel bag. The tiny icon for service blinked, cell phone code for "In your dreams." Maybe stepping outside would help.

I did. It didn't. Now what?

I was stranded at the edge of civilization with two dead bodies, and I had no idea if the killer remained nearby. I'd never felt more alone in my life.

As if in answer to the thought, a mournful howl rose toward the full, white moon. What sounded like a hundred others joined the first; the serenade surrounded me, growing in volume until I wanted to wail, too.

As suddenly as the howls had begun, they stopped. The resulting silence made me more nervous than all the noise had.

They had big wolves in Alaska; I was sure of it, although any wolf would appear pretty damn big to me. The largest canine in Manhattan was a standard poodle. Not exactly a ferocious beast—unless you took away its sparkly jeweled collar.

Standing on the back porch, with the moon all aglow, surrounded by trees so big they seemed prehistoric—hell, they probably were—I got the first sense that perhaps running off to find my mother hadn't been one of my brighter ideas.

My second hint came when twigs broke to the left, snow crunched to my right, and a thud directly in front made me reach for the gun in my coat.

I backed toward the door, but before I could get inside, a huge, hulking, furry creature emerged from the forest.

CHAPTER 3

"Big Foot?" I asked.

"Who the hell are you?" The voice, which had a Southern lilt so far out of place in this land of ice and snow that I gaped, came from the depths of a fur-shrouded hood. Was that a wolfskin coat?

Nah. Couldn't be legal.

He strode forward, and I shrank back, shoving the gun in front of me and waving it around a little. "Don't move."

Reaching out with longer arms than a person should have, he yanked away the weapon.

"Use it or lose it." He turned the thing over in his hands. "How'd you get Joe's gun?"

"He's—" I wasn't sure how to break the news about Joe, or even if I should.

I'd come upon the scene of a multiple murder, again, and now this guy had walked out of the woods. I should run for my life. Except he had the gun, and he'd probably just shoot me. Talk about being too stupid to live.

My neck had a crick from peering up at him. At five-foot-ten, I was a tall woman, but this . . . person had to top me by six inches and outweigh me by a hundred pounds. Or maybe that was just the coat.

With an exasperated sigh, the beast shoved past me and went inside, coming to an abrupt stop almost immediately.

"Shit," he muttered.

My sentiments exactly.

The man pushed back his hood as he turned.

Hello.

Tanned, rugged, with hazel eyes that held more green than brown and tawny hair shorn close to his head, he was handsome in the way of cowboys and NFL quarterbacks.

"You're the kid," he drawled. "Phoebe's daughter."

"Who are you?"

He hesitated, then glanced at the bodies and shrugged. "Phoebe had a guard and a nurse twenty-four seven. We rotated in biweekly shifts. One week new guard, one week new nurse." He scowled. "Gonna need a new one of both after today."

"You're her guard."

"No, I'm the nurse."

Sarcasm? I wasn't sure. He knelt next to the woman and set his big, blunt fingers to her wrist, checking for a pulse. Damn, I should have thought of that.

"Is she—?"

"Definitely." He switched his ministrations to the man. "Ditto. What happened?"

"I walked in; there they were." I left out the extreme case of déjà vu.

"Phoebe." He rose quickly to his feet.

"Not here. I checked."

"Not good."

"Because?"

"She's either out there alone—and your mother doesn't have the sense to put on a coat to take a walk, let alone grab one when she's running for her life—or someone took her."

"Why would someone take her?"

"You tell me. Daddy paid big money not only to keep your mother way out here but to keep her protected. Why?"

"He was paranoid?"

"I've discovered that most people who are paranoid usually have a good reason."

"Really? I've found that most people who are paranoid are nuts."

His lips twitched. I wasn't certain if I'd amused him at last or merely annoyed him even more.

"What are you doing here?" he asked.

I wasn't going to elaborate on what had brought me to Alaska. I barely knew the man. Instead, I gave the short version.

"I came to see my mother."

He lifted one brow. "Good luck with that."

God, he was annoying.

"What kind of nurse are you?" I demanded. "Army?"

"How'd you guess?"

"Your bedside manner sucks."

"Since my bedside manner usually takes place in a war zone, I can't imagine why."

I wasn't surprised to discover J.T. had hired an

Army nurse—if this guy was telling the truth, and why lie?—just another case of overkill.

"What's your name?"

"Dylan Shepard."

Didn't mean anything to me, but why should it? Until yesterday, I'd thought my mother was dead. I certainly hadn't kept tabs on her guards and nurses.

"Where'd you come from?" I continued.

"Originally or today?"

"Both."

"Alabama and my cabin."

"Which is where?"

"South of Tennessee, north of the Gulf."

"Funny guy."

"I get that a lot."

I gave him a long look.

"I own a fishing cabin about two miles from here," he continued. "Sometimes I'll stay there between shifts."

"And the other times?"

"I fly to Fairbanks and get a life."

"You're a pilot?" My voice rose with excitement.

"No, but I can call one." He frowned at the bodies again. "Right now, I think I'll call the police."

"With what?" I asked. "If there's a phone here, I can't find it."

"Extreme security. J.T.'s orders."

"What if there was an emergency?"

He lifted a brow. "Like this?"

I spread my hands.

"I have a phone at my place." He headed for the door, and I followed. When he stopped, I rammed into him, then bounced back about three feet.

"Where do you think you're going?" he demanded.

"I'm not staying here." I glanced at the bodies. "With them. I'm going with you."

"Listen, Your Highness, just because you're queen of Manhattan don't make you the boss of me."

"Actually, I think I *am* the boss of you."

"How you figure?"

"J.T.'s dead."

He didn't appear surprised. "How?"

I motioned to the bodies. "Same way."

"That's . . . weird."

I had to agree.

Suddenly, he tilted his head.

"What?" I asked.

"Shh!" He punctuated the sharp hiss with an even sharper hand gesture. Since I wasn't used to being shushed by anyone but J.T., I was shocked enough to do exactly that. I still didn't hear anything.

Shepard crossed the floor. Inching to the side of the window, he peered out cautiously, then yanked his head back just as the glass exploded inward.

"Dammit!" Ducking low, he raced for the door, snatching my arm as he went by and dragging me along with him.

"What happened?"

"Shut up and run." He shoved me outside. "Fast."

"Where?" All the trees looked alike, and there wasn't a path that I could see.

Shepard shouldered past. "Try to keep up. Try not to get shot."

"Gee, I'll do my best," I muttered.

I glanced at the house. Shadows flitted beyond the

windows. They were inside, but soon enough they'd discover that we weren't. I hurried after Shepard, who was already a hundred feet ahead.

I jogged every day, but there was a heap big difference between jogging on a treadmill with my fancy-schmancy sneakers and hoofing it through the snow, wearing someone else's boots and fearing for my life. Nevertheless, I managed to cling to Shepard's heels.

I didn't hear sounds of pursuit, probably because all I could hear were my own panicked breaths and the terrified pounding of my heart. I started to get winded; I didn't know how much longer I could keep this up.

We burst from the trees and into an open field. I cringed at the glare of the full moon off all that snow. We were sitting ducks out here.

I slid into the cover of the trees, but that only brought me closer to our pursuers, although I still didn't hear anything beyond a few crunches of snow in the distance. Shouldn't they be calling out to one another, thundering after us, making a racket? That they weren't only made me more nervous.

"Over here." Shepard jabbed a finger to our right, grabbed my wrist, and dragged me after him. Instead of running straight across the pristine white field, we skirted the tree line.

Unable to stop myself, I glanced back. The moon revealed shadows fast approaching. The angle of the light made them appear almost inhuman.

My hesitation drew Shepard's attention. "They're good," he muttered.

I'd been thinking the same thing. Shepard knew the area; we should be farther ahead than we were. Sure, we'd left tracks in the snow, but in the thickness of the forest, tracks should be pretty hard to see. Unless our pursuers had freakishly good night vision.

"Get inside," Shepard ordered.

A cabin had popped out of nowhere, reminding me of Hansel, Gretel, and the witch's house—an unpleasant image, considering the fiery death at the end, at least for the witch.

Nevertheless, I ran up the steps. The front door wasn't locked, and I tumbled inside, Shepard on my heels. He flicked the lights, revealing a one-room cabin—stove, bed, table, and chairs.

Shepard lowered a heavy iron bar across the door, then slammed wooden shutters over the nearest window. I followed his lead, dealing with the shutters at the back of the house and struggling with a similar bar on the rear door.

When we'd finished, we stood on opposite sides of the room, listening. Not a sound came from outside. They had to be out there. What were they doing?

A sudden burst of howling made me start. My heart, which had been slowing, leaped and thundered once more. It sounded as if a pack of wolves had encircled the cabin.

I figured our pursuers would shoot a few, then start shooting us, but the howls continued, rising and falling in a wild chorus. Then, just as suddenly as they'd begun, the howls stopped.

Shepard cursed. "Let's go."

Before I could ask where and why, the lights went out with a tinny *thunk*, suspending us in navy blue darkness.

"Oh, goody," I muttered. "Trapped."

"Relax," he murmured. "We aren't trapped."

"We're in an isolated cabin with wolves and bad guys all around us. Electricity's out—no phone, no lights. Feels pretty trapped to me."

A sharp creak was followed by a draft of cool air, a snick, and a faint beam of yellow light illuminating a door in the floor. Steps led downward.

"You're not really a nurse, are you?" I asked.

The flashlight splashed across his face, revealing a slight smile. Though the expression did not reach his eyes, it did soften the harsh lines of his face. He appeared younger when he smiled, and I was tempted to ask him how young, but he turned and disappeared down the steps.

I had little choice but to follow, even though dark, musty, spidery, rat-infested basements are not my thing. Shepard perched a few steps below, holding open the heavy trap door. He indicated with a jerk of his head that I should continue down.

He was big, and I wasn't exactly small; as I went by, I brushed against him, chest to chest, hip to stomach. If I leaned forward just a little, my lips would brush his throat. God, he smelled good. Like moon-shrouded snow and fresh-cut evergreens.

His smile faded; he appeared almost confused. Had it been that long since a woman's breasts had been near his chest? I know it had been quite a while since these particular breasts had been near anything but a bra.

If we weren't running for our lives, I'd be tempted to discover what lay beneath that fur coat.

All my life, I'd dated slim, rich, Yankee men whose muscles had been honed by squash or a personal trainer and whose pedigrees had been much bluer than my own. I'd been interested enough, but I'd never felt the longing for them that shot through me now. The bizarre desire to get naked and sweaty and rough with a man whose muscles were bigger than my head and had been honed amid fire and blood and death.

Logically, I knew my reaction was the result of an innate need to mate with someone stronger than me, to be possessed, then protected. As soon as I was safe again, all of the lust would go away.

Why, yes, I *was* a psychology major. A lot of people with insane parents were.

I finished sliding past, the speed of the movement only serving to rub myself more thoroughly against him. Remembering the Lycra shirt and my lack of a bra, my nipples hardened. Shepard glanced down, his hazel eyes appearing almost blue in the faint ray of light. I'd opened my coat in the warmth of his cabin, and what I felt pressing against my shirt, straining toward him, had to be visible even in this light.

I wanted him to touch me, to push me against the wall, cup my aching breasts in his big, hard hands, put his mouth over my nipples, and suckle as he unbuckled his pants, yanked down mine, and thrusted.

He gritted his teeth, tore his gaze from mine, and pulled the trap door shut behind us. My cheeks flooded with heat. What was wrong with me? I preferred my sex neat and tidy, no emotional attachments, no spending the night, the less muss and fuss, the better. But out here, with him, more things had changed than the weather.

When Shepard handed me the flashlight, his face had gone blank, as if the encounter had never happened. I wasn't sure if I should be insulted or relieved. Maybe he was gay.

I preceded him down the steps to a small earthen room. An even smaller tunnel led away from it.

"How did you do this?" I tracked the flashlight beam across the walls, the floor, the ceiling. "The ground has to be frozen solid."

"With enough money, you can do anything."

Understanding dawned. "J.T."

He lifted one massive shoulder, then lowered it. "Nothing but the best for Phoebe and her keepers."

I frowned. That didn't sound like J.T. If he'd cared so much about Phoebe, why had he sent her there? Why had he told everyone she was dead? Perhaps to keep something like this—blood, death, panicked pursuit—from happening?

Shepard began to root around a shadowy corner. Seconds later, he held out a pair of gloves and a really ugly hat.

"No, thanks," I said. "I'm trying to cut down."

He rolled his eyes. "This isn't the place for vanity, Highness. Without these, you'll get frostbite, and I don't have the time."

"Thought you were a nurse."

"You want your fingers and ears to fall off? That would not be a good look for you."

"Fine." I grabbed the gloves and the hat and put them on, while he grabbed a monstrous pack and slipped it onto his back, then headed into the tunnel.

The trip was a short one. I didn't see a single spider. Not a rat to be had, which probably had more to do with the subzero temperatures than luck. My luck hadn't been anything but bad since I'd stepped out of my apartment . . . had that only been last night?

The tunnel tilted upward, narrowing. By the time a

lighter shade of darkness appeared, we had descended to our knees, Shepard removing the pack and shoving it ahead of him, as we crawled through a very tight space. I didn't like it, but I doubted I'd like what happened if I turned around and went back any better.

"Once they're inside," Shepard murmured, "it won't take them long to figure out where we've gone and follow. If we can get far enough ahead, we should be okay."

I hadn't heard sounds of pursuit, but I'd been too fixated on the possibility of spiders and rats to pay much attention.

We reached the exit hole. Shepard flicked off the flashlight and shoved it into the pocket of his fur coat. Then he made a staying motion with one gloved mitt and crept through.

I tensed in expectation of an outcry, a gunshot. When none came, he held out a hand and helped me from the passage.

We emerged much deeper in the forest, a place where the trees were so tall and thick you could barely see past them. In the distance, shadows danced—shadows that appeared more wolflike than human.

"You think they went inside already?" I whispered.

Shepard opened his mouth—and the world exploded into sound and fire and light.

CHAPTER 4

"Was that your cabin?" I asked.

"Was," Shepard agreed. He didn't sound very concerned. "Guess they decided to do this the easy way."

"Why is that"—I stabbed a finger at the brightly burning blaze—"the easy way?"

"No shootout, no storming the door. Just *kaboom*, and they're done."

"If it's so damn easy to blow up a place, why didn't they do that at the clinic?"

"Could be they wanted to make sure they had the right place, the right person—or anyone at all. Blow someone up, and you're never quite sure."

He had a point.

"What did I ever do to have people on opposite sides of the country trying to kill me?" I muttered.

"Excuse me?"

"Someone tried to kill me in New York, too."

"That might have been a good thing to share before now."

"You think?" I mocked, then really wished I hadn't.

I'd learned sarcasm at J.T.'s knee, discovered it was the best way to fight back against a man who had no use or affection for me. Being good at being a smart ass was my only measure of control in a world where I had little. The habit was hard to break.

Around here—I glanced at the trees, the snow, the acres and acres of nothing else—I didn't have much control, either. Still, being Sarcasm Girl with the only person alive for miles who hadn't tried to kill me yet was probably not a good choice.

However, Shepard's face had turned thoughtful; he didn't even react to my comment, which made it no fun at all. "Someone tried to kill you, then they killed your dad?" he asked.

"Not the same person, but basically, yes."

"Then they came for your mom."

"Also probably not the same person; they would have needed to have a plane waiting in order to beat me here."

"Not so hard."

True, but . . . "Everyone thought she was dead, including me."

His eyebrows lifted. "Well, that explains why you didn't call, you didn't write." He glanced away. "She cried for you."

My throat tightened. I'd cried myself to sleep a lot of nights missing my mother; she'd done the same missing me. If J.T. weren't dead, I'd be tempted to kill him.

"J.T. could have told them Phoebe was alive and where to find her," Shepard continued.

"Why would he do that?"

"People will do just about anything for one more minute of life."

I liked to think I wouldn't, but I'd never had the opportunity to test the theory. I hoped I never would.

"We should go," Shepard said. "They think we're dead, but that doesn't mean they won't make certain of it."

He began to walk; I began to follow. "Where are we going?"

"I've got to stash you somewhere safe," he said. "Then I'll find your mother."

"Like hell." I stopped. "I'm going with you."

Shepard didn't even turn. "No, you aren't."

"She's my mother." He kept walking. "Hey!"

His shoulders flinched, but at least he turned. "Keep it down, Highness. The bad guys aren't deaf, and noises travel fast and far around here."

In Manhattan, noises blended. Shouting wasn't a big deal; cab drivers did it every day.

"Sorry," I said more quietly. "I just want to find my mother. I *need* to find her, to see her. To explain—"

To my horror, my voice broke. I wasn't a crier, at least not anymore. Crying hadn't brought my mother back; it hadn't made J.T. love me. Nothing could.

I cleared my throat, stiffened my spine, and met Shepard's hard hazel eyes. He said nothing, just turned and walked away.

I had no choice but to follow, and as I did, my mind picked at a single pounding question. Why had J.T. told me my mother was dead?

Not that I was shocked he'd lied—when hadn't he?—but what was the point? Why would J.T. have cared if I visited Phoebe? It wasn't as if he was competing for my affections. He'd never wanted them.

There was so much going on I didn't understand, and there was no way I was going to sit somewhere safe, wherever that was, and wait for Dylan Shepard to find my mother for me. Just once, I was going to be there for the woman who'd brought me into the world.

Shepard paused; I did, too. His shoulders were so massive they blocked out the sight of whatever it was that had made him stop. I leaned to the right, the left. Nothing. I glanced behind us, then upward. The trees were so thick I could barely discern the moon, let alone the stars.

"Are we lost?"

He shot me a withering glare. "Stay here."

Before I could argue, he strode into the forest and, despite his size, blended into the shadows.

Without Shepard, the night closed in. Logically, I knew the trees hadn't moved nearer; nevertheless, I kept throwing glances over my shoulder to check. The wind whistled through the branches, the chill of the snow crept through my boots, and the air stung my cheeks. I was the last living soul for miles.

"Phoebe's gone." Shepard's voice sounded right next to my ear, and I jumped, managing to bite off the shriek before it echoed everywhere.

"Don't do that!" I rubbed between my breasts with the heel of my hand. How could such a big guy move so quietly?

"Sorry."

He didn't sound sorry. He sounded amused, which caused me to snap, "I know Phoebe's gone. Tell me something new."

"She was here less than an hour ago, and she headed"—he pointed north—"that way."

I swallowed my childish annoyance. "How do you know?"

"Rangers lead the way. Hoo-ah."

"You were in the Special Forces?" He nodded. "Thought you were a nurse."

"Medic."

Trust J.T. to hire the best of both worlds—medical training and supreme security.

"We need to find your mother before someone else does," he said, and turned away.

I followed him to a small hole in the snow where human tracks led north.

"Abandoned coyote den," Shepard explained. "I showed the place to Phoebe once. Made it our rendezvous point, just in case something like this happened."

"You expected to be attacked?"

His eyes met mine, and I saw the man he'd been, the man he still was. "Guys like me always expect to be attacked."

Which was probably how he'd stayed alive. "If this was a rendezvous," I asked, "why didn't she wait?"

"Probably got spooked."

"Because of the continual darkness, prehistoric trees, gun-wielding maniacs with explosives, and marauding wolf packs? I can't understand why."

He studied me. "How much do you know about why your mother was sent here?"

"She had delusions."

"Did anyone ever tell you what those delusions were?"

"No."

A delusion was a delusion, as far as I was concerned. Phoebe had seen things that weren't there, heard things that didn't exist, believed things that weren't true. What difference did it make what those things were?

"Phoebe thought there were monsters after her," Shepard continued. "Werewolves, to be exact."

CHAPTER 5

"That's ridiculous," I snapped.

"There's more to this world than you think, Highness."

I doubted that. J.T.'d had no patience for tall tales. He'd set me straight on the Tooth Fairy, Santa Claus, and the Easter Bunny toot-sweet. Considering my mother's slim grip on reality, that was probably for the best.

I'd had no delusions of my own. No hope that magic would change my life. No belief that love could conquer all. I knew better.

Shepard reached into the pocket of his coat and pulled out Joe's gun. He popped the clip, removed a bullet, and held it up. "What does that look like to you?"

"Is this a trick question?"

"Look at it closely. What's the first thing you see?"

"Violence. Death. Blood."

He made an exasperated sound. "I mean physical properties." He turned the bullet this way and that, until a shaft of moonlight bounced off its surface and nearly blinded me.

"Shiny," I answered.

"What kind of shiny?"

"Silver." Shepard lifted his eyebrows, and I understood. "Joe carried silver bullets?"

"So did I before my guns were blown to smithereens."

"Why?"

"Silver kills people, too."

"Too?" I repeated. "You were *expecting* werewolves?"

"Phoebe was."

"She was insane!"

"Was she?" He snapped the silver bullet back into the clip and popped the clip into the gun. "You said J.T. was killed in the same way as Joe and the nurse—throat torn, bite marks on the hands?"

"That pretty much sums it up."

"You didn't find this bizarre?"

"There was an attack dog."

"Isn't it too big of a coincidence for J.T.'s security hound to flip out and kill three people on one side of the country and another beast thousands of miles away to do the same?"

"That explanation makes more sense than werewolves. There's no such thing. Believing there was put my mother in the nuthouse."

"Burying your head in the sand will put you in the morgue."

Now I was exasperated. "How can you stand there and tell me you believe in werewolves?"

"Because I've seen them."

I opened my mouth, shut it again. If he believed that—and I could tell he did—Shepard was as crazy as Phoebe. For all I knew, he could have been a resident of the clinic and not an employee. I only had his word that he was a nurse, a former soldier, a sane person.

"Didn't you find it odd," he continued, "that the guys at the clinic were able to follow us to my cabin so easily, hardly making a sound?"

"They were highly trained."

"They were werewolves."

"That's crazy," I said, before I could stop myself. Crazy people often got crazier when you called them crazy. One of their many quirks. "They were assassins or government operatives, maybe both."

When put that way, maybe werewolves were the better choice.

"I heard them howling, Carly. So did you. We were surrounded by wolves."

Though I knew it was pointless, I tried one more time to convince him. "You don't honestly think wolves blew up the cabin? Kind of hard to manage without thumbs."

"They shape-shifted. That's what werewolves do."

"So they became wolves to follow us, shifted into people so they could blow us up, then became wolves again? Seems like a lot of hassle to me."

"If I were in charge, I'd have some shift and some remain human. Takes care of all your hunting and killing needs."

He had a point, but I still didn't believe in were-wolves.

"If there aren't werewolves," he pressed, "why the silver bullets in the guns at the clinic?"

"To keep Phoebe from flipping out?" *And you, too,* I wanted to add, but refrained. "Why would they kill J.T. and the others as werewolves, then try to blow us up?"

"To make certain you're dead, that you won't rise again as one of them."

Though I knew he was nuts and none of this was real, nevertheless, his words made me shiver, or maybe it was just the continuous ill wind whipping my hair, stinging my cheeks, and insinuating itself through the fibers of Julie's too-light-for-an-Alaskan-winter-night coat.

"The others aren't dead?" I asked.

"Hard to say, but I wouldn't be surprised if they turned up somewhere. You said there was an attack dog at J.T.'s office. Was it a big dog?"

"Aren't all attack dogs huge?"

"Were the eyes human?"

I started to laugh. Shepard didn't.

"Werewolves retain human eyes even in wolf form. If you'd gotten a good look at the animal, you might have recognized it."

My laughter died as I rubbed my forehead. "You think the attack dog was a werewolf, the one that killed my father?"

"For all we know, it could have *been* your father."

My hand dropped. J.T. as a werewolf—now, *that* was a frightening thought.

"Tell me one thing," Shepard continued. "Were the dead people still dead when you left the building?"

My heart gave one hard, painful thump as if trying to jump from my chest, then began to patter too fast.

Shepard grabbed my elbow. "What happened?"

"The bodies were gone," I whispered. "I thought the murderer had moved them."

"Sounds like they moved themselves."

I didn't believe this. I *didn't*. There had to be a logical explanation other than dead people returning to life as murderous beasts.

"We need to keep going." Shepard glanced back the way we'd come. "At the moment, they think we're dead, but that won't last forever."

"Why not?"

"Werewolves possess the physical abilities of wolves." At my blank expression, he elaborated. "Superior senses of sight, sound, and scent."

In other words, they'd be able to smell us out here, if they didn't hear or see us first. I glanced over my shoulder, too. "We should have a good head start."

"Won't last. Wolves can run forty miles an hour. They've been known to range a hundred twenty-five miles in a single day—although forty is average. They'll chase a herd for miles just to tire them out, then accelerate. Combine all of that with human intelligence . . ." He spread his hands.

I wasn't buying this, but it wasn't doing me any good to stand there, either. "Okay, let's go."

We began to walk again, Shepard leading the way, breaking a path through the snow so I could follow. Every once in a while, he stopped, pointing to my mother's footprint. I only had his word that the prints were Phoebe's, but who else would be walking around the Alaskan wilderness alone?

The longer I followed Shepard, the more nervous I became. He was leading me Lord knew where, for God only knew what reason. He'd walked out of the forest right after I'd found dead bodies. He could have killed them.

Of course, he could have killed me, too, if he'd wanted to. Why wait?

Why did a crazy person do anything?

Surreptitiously, I took out my cell phone and nearly dropped it when I saw I had a signal.

"I—uh—" Shepard stopped; I slipped the phone into my pocket as he turned. "Need to go." I jerked a thumb at a nearby tree, and Shepard nodded.

As soon as I was out of sight, I increased my pace. As soon as I was out of earshot, I ran.

Stupid, really. Shepard had been tracking Phoebe; he could easily track me. But I had the crazy idea that if I could make a phone call before he caught me, the cavalry would arrive. Except, how would any cavalry find me in this vast wilderness, especially when I had no idea where I was?

I paused, breathing hard, wondering if I should zig to the right or zag to the left. Then the crackle of feet atop hard snow made me turn.

The wolf was huge, its fur both silver and black, enough like Shepard's coat to make my skin prickle. Wasn't there a legend about shamans who donned the skin of a wolf and became one?

It advanced as I retreated. The shape and shade of its eyes were difficult to determine in the night beneath the canopy of trees. Something light, perhaps hazel?

The beast growled, low, threatening, and I stumbled,

nearly falling before managing to stay upright. What was it waiting for?

My boot slid as if I'd stepped on ice. I glanced down. I *was* on ice. My gaze returned to the wolf, which appeared to be grinning. But why?

That became evident as a sharp crack split the night, and the ice gave way beneath my feet.

CHAPTER 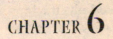6

The shock of the water made me cry out. The wolf surged forward, and for the first time, I saw its eyes clearly. They *were* human.

Fear made me flail. Broken ice bobbed around me. My mouth filled with water so cold my teeth hurt. I needed to calm down, take one disaster at a time.

First, don't drown.

Second, get out of the water—fast.

Third, don't get eaten by the werewolf.

I managed to tread water despite the weight of my boots, clothes, and coat, but I wouldn't be able to do so for long. I lunged at the side of the hole, my gloved hands scrabbling for purchase, and the wolf snarled, then snapped at my fingers. I let go and went under again.

What was going on? If the beast wanted me dead, there were faster ways than drowning me.

When I bobbed up, blinking water from eyeballs that burned with cold, the wolf lay on the ice, nose on its forepaws, staring right at me. This close, I could see the eyes quite clearly; I didn't know them.

Nevertheless, I was screwed. If I tried to get out, the werewolf would attack; if I stayed in, I'd drown or freeze to death. Already, the lethargy that preceded hypothermia slowed my movements. My lips froze together, and my eyelashes dripped with teeny-tiny icicles.

Suddenly, the beast lifted its head. Something was coming. By the sounds of the approach, something big. Maybe a bear.

Would that be better or worse?

The figure that shot from the trees wasn't a bear but Shepard. The wolf scrambled to its feet.

"Dylan." I tried to shout, but my voice had gone hoarse from the cold. "It's—"

I meant to say "a werewolf," but Shepard finished the sentence with a single word: "Joe."

The animal charged. Shepard drew his gun and pulled the trigger in a smooth, practiced movement that reminded me of old westerns and gunslingers—although I'd never seen one where the gunman wore fur.

The werewolf exploded, flames shooting so high I feared the trees might catch fire. Huh. The assassin in New York must have been a werewolf, too.

Shepard hurried past the burning ball of fire without even giving it a glance. "Why did you walk on the ice?" he asked, pausing at the edge. "It isn't stable."

"Like I'd know stable ice if it bit me on the ass." I wasn't making sense, but can you blame me?

Shepard dropped to his knees, then stretched flat, inching onto the surface, but every movement caused more cracks to race between him and me. He stopped, worry etching furrows in his face. "We've got to get you out of there. Fast."

I didn't have the energy to say something sarcastic, which bothered me more than the cold.

Behind Shepard, shadows emerged from the trees. I blinked several times, and enough of the icicles fell away so that I could see clearly.

"Wolves," I whispered.

Shepard scooted backward so fast the ice crackled threateningly, but he managed to reach solid ground and draw the gun. This time, however, he didn't shoot. The wolves were actually wolves, their eyes devoid of the whites that marked both a human and a werewolf.

The animals skirted Shepard, slinking nearer to me, their manner nonthreatening. A large black male paused at the edge, then hunkered down and crept forward in a movement that mimicked Shepard's. Except that the wolf weighed less than I did, so the ice did not protest. It reached me and bent its head as if in submission. I wasn't sure what to do.

"Grab on," Shepard said quietly.

I hesitated, not wild about going anywhere near the powerful jaw and sharp teeth, but the cold had gotten so bad I didn't much care how I died. So I used the last of my energy to make a final lunge, and my fingers found fur.

I clutched, pulled, then wrapped my arms around the wolf's neck and hugged with all my might. The animal inched backward until we were both on solid ground, and I let go.

The wolf stood and shook itself. Bits of ice, snow, and water sprayed everywhere, and the world began to fade.

A chorus of growls snapped me back. The wolves stood between Shepard and me. Shepard pointed his gun at the nearest one.

"No," I managed. "They're trying to help."

"I have to get you warm, or your heart will stop."

As if they'd understood, the wolves closed in, encircling me, snuggling close, sharing their heat.

The last thing I heard before I passed out was Shepard muttering, "I'll be damned."

When I awoke, I still lay beneath the stars, surrounded by wolves. I began to shiver so violently my back ached with it. Would I ever be warm again?

"Let's get inside."

Inside? Where? How? I didn't know. But the idea was so appealing I struggled to sit up.

My movements woke the wolves, and I stilled. Would they turn on me now?

One by one, the animals unwound themselves from the pile. As they did, they brushed my hands and face with their noses, gently, like a kiss, then faded into the trees.

"Were they real?" I breathed.

A single howl was answered by several more. The sound no longer made me feel sad and lonely but accepted, as if I were one of them.

Shepard lifted me into his arms and strode away from the broken river. Farther downstream, with the shelter of snow banks on three sides, he'd pitched the tent he must have been carrying in the huge backpack.

Inside, a small stove warmed the air. He set me on

what appeared to be a deer hide so he could tie the flap, then turned. "Strip," he said.

I blinked stupidly.

"You have to get out of the wet clothes, Carly. You'll never survive in them."

I was too cold to be modest; I was also too cold to be naked.

He released the buttons of my coat more quickly than I could have with my numb fingers, helping me slip out of it and the rest of Julie's things as if I were a child. When I was naked, he threw his wolf coat around me. Oddly enough, the warmer I became, the more I shivered.

Dylan began to undress, too.

"Wh-wh-what are you d-d-doing?" My teeth chattered so much I was afraid I'd bite off my tongue.

"Skin-to-skin contact is the quickest way to offset hypothermia."

He yanked off his shirt. Muscles rippled in the firelight, sleek and golden. Perfect. If I weren't dying, I'd be tempted to lick him all over.

His boots, socks, and pants went the way of his shirt, then he scooted beneath the coat before I could get a decent look at anything else. I did, however, feel it.

He slid his body along mine, urging me to turn over. "Spoon, Carly, like this."

My back to his front, we fit together like spoons in a drawer, something I'd heard about but never done. When you sleep with a guy just for the sex—my standard modus operandi, as I'd trusted no one long before J.T. had suggested it—spooning isn't included. A damn shame, too. Spooning was nice.

My head rested beneath his chin; his arm lay heavy across my hip. Our feet tangled together, his so much warmer than mine.

"How did you know the wolf was Joe?" I asked.

"Same eyes, and Joe's hair was black, with just a little gray."

In other times—like yesterday—I'd have scoffed at that explanation. But yesterday I hadn't seen human eyes in an inhuman face.

"He herded me onto the ice. After it cracked and I went in, he wouldn't let me climb out."

"That makes no sense. Werewolves like to kill in the most bloody, destructive way possible. They don't try to drown or freeze their victims to death. They don't have the self-control." Shepard's breath drew in, then sifted out, the movement pressing us more intimately together. "These aren't behaving normally, and I don't like it."

"You'd prefer they tore me limb from limb?"

"Of course not. But they're up to something, and it can't be good."

I had to agree. "In New York, the man who tried to kill me exploded when my bodyguard shot him."

"Your bodyguard carried silver bullets?"

"Apparently so." I wondered if they always had.

"If J.T. expected the werewolves to come, why didn't he keep you in a glass cage like Phoebe?"

"I wouldn't have stayed."

Dylan went silent, tugging me closer, sharing his warmth. I would have liked to ask more questions, but in the aftermath of another brush with death, that urge to feel alive was back, much stronger than it had been on the steps of his cabin, when guys with guns

were chasing us, before I'd ever heard about werewolves, before I'd ever seen one.

I arched my back, and his penis leaped, pressing
against my spine.

"Carly." Dylan's voice was low, warning.

I turned to face him. "What?"

"This is about staying alive."

"Exactly," I said, and kissed him.

CHAPTER 7

Dylan's lips were cool, his mouth so warm, his skin soft over the hardness of bone and muscle. I sank into him—tasting, touching, needing the heat of his embrace in more ways than one.

He held back, believing I was fragile, dying, and maybe I was, but if this was my last night, I didn't want to spend it cold and alone.

I swept my tongue into his mouth, grazing his teeth, the jaggedness of their edge a delicious sensation. My fingers explored his chest, all muscle and sinew and smooth, smooth skin. My thumbs ran along the hollow of his collarbone; my palms skated over broad shoulders.

"Carly, no." His words vibrated against my lips. I lifted my head, searching for the truth. Did he truly mean no?

His eyes said the same thing as the erection pressing against my stomach. He wanted this; he wanted me, as much as I wanted him.

"It's all right, Dylan." I wrapped my hand around him—cold to warm, soft to hard. "Didn't they ever tell you in nursing school about the best way to heat the blood?"

"They might have mentioned something," he drawled, his accent more pronounced than ever before.

I leaned in, my mouth hovering over his as I let our breath mingle, let him think I might kiss him, then again I might not. The dip in ice water seemed to have hardened my nipples permanently. They grazed his chest, and I had to fight not to rub myself against him and purr.

Meanwhile, I stroked him, milked him, made him groan, pulse, nearly come before he grabbed my wrist and held me still.

"I want this." I stared into his eyes, letting him see that I did.

He surrendered with a curse, his mouth capturing mine in a kiss that raised the temperature beneath the wolf coat several degrees in an instant.

He made love to my lips, gently at first—nibbling, then stroking. As the heat spread both through and around us, the kiss hardened, deepened. His teeth nipped; he enticed my tongue into his mouth, suckling just the tip, and his hands . . .

They were everywhere. I'd never felt a working man's hands on my body. I'd never considered how arousing they might be—the subdued strength, the contrast of callused palms to skin pampered daily by lotions and potions. Every brush was a delight, every scrape an enticement. Shivering, I pressed myself against him, silently begging for more.

"Shh," he murmured, tracing his lips from my

mouth to my cheek, then my eyebrow. "I'll make you warm."

In the rush of desire, I'd forgotten the icy river bath, the pain in my extremities, the near-death experience, which had been the whole idea.

The firelight danced across his face, and I followed the flickers with my fingertips. His eyes opened, hazel darkened to evergreen, and he smiled. The expression did something odd to my heart.

He flipped the coat over our heads, and the world receded; everything important lay within the cocoon of heat created by our bodies. He walked his lips over my neck, then down to my breasts.

One slight flick of his tongue, and sparks ignited. A moan escaped. I couldn't help myself. Nothing had ever felt this wonderful in my life.

Taking the sound for the encouragement it was, he drew me into his mouth; my hands tangled in his hair, showing him a rhythm.

I'd never been aroused by attention to my breasts. Perhaps because most of my dates said hello with their eyes locked beneath my neck and spent the better part of those dates the same way. Most men I'd slept with pawed and poked as if conducting a science experiment.

Dylan did none of these things. He treated my breasts as he treated the rest of me, with a respect bordering on reverence. Because of that, I opened myself to him in every way.

The pull of his lips caused my hips to arch in response, and his palm lowered, heat in my belly both without and within.

The pull of his roughened fingertips was a contrast

to the gentleness of his touch. The scent of him, snow and evergreens, the land, the wind, the night . . . I'd never smell any of them again without thinking of him.

He kissed his way down my rib cage, tongue running along each curved bone. He rubbed his face against my belly, the scratch of his beard making me jerk, then the press of his lips grounding and settling me.

My hands drifted over his shoulders, across his back, then hesitated at what I felt there. But when I began to explore, he slid lower, flicked his tongue over me once, and I forgot everything else as he kissed me where I'd never been kissed before.

I cried out, as much from the shock as from the sensation. I'd never accepted oral sex, never been interested. To me, the act was more intimate than intercourse, and I wasn't much for intimacy. But here in the land of eternal midnight, with a man I'd only just met—a man who'd saved my life several times—I could no more deny him that than I could deny him anything. I didn't want to.

I wanted to learn everything he had to teach, both in the darkness and in the light. I wanted to be with him, to hold him, to welcome him into my body and my life.

My legs trembled. He ran his fingertips down the quivering muscles, then up again, urging me without a word to relax. His mouth did clever, amazing things, soft flickers of his tongue, hard, open-mouthed kisses. He tasted me deep inside, riding his thumb on my throbbing center until I convulsed, fighting to be free, even as I ached to become one with him.

He understood my need and met it, rising over me with one sleek, powerful surge and plunging inside as the orgasm rolled over me, and I cried out unintelligible words that ended in his name.

The coat fell away, revealing his face in the firelight, stark, open, and I got that funny feeling again just below my breastbone. Reaching up, I touched his cheek, and he opened his eyes, staring into mine as he came.

When the last shudders died, he buried his face in my neck and kissed me, then rolled aside, spooning us as he stroked my hair.

Now was usually the time when either I left or they did. Except there was nowhere to go, and I wasn't sure what to do.

"Sleep," Dylan whispered, and, amazingly, I did.

When I awoke, the flame in the small stove still burned merrily, sending shadows dancing across the canvas walls. Dylan was no longer wrapped around me; the tent had become quite toasty.

He lay on his stomach, fast asleep. His eyelashes created a shadowy crescent against his cheeks, the stubble of his beard making him appear paler than I knew him to be. Perhaps the pressure of dragging me along as we ran for our lives was wearing on him.

But shouldn't he be used to pressure? He'd said he was in Special Forces—a Ranger. They fought for their lives all the time.

He'd also said he was a nurse. Was that truth or fiction? I knew so little about this man, and I wanted to know everything.

Reaching out, I ran my palm across his shoulder, down his back, and I felt again what I'd felt last night: deep ridges across what should be perfect flesh.

I propped myself on one elbow, drew back the makeshift blanket, and winced. Raised white streaks marred one shoulder.

Frowning, I leaned in close, but I didn't need to see any better to know that claws had made those scars.

CHAPTER 8

When I lifted my gaze, Dylan's eyes were open. The stillness of his expression revealed that he hadn't wanted me to see, even before he shifted and pressed his shoulders to the ground.

"Who did that to you?" I demanded.

"Not who. What."

"A werewolf," I murmured. "Tell me."

"Not relevant."

"We're being chased by werewolves that want me dead. You don't think scars from a werewolf are relevant?"

"One has nothing to do with the other. The werewolf that did this to me isn't after us."

"How can you be so certain?"

"Because he's a coat."

My gaze flicked to the wolfskin. "Good."

He stared at me for several seconds, then shook his head. "You don't want to throw it off while you make girlie, grossed-out noises?"

"Maybe later."

A surprised bark of laughter escaped him. "You're amazing."

"Right back atcha."

I was tempted to pull him into my arms and make him forget what haunted him, except I was pretty sure what haunted him was chasing me—or something very much like it. I wanted to know everything Dylan did about the creature that shouldn't exist.

"Tell me," I repeated. "Please."

Maybe if I knew more, I'd be afraid less. Probably not. But knowledge is power; knowing more definitely couldn't hurt.

Dylan stared at the roof of the tent as if he could see through it and into the night. Would the sky lighten even a little to signal the dawn?

I had no idea what time it was anymore, I didn't know what day it was. My world had narrowed to Dylan and this place, and maybe that wasn't so bad. Out there, people—make that things—were trying to kill me. In here, there was only us.

"I was in Afghanistan," he began. "Place was mostly a wasteland even before we arrived. We searched those caves endlessly."

"For Bin Laden?"

"Among others. There's no shortage of nuts there— or anywhere else, for that matter. People in the U.S. think they understand what's going on outside our borders, but they don't. Not really. The majority of the world would be happy to see America fall like the Roman Empire, and we might. All the signs are there."

My eyebrows lifted, my interest piqued, but I let

it go. Werewolves first, Roman Empire comparisons later.

"We had constant intel about this terrorist or that whack job," he continued. "Every day, every night, a new mission to check out a new cave. The things are like an endless honeycomb. I still see them when I close my eyes. When I sleep, I see what came out of them."

My skin prickled. "Werewolves?"

He took a deep breath and let it out slowly. "A whole pack. The moon was dark—"

"Dark?" I interrupted.

"New moon, or no moon, although the moon's always there, we just can't see it. Dark moon is the best time for an op. No shiny silver flares off the guns."

Made sense, or at least as much sense as anything else he'd been saying. "I thought werewolves only came out under the full moon."

"Under a full moon, they're possessed by a blood lust so strong they can do nothing but kill. Under any other moon, they kill just for the fun of it."

"Fun?" My voice wavered.

"They're monsters, Carly. Once bitten, pure evil takes over—the love of the kill, the thrill of having power over life and death.

"That night, our intel said the usual: terrorists in a cave at such-and-such longitude and latitude. We'd bomb the hell out of that particular section, then we'd go in and check what was left of the bodies and hope like hell we'd find Bin Laden or at least a large enough part of him to be sure."

"But that night, you found something other than terrorists?" I asked.

He shrugged. "I don't know who the men were who came out of those caves in the shapes of wolves. The night was so dark," he continued, his voice low, hoarse, his face still, eyes distant. I laced my fingers with his. He didn't seem to notice, but I held on anyway.

"Before, whenever we reached the bombed-out caves, nothing moved; everyone was dead." He took a deep breath, then another. "But not this time."

"What happened?"

"No silver bullets," he said simply.

The scene spread out in my mind. Wolves climbing out of the rubble, slinking shadows beneath the ebony sky. Coming closer, their forms solidifying into snarling, slavering beasts. The soldiers emptying clip after clip into them, and still they advanced—an army of wolves with human eyes. I shuddered.

"Hey." Dylan tugged me into his arms, and I let him. "You okay?"

"I need to hear this. I have to know."

Being held against him helped. He'd fought werewolves before and won. He'd do so again. We'd beat them; we'd survive. Together.

"How did you get out of there alive?" I asked.

"Pure chance, dumb luck. All of the others were killed. Kind of."

"How can you be kind of dead?"

"Killed, not dead. Or at least, not dead completely, or maybe dead and then risen again."

"Isn't that a zombie?"

My voice was flippant; once again, he didn't laugh. "There are more monsters in this world than you realize."

We went silent for several seconds. I decided I didn't

want to know about the "more" right now. I had all I could handle with the werewolves.

Dylan's chest rose and fell against my cheek, the movement already familiar and comforting.

"The first wolf knocked me aside," he continued. "I flew several yards, fell down an incline. My shoulder burned. Didn't realize how bad it was until I tried to climb out of the hole and passed out. The screams brought me back."

He swallowed, and his throat clicked loudly in the sudden silence. "I made it to the top. By then, the screams had stopped, and the wolves milled around among the bodies. I still thought they were wolves." He shook his head. "Even though hundreds of bullets had plowed into them and they'd kept coming. One of them sensed me, lifted its head, and I saw the eyes. There was no mistaking them for just wolves after that."

"No," I agreed. I'd seen one, too.

"I knew they'd come for me. I didn't plan to go easily, but all of my weapons were useless."

"What did you do?"

"I didn't have to do anything. A howl sounded in the distance, and they disappeared."

"Like that?" I snapped my fingers.

"No." The ghost of a smile tilted his lips. "They left on four paws. Called by their leader, I think. I started to climb out of the hole again. I needed to check if anyone was alive, though I doubted it, then make sure they had proper burials back home where they belonged." His accent became stronger, sounding as deep as the South where he'd been born. "But before I could, they began to change."

"Change?" I whispered, but I knew what he meant.

"They rose again. First as men, completely healed of all the wounds that had killed them. Then they became wolves and followed the others into the night."

"And then?"

"I called for help, and when they came, I told them I was the only one left. My shoulder was wrecked. Even with surgery, there was too much damage for me to stay in active service."

"Did you ever see . . ." I trailed off, uncertain what to call the other Rangers anymore.

"I hunted down every last one, and I killed them."

I started. "What?"

"I couldn't let them wander the earth like that," he whispered.

I laid my palm against his cheek, and he put his hand over mine, holding me to him.

To hunt down his friends and kill them had to have been the hardest thing Dylan had ever done. But he'd done it. For them. He was the strongest person I'd ever known.

Dylan kissed my forehead, then tucked my head beneath his chin. "It'll be dawn soon," he said. "We'll have to get moving."

I didn't want to. I wanted to stay there forever, safe in our own little world. But we wouldn't *be* safe. We might never be safe anywhere again.

"How did you figure out what they were?" I asked. "How did you learn what you needed to kill them?"

"I listened to the local legends, which were unsurprisingly full of werewolf tales. Then I went to Kabul and bought as much silver as I could and used it to make bullets."

Dylan went silent after that. I guess there wasn't much else to say.

I touched his arm, and he glanced up. "You were medically discharged?"

He nodded. "When I came back stateside, I decided to devote myself to medicine—saving lives instead of taking them. Then maybe I'd stop dreaming of wolves with the eyes of my friends."

"Did you?"

"No."

"How did you end up in Alaska?"

"Everyone who worked with your mother had to believe in werewolves."

I bet those had been fun interviews. "Why?"

"Keep her calm?" He shrugged. "Or maybe J.T. wanted to make sure we were prepared when they came calling. Not believing can get you killed."

"J.T. didn't believe in werewolves."

"You sure? He did require all of his underlings to carry silver bullets."

Had J.T. believed, or had he only been covering his bases? If he did believe, then why hadn't he told me the truth once I was old enough not to panic?

Then again, was there ever an age when learning werewolves were real would not cause panic?

As Dylan had pointed out, not telling me might have gotten me killed. However, J.T. had made certain I was protected, and really, not a werewolf in sight for more than twenty years—as far as I knew.

I sighed and rubbed my forehead. Trying to understand my father's motivations for anything was always good for a headache.

"Even if J.T. didn't believe at first," Dylan said, "I bet he changed his mind at the end."

Phoebe, you were right.

Aha!

"How did J.T. recruit people who believed in werewolves?" I asked.

Dylan's lips curved. "Your father had connections everywhere. I've heard whispers of a government agency that fights monsters."

My headache was back.

"I'm sure for J.T., it was a simple thing to locate those who'd had close encounters of the wolf kind and survived," Dylan continued.

Knowing J.T., he was right.

"We need to go," Dylan murmured.

Moments later, we stepped out of the makeshift shelter. Snow had fallen while we were inside, just enough to obscure any tracks there might have been. Good news/bad news for us. On the one hand, maybe the snow had obliterated our scent, too. On the other hand, it had covered any trace of Phoebe.

Caw. Caw. Caw.

Several crows swooped out of the trees, dipping low, nearly brushing the tops of our heads, then flying upward. They headed north for a few seconds, came back, and dive-bombed us again.

"Is that normal?" I asked.

"No." Dylan studied the birds. "Seems like they want us to follow them."

"Because crows are capable of that level of thought?"

"Got me." Quickly, we struck the tent and packed

up. The crows still circled. Once we were ready, they continued on a path only they seemed to know.

"Is following them a good idea?" I asked.

"I don't have another one."

We walked steadily north for hours. The only other animals we saw were a pair of very jumpy coyotes. The two dashed out of the forest so close to me I gasped. They froze, then cowered, abasing themselves at my feet.

"What the—" I began, and the two yelped and ran as if I'd pulled a gun and started shooting.

Dylan and I watched their gray tails wave between the trunks and eventually disappear.

"Maybe they've never seen humans before," Dylan murmured.

Out there, such a thing was possible; nevertheless, the encounter was disturbing. What was it about me that made wolves protective and coyotes terrified? What made all the werewolves want to kill me?

The crows flew ahead. They seemed to know exactly where we were going. Or at least, where they were going.

With the constant repetition of tree after tree that looked exactly alike, the blue-black sky, and the exhaustion of trudging through knee-deep snow, I began to zone out. The first sight of the wolf sailing through the air only made me pause and stare.

Until the beast hit Dylan broadside, and the two slammed into the ground. With the huge pack on his back, Dylan couldn't maneuver.

He got one arm around the wolf's throat and reached for the gun with the other, but in the struggle, the weapon skittered away. The animal lunged, and

Dylan was forced to use two hands to keep from getting mauled.

I dived for the gun, and as my fingers closed on the grip, the wolf swung around, jaws snapping, teeth catching the meaty area below my thumb. A quick spark of pain, and it released me.

But that one instant was enough. Blood dripped onto the snow, bright red against stark white, the sound a patter of rain in the sudden silence.

I lifted my gaze and stared into familiar, human eyes.

"J.T.?"

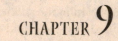

The wolf with my father's eyes jerked back. No recognition, no remorse—not a big shock in either the man or the beast. He swung his huge, furry head toward Dylan, and I shot him.

Fire sent me stumbling back. Dylan threw the animal off and scooted away from the flaming, howling thing.

I dropped to my knees, the gun sliding from my limp fingers and onto the ground. Dylan crawled across the snow, yanking the pack off his back and pulling a first-aid kit out of a zippered pocket.

I took one look at the tiny blue box with the red cross on top and began to laugh. "I don't think anything in there can help me now."

He grabbed my injured hand, yanking off the torn and bloody glove. "Why didn't you run?"

"You think I'd leave you behind, let J.T. tear out your throat?"

In the middle of hunting through the jumble of tiny tubes and bottles, Dylan glanced up. "J.T.?"

"Didn't you see his eyes?"

"I was a little more worried about his teeth."

"It was him," I said firmly.

"I'm sorry you had to shoot your father."

I remembered what I'd seen in those eyes. Not that J.T. had been warm and friendly, but he'd never been a stone-cold killer—until he'd turned furry.

"That wasn't my father. Not anymore."

Dylan found a small bottle of alcohol. "This is going to sting," he said, and doused me.

I hissed as the liquid hit the punctured flesh, then gritted my teeth while he rubbed in antibiotic ointment and bound the wound.

"Will that help?" I asked.

"Won't hurt."

He wouldn't meet my eyes. I reached out with my good hand and lifted his chin. "I'm going to change now."

"Yes," he said simply.

"You'll kill me then?" He winced. "Do for me what you did for your friends, Dylan. Promise."

He gave a sharp nod—he'd do what needed to be done—then leaned forward and kissed me. Gently at first, then harder, more desperate, as if he could stuff an entire lifetime of embraces into the hours we had left.

I wrapped my arms around his neck, and he dragged me into his lap. I lost myself in the scent, the taste, the heat of him. Images tumbled through my mind—naked, sweaty sex atop the snow. If we did it right now,

I was certain we could finish before I turned into a wolf and tried to kill him.

I pulled away, though it wasn't easy, but I wasn't sure how long I had, when I'd begin to want more from Dylan than his body. When would I begin to want his blood?

We were both breathing heavily. His lips were swollen, and I'm sure mine were, too. A vein pulsed in his throat. I couldn't stop staring at it.

I had a sudden image of him rising above me, plunging into me, again and again, and at the final moment, when the orgasm rushed over us both, I would bite down and let his life blood spill free.

I scrambled off Dylan's lap and scooted away, wiping my mouth, staring at my shaking hand, relieved to discover it wasn't covered in blood. "Maybe you should just shoot me now, before . . ."

"No."

"What if I hurt you? What if I kill you?"

"I know how to stop a werewolf, Carly."

That he was talking about me, or what would soon be me, sobered us both.

"How long?" I asked.

"Within twenty-four hours."

"When the moon comes up?"

He shook his head. "Day, night, full moon, or new— the first time, it doesn't matter."

"What will happen?"

"Carly—"

"I want to know!"

My voice was too loud in the suddenly silent forest. Even the crows had deserted us. I took a deep breath and tried again. "I'm sorry. It would help if I knew what to expect."

Dylan pressed his lips together, as if he wanted to keep the words in. Then he sighed, and they tumbled out.

"Lycanthropy appears to be a virus, passed through the saliva. You'll become feverish, delirious. You'll remember things that haven't happened—at least, to you. A kind of collective consciousness that gets passed like a germ. You'll experience the thrill of the hunt, the love of the kill, the taste of the blood."

Oh, hell, that was happening already.

Dylan stood and began to set up camp.

"What are you doing?"

"I can't let you—" He yanked the tent free in one angry movement. "You should be inside when—" He broke off.

Where I was when I died didn't matter to me, but it seemed to matter to him. At least, setting up camp was something to do. Until I grew a tail.

"Why do we seem to be running into one at a time?" I asked. "If the werewolves want me dead, wouldn't it be simpler to send a whole pack and tear me limb from limb?"

"Who knows what's in their mind? Joe and J.T. might have been scouting. The pack may have split up to cover more ground." His gaze drifted over the prehistoric trees. "There's a lot of ground."

Which reminded me of what we'd been doing out there in the first place.

"When this is over, you have to find Phoebe."

He frowned. "Of course, I'll find Phoebe."

"Tell her I love her. That I always have." My voice broke. I'd really wanted to see my mother again, to explain that I hadn't deserted her. "Tell her I'm sorry." I glanced at the still-smoking wolf. "About J.T."

Dylan took my good hand. He didn't seem able to bring himself to touch the one that throbbed and stung and radiated heat. I couldn't blame him. "You had to."

"Remember that. When *you* have to."

He pulled me into his arms. His grip was bruising, but his cheek against my hair was gentle.

I clung to him. I couldn't help myself. I wanted Dylan's embrace to be the last thing I remembered before the virus took me.

I got my wish.

Heat flowed over me like lava, burning away the last vestige of myself. My skin became too small for my body. I wanted to burst free, to run through the trees, roll in the snow, chase something human.

Images spilled into my mind—places I'd been, people I'd known, then eaten. I should have been horrified; instead, I was energized. Strength, power, the world was mine.

I could run for hours and never be tired. I could chase things and catch them. I was no longer alone. I had the pack. Soon I would join them, and everyone would be afraid.

I howled as ravenous hunger thundered in my head and pain tore through my soul. Something was coming, and that something was the dark side of me.

CHAPTER 10

Hell isn't hot or fiery red or full of lost souls. Hell is cold, black, silent, and lonely.

The darkness was a cool, velvet cloth across my face. Something stirred there, a scratch, a swirl of movement, and I skittered back, cringing.

The snick of a match, and my eyes closed tight. I didn't want to see what awaited me on the other side.

"Carly?"

Dylan's voice. That couldn't be right, unless I'd—

My eyes snapped open, terrified I'd find him covered in blood and gore, because of me. But he appeared exactly the same as the last time I'd seen him.

He finished relighting the stove, which had gone out. Soft firelight lit the tent. He looked as tired as I felt.

"You okay?" he asked.

I glanced down, patted my naked chest, my face, tested my teeth. I held my hands out in front of me. No fur, no claws, no fangs.

"What the hell?" I asked.

Before I finished the last word, Dylan dragged me into his embrace. Then we both held on.

"I had the gun in my hand," he whispered. "You were growling, snarling, saying terrible things."

"I was seeing terrible things." Although at the time, I'd kind of liked them. I trembled.

"Cold?" He rubbed my arms, then leaned away, returning with the wolfskin and settling it around me like a cloak.

"What happened? I—" Sounds and images flickered through my mind. What was real? What was not? Why was I still alive?

"You didn't shoot me." I sighed. "You really need to shoot me."

"You didn't shift, Carly."

"The night's still young." I frowned. "Isn't it?"

"The night passed. And another day, and now it's night again. It's been thirty-six hours since you were bitten, and you're still you."

"I'm not so sure about that." I felt different somehow—stronger, calmer, more *me* than I'd ever been.

"Any desire to rip out my throat, drink my blood, rule the world?"

"No." Although all this hugging in the dark was making me desire other things.

"I don't know what happened," he continued, "but you're not a werewolf."

"Just because I didn't change yet doesn't mean I won't."

"Everything I've learned about lycanthropy, every person I ever spoke with was adamant about one thing: first change within twenty-four hours. It's inevitable."

"Or not."

"I touched you with silver. Not even a wisp of smoke."

I yanked the bandage off my hand. Only faint red marks remained where J.T. had bitten me.

"None of this makes sense."

"Does anything about werewolves make sense?" He pulled me into his arms again. "Let's just enjoy the miracle."

I snorted.

"Hey." He leaned back to peer into my face. "Miracles don't happen every day."

"In my experience, they don't happen at all."

"Poor baby," he murmured, his lips trailing from my temple to my cheek, then hovering over mine. "No magic in your life. I can fix that."

"Promise?" I whispered, our breath mingling.

In answer, his mouth crushed down. Our teeth clanked, our tongues mated, our clothes flew every which way. This was the miracle—what we'd found together, what we felt for each other. I never wanted to let him go.

The tent was cool, but the wolfskin was warm. Burrowing beneath it was like coming home. Just as making love with Dylan was like finding my mate.

I stilled. Occupied with nibbling his way from my lips to my chin, down the slope of my neck to my breast, he didn't notice.

Mate. What a strange thing to think.

His mouth closed over my nipple and tugged. I forgot all about it.

His warmth spilled over me like a wave. His body covered mine; he was already hard against my belly.

My fingers fluttered over his back and stilled when they encountered his scar.

Fury flowed through me, heating from within. No one touched Dylan but me. No one marked him, ever. If he hadn't already killed the wolf that had dared, I would have.

Anger pulsed in my blood, fueling the desire. I rose up, pushing him onto his back. He flipped over with a grunt. I guess I'd shoved a little hard.

I wanted to do things with him I'd never done with anyone else, things I'd never wanted to do. Lowering my head, my hair cascaded over his skin, a curtain between myself and the world. He sighed at the sensation, his breath catching when I rubbed my cheek over his belly, then my tongue over his tip.

"Carly," he began, then gasped when I scored him with my teeth and drew him into my mouth.

He leaped in response, seemed to grow and pulse. The power flowed through me. I was in charge. He could do nothing but submit—on his back, vulnerable, clutching, begging, needing what only I could give. I was so turned on I moaned.

The sound vibrated against him, around him, and he shuddered. His fingers, which had been in my hair, tightened as if he meant to pull me away. I didn't want to go. I wanted to seize control, to dominate, to make him come.

Slowly, I began to move, taking him in to the hilt, then withdrawing to the tip, hesitating as if I meant to release him, then plunging back once more. When he was perched on the edge, I rose up and over him, my hips repeating the motions of my mouth—plunge, release, accept, withdraw. Faster and faster, harder and deeper. My arms lifted, a glorious exultation to the night as I arched, clenched, then held my breath.

The orgasm flowed between us, the convulsions of one increasing the tremors of the other. I cried out; he did, too, and we both tumbled together into the light.

When the last tingles had made their way to my toes, I found myself draped over him. His palm cupped my hip; my hair shrouded both our faces.

"Whoa," he said. "You really know how to take charge."

I stilled. "Is that a problem?"

"Do it again."

I laughed, and so did he, but the lighter mood didn't last long. We weren't in this tent for a camping trip. We had big problems awaiting us. Problems that hadn't disappeared because I'd dodged the silver bullet.

There were still werewolves out there trying to kill me, and I didn't know why. My mother was still missing.

Dylan sensed my withdrawal. He shifted, slipping out of my body and my arms. I felt his loss as an ache in my chest. I reached for him, and our fingers entwined as if we'd been holding hands for an eternity.

"Today," he promised, "we'll find her."

Half an hour later, we were dressed, packed, and confused.

"No tracks. No crows," Dylan muttered. "Where are they when you need them?"

"Crows rarely fly at night. They roost."

"They *what?*"

"Gather in communal nests."

"How do you know that?"

I blinked. "I'm not sure."

He cut me a quick, suspicious glance. I couldn't blame him. What Manhattan socialite knew the habits of crows?

I'd never been a whiz at Trivial Pursuit. I remembered things that applied to my work and myself, no problem, but other bits of info went right out of my head. So when, and why, had I learned any information about crows?

Dylan stared at the sky. "Which way should we go?"

I lifted my face to the night and closed my eyes. The breeze filtered over my skin, cool like a river, and on it I caught the scent of—

"Mother."

CHAPTER 11

"Where?" Dylan asked.

I opened my eyes and pointed to the navy blue shadow of a distant mountain.

Dylan gave me a wary glance. I didn't blame him. I was acting weird.

So why did I feel so damn good? What in hell had happened in that tent, besides great sex and a miraculous recovery from a werewolf attack?

My mother was close. I could feel her, smell her. I practically ran through the trees—this time, I led the way—bursting free of them and into a snow-shrouded field. Ahead lay the mountains, and circling over one tall peak was a flock of crows.

The sky had lightened almost imperceptibly. But the crows felt the coming of what passed for dawn, and so did I.

Dylan and I crossed the field. We'd reached the opposite side and started up the incline when a chorus of howls erupted. I spun around, cursing at the sight of the wolves loping after us.

"Friends or foes?" Dylan murmured.

I couldn't see the whites of their eyes, but just as I knew my mother was near, I also knew what they were. "Werewolves," I said. "Run."

However, running wasn't an option while climbing a steep, craggy mountainside. Luckily, climbing isn't on a werewolf's top-ten list of talents. The pack fell farther behind, but they would catch us eventually, and we didn't have enough bullets left to kill them all.

"Go," I said. "I'm slowing you down."

He actually laughed in my face. "Yeah, that'll happen."

"Dylan, please. I—"

"Carly." His attention focused behind me.

I turned, terrified I'd discover the pack of werewolves had materialized right behind us. But when I followed his gaze, I discovered that dawn had arrived with just a slight graying of the horizon, and with it, our salvation.

The wolves dropped to the ground, writhing. Some of them skidded several feet down the mountain. Others slid off the side and into the abyss. The fall wouldn't kill them, but it would certainly slow them down. So would the shape-shifting. Even in this land without sun, the werewolves could not hold their wolf form at daybreak.

"Let's make some time," Dylan said.

An hour later, we reached the peak where the crows circled. The wolves had disappeared; the men they'd become had not yet materialized.

We dragged ourselves over the last summit to find

a shadowy oval carved into the side of the mountain.

"Shall we?" Dylan said, and started forward.

I grabbed his arm. "Me first."

"Like hell."

"Why don't you both come in at the same time?"

My head snapped up. My eyes began to tear at the sight of the woman standing in the mouth of the cave.

"Mom?" I whispered. Then I didn't know what else to say.

In the end, no words were necessary. She opened her arms, I went into them, and it was as if I'd never left.

Much too soon, Phoebe murmured, "We'd better get inside," and I was forced to let her go.

"I thought you were dead," I blurted.

She cupped my cheek with her palm. "None of that matters anymore."

Inside was as I'd expected—dark, cold, stone, and ice. Dylan pulled out his flashlight, and Phoebe led the way. The cave continued back much farther than I would have believed possible. We passed several small, dark caverns. In one, I could have sworn I saw a body or two hovering at the edge of the light.

"What is this place?" I asked, my voice hushed.

"You'll see," Phoebe said.

Eventually, the narrow passage widened into a cavern. A backpack lay against the wall. Several discarded food wrappers were piled nearby.

My mother stared at me, as if she couldn't get enough of the sight. I knew how she felt.

"You look exactly the same," I said.

Tall, slim, with long, silky black hair and a dark gaze that made her seem exotic, I could understand how

J.T. had fallen in love with her. What I could never understand was how he had fallen out.

"You don't." Her eyes filled. "I missed everything."

"It wasn't your fault."

"Your father couldn't help it. He didn't understand."

"I hate to interrupt," Dylan said, "but *what* is going
on, Phoebe? You know there are werewolves after us?"

"Of course. I sent the crows to bring you to me."

"You *sent* them?" I repeated.

"How else would I get you here?"

"I think we need to get out," Dylan muttered, glancing back the way we'd come.

"We will," Phoebe soothed. "But first, I'll explain."

"Explain quick," Dylan said.

She smiled. "I always liked you the best of any of my
jailers, Dylan."

He winced at the word, and she patted his hand. "As
I said, that's all over. I'm glad you weren't there when
they came for me."

"How did you get away?" Dylan asked.

"I felt them coming before they arrived."

Dylan glanced at me. I shrugged. I'd known the
wolves were werewolves before I'd been close enough
to see them. I'd felt my mother from very far away.
Things that used to be crazy suddenly weren't.

"How did they find you in the first place?" I asked.

"I have no idea. Your father was the only one who
knew where I was."

Something must have shown in my face, because
she paled. "He's dead."

"Yes." He was now, thanks to me, but I wasn't going
to get into J.T.'s dual demise.

"J.T. wasn't the only one who knew where to find you," Dylan said. "Over the years, there've been quite a few guards and nurses."

"Fewer than you'd think. Everyone was like you, Dylan. They'd seen werewolves, and they believed. They were safer here; they didn't want to leave." She laid her hand on his arm. "Would you sell me out to the beasts?"

"Of course not!"

She patted him. "Exactly. J.T. wasn't a nice man, but he was a smart one."

I saw what she was getting at. In hiring people who'd seen what she'd seen, J.T. had protected Phoebe in the best way possible. Those who knew what werewolves could do, those who'd been hurt by them or lost loved ones to them, would never turn anyone over to the common enemy.

"Did J.T. believe in werewolves?" I asked.

"I'm not sure if he truly believed. He never saw one." Until the end.

"He sent you here," I said. "He divorced you."

"To keep me safe. Telling everyone I was insane kept people from wondering. Telling everyone I was dead kept them from searching."

"You knew he told everyone you were dead?" I took a breath. "Even me?"

"I'm sorry, honey." She brushed my hair away from my eyes. "It was for the best."

Debatable, but now was not the time for that debate.

"If everyone thought you went insane and killed yourself, why the sudden search-and-destroy mission?" Dylan asked.

Phoebe winced. "I made a mistake. I wanted to know

more about where I came from. I bribed the other nurse to get information about my adoption."

"Red flag," Dylan muttered.

Phoebe nodded. "First, some government yahoo showed up. The werewolves weren't far behind. But at least I discovered how my parents died."

"Wolf attack?" Dylan guessed.

"Yes and no. A pack of wolves ran onto the road, and my parents' car went out of control. I survived, but my guardians made sure everyone thought I hadn't. Then they sent me as far away from here as I could get."

"Why?" I asked.

"We're the last surviving members of a tribe descended from wolves."

"Mom," I said patiently. "That's impossible."

"I'd think you'd know by now that nothing is impossible."

I *had* seen the eyes of my father in the face of a wolf. I'd seen wolves change into people. I'd seen people and wolves explode into flames at the touch of a silver bullet. Impossible just didn't mean what it used to.

"There are many Native American tribes who believe they're descended from animals," Phoebe continued. "The Ojibwe, for instance, are divided into clans by the animals they are descended from. It's a common enough origination legend."

"Legends aren't real."

"Werewolves are considered a legend," Phoebe said.

I gave up. "Fine, we're descended from wolves."

Which kind of explained why the real wolves had come to help me after I'd fallen in the frozen river. They'd known I was one of them, even though I hadn't.

"If we're part wolf, wouldn't that make the werewolves our brothers or our cousins?" I asked. "Why do they want us dead?"

"Because something in our blood or our DNA makes us immune to lycanthropy."

"Which explains why you didn't shape-shift," Dylan pointed out.

"You were bitten?" Phoebe's hands fluttered, her face flushed, and she began to hyperventilate. "When? How?"

"Calm down," I said. "If we're immune, what difference does it make if I was bitten?"

I certainly didn't plan to tell her by whom. That info might give her a stroke.

"You're right." She took a deep breath, let it out slowly. "Just the thought of you being attacked . . ."

"I'm fine. A little nip, healed right up."

I showed her my hand, which was now completely void of any mark at all. She smiled. "You're living proof that the legend is real."

In the next instant, her smile disappeared, and the agitation returned. "They'll want us more than ever now. The werewolves want us dead, and the government wants to put us in a lab and discover what makes us tick. I'm sure one of their Men in Black was right behind the werewolf assassins in Manhattan."

I shuddered. If I hadn't hopped a plane, I'd have been in a government-sanctioned cage by now, being poked and probed. I'd rather be here.

"Why did they attack J.T.?" I asked. "He wasn't immune."

"They don't like to leave loose ends," Dylan answered. "They were going after Phoebe and you. If they left J.T. behind, he'd raise a ruckus. With his kind of money, he could hunt them down for decades. If all three of you were gone . . ." Dylan spread his hands. "Retribution would most likely end there."

"Why do the werewolves care if we're alive or dead? It's not like we can repopulate the world with anti-lycanthropy children."

"No, but if whatever it is that makes us special is isolated," Phoebe said, "perhaps made into a vaccine, all of their fun is over. If they can't make new werewolves, sooner or later, they'll die out."

"That sounds like a good thing to me."

"Are you willing to give up your life for it? Live in a lab like a rat? I just spent the last twenty years in a cage, Carly. I don't recommend it."

"You may not have a choice," Dylan said. "If we can manage to get away from these werewolves, there'll be others. They won't stop. Maybe you'd be better off with government protection."

"I know a place that's safe for us. Where we can live free, together." Voices sounded near the mouth of the cave, and Phoebe's expression darkened. "We have to hurry."

I glanced at Dylan. I still wasn't certain how sane my mother was, although what she'd said made sense of a lot of things that hadn't.

I guess anything was better than waiting there for the werewolves.

We followed Phoebe into the passageway, then turned away from the entrance. The narrow path twisted and turned, dipped, then inclined. We walked for at least ten minutes before a lighter shade of darkness appeared. Five minutes more, and we emerged into another world.

Still bound by ice and snow, the land was flatter, more tundra than forest, with miles of white on white, trailing into the darkness.

"We're about a hundred miles from Barrow, inside the Arctic Circle," Phoebe explained. "There's a village here for people who need to hide."

My gaze wandered over the barren landscape. "Are you sure?"

"The crows wouldn't lie."

I rubbed my forehead, wondering again if Phoebe was completely sane, despite the truth in her werewolf delusions.

"I'm not crazy," she said. "Eventually, you'll understand the crows, too. Along with our immunity, we also come into a little bit of magic."

"Magic," I repeated dully, now rubbing the bridge of my nose.

"You sound just like your father." Phoebe made a *tsk*ing sound. "You've seen werewolves. If that isn't magic, what is?"

She had a point. I dropped my hand. "What kind of magic?"

"You'll gain some of the powers of a wolf," Phoebe explained. "You'll be able to smell, hear, and see much better than any human."

My eyes widened. "I already can."

Phoebe cast a quick glance at Dylan, then returned her gaze to mine. "Why didn't you tell me?"

"I thought I was nuts. Instead of shifting when we're bitten, we get these powers?"

Phoebe shook her head. "I was never bitten, Carly."

"But—"

"You're expecting a child."

I started as if I'd been stuck with a cattle prod. I could do nothing but open and shut my mouth; no sound came out.

"Creating a child is magic," she continued, "so it brings out the magic in us."

I couldn't look at Dylan. Every time we'd been together rushed through my mind. There hadn't been that many, but one was all it took. We'd neglected, in our mad rush to avoid the werewolves, to bring along a condom. I hadn't even thought of the lack until just that moment.

My heart raced; I felt dizzy. Dylan and I had only known each other a few days. Sure, extreme danger brings people closer, but does it keep them together forever? Did he even want children?

Dylan touched my shoulder. I glanced into his eyes, and suddenly everything was all right.

"I told you there was magic in the world," he whispered, and kissed me.

There was definitely magic right here and now between us.

When he lifted his head, determination filled his face. "You two go ahead. I'll make certain they don't follow us."

"You can't fight them all," I said.

"Sure I can."

"They're werewolves, Dylan. Not terrorists."

"Same thing," he muttered.

With my enhanced senses, I heard them on the other side of the cave—thumping, scrambling, muttering. They were definitely up to something.

"We need to go," I said.

I didn't want to watch a pack of werewolves come

out of *this* cave. I certainly didn't want Dylan to face his nightmare all over again.

"Relax," Phoebe murmured. "They're still ruled by the sun and the moon. They can't shift for hours yet. Whatever they're up to, they'll be up to it as men."

The three of us headed down the other side of the mountain. We'd no sooner reached the flatter frozen land than a huge *kaboom* rent the air. A sharp crackle, then a whoosh sounded. When we turned around, all we saw was a puff of white shooting up from the other side of the mountain.

"Avalanche," Phoebe murmured. "That's what you get for using explosives near that much snow." She shook her head. "They're so predictable. Always blowing people up whenever they can't eat them. By the time they dig their way out, if they even can, they'll think we're dead."

"What if they search for us?"

"All they'll find are body parts. There were several frozen hikers in the caverns."

I recalled the shadowy image of bodies hovering at the edge of the light as we'd hurried toward the exit.

"This place is dangerous if you aren't careful." Phoebe turned her back on the mountain, and her face took on a gleam of anticipation as she looked forward.

I wanted to as well, but first, I had to make certain of something. Taking Dylan's hand, I drew him away from my mother.

"You don't have to stay here," I said.

"Did the cold freeze your brain? You think I'd walk away from you?" His face gentled. "From our child?"

"You didn't ask for this."

"Neither did you."

"Living in an icebound wasteland village isn't what you wanted out of your life, Dylan. You wanted to help people."

"If what your mother says is true, I've found the best possible place on earth to use my skills. The werewolves might be put off for a while by the explosion and the avalanche, but they'll be back. People here will need someone like me."

I took a deep breath and said what was in my heart. "I need you."

A shadow passed over his face. "For the baby?"

"For me. I don't know how it happened or when, but I fell in love with you."

"It probably happened at the exact same moment I fell in love with you." He smiled. "Like magic."

And speaking of magic . . .

"I'm descended from wolves, Dylan. Can you deal with that?"

He entwined our fingers, rubbing his thumb over my palm. "You're wolf, not werewolf. You'll never *be* a werewolf, Carly. That's a comfort to me."

After everything we'd been through, it was a comfort to me, too.

"They've come to welcome us," my mother said.

People had materialized from Lord knows where. Tall, short, young, old, men, women, white, brown, red, they trailed across the frozen land in our direction.

"I still think we should help the world fight the werewolves," I said.

"We will." Phoebe lifted her arm and greeted the others. "In that group are some of the most brilliant scientists on earth. They came here to work in peace and not be hounded by anyone. We can be safe while we find the cure; then we can release it to the world. Someday we can go back."

The hope of returning to a land without so much ice and snow flooded me with relief. I was thrilled to have found my mother, ecstatic to have found Dylan, but the thought of Manhattan being lost to me forever had been a dark blot on an otherwise stellar future. It was a fact of life—sometimes a girl just needed to shop.

"You think of everything, don't you?" I asked.

"That's what mothers do." Her eyes met mine. "Ready?"

In answer, I reached for Dylan with my right hand, for my mother with my left, and together we walked into the chill twilight of a whole new world.

CRAZY
FOR THE CAT

Caridad Piñeiro

This story is dedicated to Celsina and Peter for all your support, understanding, and laughter.

PROLOGUE

The stillness of death replaced the noises of the night.

Gone were the chirps of the tree frogs and the chatter of the small monkeys in the nearby jungle. Even the low slap of the water against the dock near the river seemed more muted.

Victor Chavez raised his head from the field notebook where he had been writing intently, describing the plant the tribal shaman had showed him a few days before. Carefully packed inside his duffel were a number of slides and specimens from the unusual vegetation, materials he and his colleague, Jessica Morales, would test when he returned to New Jersey.

New Jersey, the Garden State, but the night in Jersey's farmlands was never as quiet as it was here in the Amazon rain forest . . .

It's too quiet, he thought.

He rose from the hand-hewn desk and crept to the square hole cut into the wooden wall, which served as a window in his modest hut. He pulled aside the light canvas shade that had been closing it off.

As he stood at the opening, Victor wondered what it was that had created such a dearth of noise in the rain forest outside. Peering through the crude window, he thought he saw something shifting through the underbrush close to the edge of the village.

A man? he wondered, searching the shadows, where he again caught a glimpse of a shape—definitely something human. Dark and large. For a moment, the silhouette seemed familiar, but only for a moment, as the underbrush stirred again, and instead of a man, a large black jaguar came into view.

For days, Victor had felt the presence of the cat, had thought he had seen the animal stalking him. Now here it was, right out in the open, seemingly without fear.

The black jaguar was magnificent, one of the biggest he had ever seen. Moonlight bathed the animal as it moved farther out from the jungle. Beneath the glistening midnight black of its fur, he could barely make out the distinctive darker rosette patterns of a regular jaguar.

The black cat's thick muscles bunched, elegant and lethal as it moved, but not away from the huts as he expected. It stalked closer and closer to the village, as if with a purpose.

Cold fear seized Victor when he made eye contact with the animal. An eerily human gaze locked with his, and in that second, he knew the cat was coming for him.

He rushed back to the center of the hut, searching wildly for anything he could use as a weapon. He was a scientist and not a hunter. *Ill equipped to fend off a black jaguar*, he thought as he grabbed the chair from his desk, thinking he could use it to keep the animal at bay until help came.

He heard rustling outside, then the jaguar flew through the crude window opening and landed before him. Victor screamed. He called out repeatedly for help as he jabbed at the black cat, but with one swipe of its massive paw, the cat ripped the chair from his hands. The jaguar lunged at him, landing solidly on his chest and knocking him to the ground.

Pain seared through Victor's shoulder and neck as the animal bit him. Deep, sharp fangs easily pierced skin and muscle. His screams turned to a sickening gurgle and a hiss leaking from his ravaged throat.

The cat wasn't done.

With a shake of its immense head, the jaguar jerked Victor back and forth, as if playing with him. It tossed him aside, then sauntered away from him and roared with delight, even as the cries of the villagers indicated they were on their way.

Eyesight fading as his life bled from him, Victor met the cat's knowing gaze, saw the glee there. Human glee and satisfaction. A rumble came from the black jaguar's mouth, almost like laughter.

The animal approached him again, its breath hot against his face. Midnight-black fur soft as it brushed his cheek a second before the cat took Victor's head into its large mouth.

Victor tried to scream again, the sound echoing only in his brain as the black jaguar delivered its killing bite, crushing his skull as if it were a papier-mâché piñata.

CHAPTER 1

One month later

Thick vines crept along the jungle floor, creating a tangle from which ferns and other low-lying ground cover sprouted. Irregular shapes beneath hinted at fallen trees and branches overrun by vegetation, slowly rotting in the heat and humidity of the Amazon rain forest.

The air sat heavily on all the creatures within the rain forest's embrace. Their chirps and calls created a cacophony of sound and fury until the animals sensed its approach. The rain forest fell silent at once.

The massive black cat slinked through the underbrush, sure-footed and eager for the hunt. Strong muscles shifted beneath ebony fur as it moved along. The cat's mouth hung open, pink tongue swiping away at the remnants of an earlier meal. A soft snuffle erupted from its nostrils as it sought the scent of another animal.

Or maybe of a human.

With a loud snarl, the animal launched itself toward its prey . . .

Jessica Morales bolted upright in bed, the dream so real she had almost imagined herself in the rain forest watching the approach of the magnificent black panther.

She corrected herself: not a black panther, a black jaguar. The gene for melanism was dominant amongst the South American cats, creating jaguars that had coats ranging from the more familiar black and gold fur to animals that could appear almost entirely black. She had discovered this while doing research to try to make sense of Victor's death a month earlier. She also learned that jaguars were the only cats big enough to kill a human being.

Lying back against her pillows, Jessica considered that her colleague and former lover had described the black jaguar quite well in the field notebook that had recently been returned to their employer. After determining that Victor's death had been an unfortunate accident, the Brazilian authorities had forwarded Victor's duffel bag with the enclosed notebook to his family, who had in turn sent it to the pharmaceutical company where she and Victor had worked together.

The bloodstains on the bag and the protective leather cover of the field notebook taunted her about not having gone with Victor on this assignment. Instead, as the company's top ethnobotanist and pharmacologist, she'd had to remain in New Jersey to present a seminar to a group of prospective investors.

Maybe if she had been with Victor, he wouldn't have been killed . . .

But maybe not, Jessica thought, recalling the details Victor had jotted in the notebook about the immense size of the black jaguar he had seen while out on a specimen-collecting trip with a local shaman and guide from one of the tribes along the Rio Galvardo. Victor had not worried about the animal since his guide had been armed, but after having the animal follow him for a few days, Victor had gotten spooked. His fear had conveyed itself to her as she read through his notes, trying to understand his seemingly inexplicable death.

A series of normal entries in his field journal had deteriorated into an increasing number of anxious notations about the almost constant presence of the large cat and Victor's troubling encounters with logging-crew members who were cutting down trees in the areas close to the tribal reservation.

One of the last records in the notebook had been Victor's description of a native plant responsible for some nearly miraculous healing he had witnessed when the shaman had placed the crushed leaves on the wounds suffered by a few of the villagers after a violent encounter with the loggers.

Wide awake and more alert than anyone should be at three in the morning, Jessica decided that trying to return to sleep was futile. Based on what was in Victor's notebook, she had begun a simple trial, treating a series of cultures with a diluted titration of the suspension from the test tube in Victor's bloodstained duffel.

If the plant's properties were as strong as Victor had noted, she should have results by now.

Rising, she quickly showered, dressed, and made the short drive from her riverfront condo in New Brunswick to her nearby office and lab facilities. Her mother despaired that Jessica's proximity to work would forever rob her of any grandchildren.

Maybe that wasn't far from the truth.

With thirty barely two years away, Jessica's personal relationships with men had been few and far between, usually because of the demands of her job. Her visits to her family home were always difficult, because her mother inevitably hounded her about settling down and having kids. In the back of Jessica's mind was the constant awareness that if her sister were still alive, her *mami* would probably already have grandchildren.

But her older sister, Rachel, had died many years earlier from an infection that no available antibiotic had been able to stop. Jessica had been just sixteen at the time, her sister twenty. She had sat by Rachel's bedside, waiting for a miracle as the infection ravaged her sister's body.

Feeling useless, Jessica had tried to comfort Rachel by reminding her of all the fun times they'd had as children. The trips down the shore and amusements along the boardwalk, the surrey ride during which they had pedaled furiously to catch up to a cute group of boys.

Rachel had smiled at that recollection, but moments later, with a last gasping breath, she had passed away.

Jessica had made a promise to Rachel that day that she would dedicate her life to keeping others from suffering the same fate. More than a dozen years later, she had let nothing get in the way of keeping that promise. Not the many years to obtain her various degrees, the late nights in the lab, or the time spent away from her mother and father as she traveled the world in search of other cures.

Her many journeys had resulted in a treatment that

was now the subject of a new drug application being evaluated by the FDA. Maybe her drug would save the life of someone else's sister and, if not that drug, maybe one of the other medicines she was hoping to discover and develop.

As she wheeled her hybrid SUV into the parking lot of the pharmaceutical house where she worked, Jessica remembered fondly how Victor had been with her during her many journeys to discover new medicines in some of the world's most unique and sometimes endangered ecosystems.

In her office, her gaze settled on some of the photos she had taken during those trips. One was of her hiking up a mountain in the Himalayas, beside another one of her and Victor standing close to blazing-hot lava fields in Costa Rica. They had been lovers then but had ended the relationship shortly thereafter, once they had realized that the most they could be was friends with benefits.

She picked up the photo and tenderly ran her hand across Victor's handsome, smiling face. A dimple peeked from one cheek, and the boyish grin reached up into dark brown eyes glittering with merriment. She would miss his gentle ways and his sense of humor and daring, a daring she had shared with him and which she wouldn't set aside even now. She believed strongly that her adventures made a difference, even if they brought with them the possibility of death.

Jessica hoped that the results from her simple trial would at least demonstrate that Victor's death hadn't been in vain, that the plant Victor had brought back from the jungle could save people's lives.

Flashing her security badge against various doors

granted her access to her lab. The cultures she had treated were in a clean room, and she went through the required process of suiting up and making sure she was sterile before entering. At the bench to one side of the room rested the half-dozen petri dishes to which she had administered the plant titration.

She walked over, pulled up a stool, and prepared the first slide. Beneath the magnification of the microscope, the results were clear: no bacterial organisms remained.

Repeating the procedure for each of the five remaining petri dishes, the trial yielded the same result, even for the last dish, which had contained a rather antibiotic-resistant strain of staphylococcus.

One similar to the infection that had killed her sister.

After leaving the clean room and returning to her office, Jessica recorded her observations and results in her lab book. She had to make the arrangements for getting herself to Brazil soon. Victor had clearly found something of great importance, and judging from the notes in his field journal, the habitat for the plant was in danger from the encroachment of the loggers.

Jessica didn't want to wait too long and risk losing the seeming miracle drug that had cost Victor his life. In addition, in two weeks' time, she was scheduled to speak before the company's shareholders at their annual meeting. Her boss would not appreciate her skipping out on the command performance, so her trip to the Amazon would have to be a quick one.

As soon as possible, she intended to contact Javier Dias da Costa, Victor's guide at the tribal reservation. Dias da Costa was one of the few guides permitted at the reservation and, according to comments in Victor's journal, none too pleased that the tribal elders had allowed strangers into their midst.

Jessica didn't know why he disdained foreigners, and she didn't much care. She had made a promise to Rachel years ago, and now she silently made another to Victor.

Your death will not be in vain, mi amigo, she whispered as she lovingly ran her hand over the blood-stained duffel bag resting on her desktop.

Javier Dias da Costa paced in front of the dock like a jungle cat imprisoned in a cage, restlessly shifting back and forth, back and forth, along the cement wharf as he waited for the *americana louca* who had woken him out of his first pleasant slumber in more than a month. She had called him using his private cell-phone number in the wee hours of the morning, demanding that he take her upriver to the reservation. He hadn't been able to rest well since finding the remains of the annoying *Americana*'s colleague.

Even now, the images were fresh in his brain, but that wasn't what kept him awake.

Guilt refused to let his mind rest.

Guilt and concern that the killing wouldn't end.

He stopped and searched the wharf for any signs of the woman, hoping she would change her mind and decide not to follow her colleague. Javier already had enough problems. The loggers, led by an ex-tribe member, Armando Ruiz, were a violent, troublesome bunch.

The last thing he needed in the mix was this obviously irrational and selfish American scientist, who called people in the early hours of the morning to say she would be arriving any day. No "Are you available?" or "Are you even interested?" Instead, he had gotten a call on his private number, demanding that he take her to the tribal shaman.

Not that the shaman would object, Javier thought.

When he had gone upriver to tell the tribal elders of the *americana's* demand, the shaman, his uncle Antonio, had been eager for the *americana* to finish what her colleague had begun. His *tio* hoped that the discovery of the healing plant would finally give the court reason to enforce its orders that Armando cease logging. An order he and his loggers were blatantly ignoring. Javier, however, suspected that Armando would not stop until he had completed his quest for revenge against the tribe, and Javier's family in particular.

As he glanced up from the dock, Javier caught sight of a tall, very attractive woman waiting up at street level. Snug jeans hugged an ass he could wrap his big hands around, and as she turned in his direction, searching the street for something, his mouth watered at the way her T-shirt embraced her generous breasts. He drew in an appreciative breath as he caught sight of the intriguing face framed by thick, chestnut-colored, shoulder-length hair.

Unfortunately, the approach of an older, heavyset American woman with a camera slung around her neck and a knapsack across one shoulder precluded further observation.

"Senhora Morales, I presume?" he asked the woman, dipping his head in greeting as she paused before him, her thick fingers wrapped around a carefully folded map.

"If you're her guide, I might say yes," the woman teased with a smile that brightened her heat-flushed face.

"You're not Senhora Morales."

"Unfortunately, no. I'm looking for the *ponte pensil* to the ecological preserve," she explained.

Javier efficiently told her the quickest way back upriver and toward the small footbridge to the city's reserve. Then he turned his attention back to the task at hand and scanned the area again for the American scientist. He resumed pacing but nearly knocked over a woman who had snuck up behind him—the beautiful one from up on the street.

As he met her determined green-eyed gaze, it occurred to him that major trouble had just landed at his door.

"Senhora Morales?" he asked tentatively, praying all the while that she would say no.

"I'm not married," she replied coolly.

"Senhorita Morales?"

She smiled sexily, lips full and teeth perfectly white and straight. He swiped at a trail of sweat as it slipped down the back of his neck.

"Actually, I haven't been a *senhorita* in quite some time. Doutora Morales will do or, maybe better yet, Jessica."

Warily, he said, "*Fala portuguese?*"

"I don't speak Portuguese, but with my Spanish, I can understand a great deal. It's a pleasure to finally meet you, Senhor Dias."

She stuck out her hand in a no-nonsense gesture, and he reluctantly shook it. It wasn't soft as he'd expect from a scientist, especially a female scientist who was built to be pampered like this one. Shaking off that thought and eager to put distance between them, he said, "Doutora Morales. I was hoping I could get you to reconsider—"

"Guess again, Senhor Dias."

"Javier, *por favor*."

"Javier, I intend to finish what Victor started," Jessica said firmly. She glanced over Javier's shoulder and noted a small group headed their way. In the lead was a man she had spotted hanging out in the hotel bar the night before when she had gone to get a drink. With the trip upriver taking six or seven hours, it had been impossible to head to the reservation the day before, as she had landed in the late afternoon, and night travel on the river could be dangerous.

Javier had offered to meet her at her hotel that morning. She had suspected his offer had more to do with persuading her to go back to the States rather than making her trip more comfortable, so she had opted instead to meet him at the docks from which his company ran its tours, thinking it would make it harder for him to refuse once she got her things near his boat.

"Who's that?" She gestured toward the approaching group, and Javier turned. He muttered a colorful curse beneath his breath.

"Trouble?" she asked.

"*O diabo ele mesmo*," he muttered.

Jessica could believe his comment. The devil approaching had a good half a foot on Javier's six and almost that much more across the width of his shoulders. In contrast to Javier's rather pleasing golden color, this man was dark everywhere. His hair, skin, and eyes were all as deep a brown as one could imagine before becoming black. A glower furrowed the sweat-shiny planes of his forehead as he stalked their way.

"*Comecando o problema outra vez*," the man called out, fists the size of large hamhocks clenched at his side.

"No problems at all, Senhor." She held out her hand, but the man ignored her.

"Didn't you understand the last time, Dias?" he said in Portuguese, and jabbed Javier in the chest, rocking him back with the poke.

Javier shot her a glance, clearly controlling his response on her account. The brute was about to touch Javier again, but Jessica snagged his wrist in midair. The dark man laughed and jerked his hand out of her grasp, seemingly as interested in her as he might be in a small gnat. Angered, she took a step toward the bully, but Javier eased his arm across her body to keep her back.

"Armando, we don't want any problems, *compreenda*? Senhorita Morales is just a friend of a friend I'm taking for a day trip," he said. Armando finally looked at Jessica. His gaze turned to a leer as he took in her womanly figure and snug jeans.

"Senhorita? Well, I can help take care of that," he said, and groped himself, eliciting a series of catcalls and jibes from the trio of men behind him.

"*Basta*. We'll be on our way now," Javier said, and held his hand out to indicate Jessica should head to the end of the wooden dock, where a small river boat was moored.

She hadn't taken more than a step toward the dock when Armando snagged her arm and jerked her back. She stumbled for a moment before righting herself.

"Don't touch me again," she warned, but Armando merely threw back his head and laughed. His trio of hyenas joined him loudly enough to attract the attention of passersby along the wharf and the nearby street.

Javier tried to place himself between her and Armando, but Armando lunged at her once again. She neatly sidestepped him, and with a quick grab of her own, she bent Armando's arm back and up, applying hard pressure to drive him to his knees.

"I told you not to touch me agian," she pointed out calmly.

Armando fought to jerk free of her grasp, and when he couldn't, his three minions came at her.

"*Filho da puta*," Javier cursed beneath his breath, and threw himself at the trio, fighting them off while she struggled to keep her hold on the brute she had pinned on his knees. If he got free, there was no way she and Javier could fight off the group of violent men.

The sounds of fists striking flesh and the sickening crunch of bone suddenly gave way to a shrill whistle and thudding footsteps. The police were coming to break up the fight.

All three of Armando's men lay on the ground, groaning while Javier stood above them, slightly winded but apparently unscathed. As he met her gaze, he shot her a vicious look and commanded, "*Diexe-o ir!*"

She released Armando as he had instructed, looking up at the approaching policeman. Armando glared at her, then shouted curses at his men and ordered them to get back to work. They scrambled to their feet and rushed away in the direction of a large tugboat at the far end of the wharf. In front of it was an immense load of timber.

When the officer was satisfied that the dispute was over, he left the dock.

"Let's go," Javier said, and snagged her arm. She dug in her heels, forcing him to stop.

He faced her then, and she noticed the raw-looking scrape along one high cheekbone. It would be bruised by morning, and she winced, feeling guilty that she'd put him in the position to get hurt. "I'm sorry."

"Sorry? Doutora Morales, you'll know the real meaning of sorry if you get in Armando's way again."

Pulling back her shoulders and raising her head at a defiant angle, Jessica snapped, "I can take care of myself."

Javier snorted and crossed his arms. "Really? Then I guess you can manage those bags all by yourself," he said, motioning to her two heavy suitcases sitting on the dock nearby. "Let's go," he added, and walked away.

Jessica glared at his retreating back. She readjusted her knapsack and slipped it over both shoulders before picking up her bags and following him.

"*Come mierda,*" she muttered in Spanish beneath her breath as the weight of the bags dragged on her arms, but it wasn't enough to keep her from noticing that the jerk had quite a nice ass.

CHAPTER 2

Javier didn't address Jessica directly once she was onboard, except to advise her that they would arrive at the reservation by late afternoon. Perfect by her. It let her turn her attention to the many sights to be seen and captured with her camera along their lazy ride upriver.

The boat was wide and flat-bottomed, with a thick canvas canopy to diffuse the strong rays of the sun. The craft was clearly intended for short river cruises and not the prolonged overnight stays that Javier's company offered on the larger passenger ships docked back in town. A trio of benches filled the center of the boat, but toward the stern was an open space. Two hammocks swung there lazily, probably for a mid-afternoon siesta.

The boat chugged lazily through the nearly black water of the Rio Galvardo, which moved more briskly than that of the Amazon. The dark coffee color was a byproduct of the tannins leaching from the bark of nearby trees. It had a rather beneficial effect: the tannins killed bacteria and mosquito larvae.

So far, Jessica hadn't been bitten even once, and as she saw natives drinking and collecting water from the edges of the river, she assumed the tannins made the water potable as well.

The natives moved in and around huts that rose from the river on stilts to keep their floors above water during flood season. Some of the natives waved to the boat. A canoe or two ventured out into the deeper waters, intent on fishing.

A couple of hours later, Jessica noticed a large tugboat lumbering downriver and pushing a large barge loaded with cut timber. She recognized the emblem on the tug as the same one that belonged to Armando, which she had seen earlier at the dock. As it passed, she called out to Javier, "Why are they still cutting?"

Javier stood at the wheel of the boat, his too-broad shoulders stiff beneath the sweat-stained khaki shirt he wore. "The logging crews are far removed from the courts and their orders."

She thought of the comments in Victor's field journal about the fights with the loggers and his concerns that they would soon be at the location of the miraculous healing plant to which the shaman had guided him. If the loggers cut down those trees around the plant's delicate habitat, a valuable and unique resource might be lost. She thought of her sister and others like her who would suffer for it.

She couldn't let that happen.

Walking to the front of the boat, she stood beside

Javier. Her lightweight cotton shirt was sticking to her from the heat of the day, and she stripped it off, revealing the tank top beneath.

He shot an appreciative glance at her body from the corner of his eye but didn't face her. "Are you hungry?" he asked.

She'd been so busy taking in the scenery that she hadn't noticed, but now her body awakened, and her stomach issued a noisy growl.

He smirked, and with a quick jerk of his head toward a cooler at his feet, he said, "There's some sandwiches there. Soda as well. Help yourself."

She bent and removed two of the paper-rolled sandwiches, offering one up to him. He lashed the wheel of the boat in place with a rope and grabbed the sandwich. He laid it carefully on the wood of the cockpit and peeled off his shirt. Like her, he wore a tank top beneath, exposing the powerful muscles of his chest and arms. She dragged her gaze away from all that enticing masculinity.

Leaning on the edge of the captain's cockpit, Jessica unwrapped her sandwich and opened a bottle of soda. The sandwich was simple: spicy *chourico* sausage on crusty Portuguese rolls. She took a bite and murmured, "Delicious. *Obrigado.*"

"You're welcome," he said with a smirk at her use of Portuguese.

Anger rose up swiftly at his condescending attitude. "You've obviously got a problem with me, so what is it? Have I done something to offend you?"

Javier ripped off a large chunk from his sandwich and chewed slowly, thoughtfully, before swallowing and turning his green-gold gaze on her. "You think that because you can say a few of our words, you understand us. That you have the right to barge in where you're not wanted."

"Where I'm not wanted? The shaman said—"

"The shaman thinks your pharmaceutical company will help him stop Armando from continuing his logging, but he forgets the risk that outsiders bring to our tribe." He bent over and pulled a bottle of soda from the cooler.

Outsiders like me, Jessica thought sadly. It wasn't an unusual attitude. She had faced it more than once during her travels. Locals who feared her research would change their way of life were always suspicious. She just wished she could learn to stop taking it so personally. "I won't interfere in your ways."

Javier snorted and took a long chug of soda before facing her. "But that's exactly what they want you to do—to interfere, to get FUNAI and the courts to stop Armando, only . . ."

He shook his head and shrugged his broad shoulders. He eyed her up and down, the look mixed with annoyance and possibly attraction. "Get your samples, and then get out."

She jerked back as if he had hit her. She fought to keep from slapping the arrogance off his handsome face. "You can't order me around, Mr. Dias. I've got a job to do, and I'll go when I'm ready to go."

Grabbing what remained of her sandwich and soda, she stormed to the back of the boat. Whenever Javier glanced back at her over the next few hours, she glared at him. He cursed under his breath and focused on steering the boat down the dark river.

At close to four in the afternoon, Javier cut across

the wide breadth of the river toward the shore. She saw a modest dock sticking out into the water. Well beyond it, nestled into the canopy of the rain forest, was an assortment of thatched huts and buildings. She realized this was the main settlement of the tribal reservation.

The boat bumped against the wooden dock, which creaked and groaned as Javier reversed the engines to force the craft closer. Natives from shore rushed forward to help secure the boat in place. Jessica stood at the back of the boat, feeling uncertain, while the natives showered attention on Javier.

He smiled and hugged some of them, jovially speaking with others. Both men and women were bare-chested and sported an assortment of tattoos and markings on their bodies. The bright red designs on their faces and bodies and on the palm headbands the men wore were probably *achiote*, Jessica realized. The men also wore strips of palm around their chests, waists, and foreheads.

At odds with the tattoos and palm adornments were the contemporary designs in the fabrics of the women's skirts and shorts and the modern pants most of the men wore. The modern world had already touched them even in this most simple of ways, Jessica realized. *No wonder Javier has concerns about outside visitors*, she thought.

The natives eyed her just as curiously, pointing at her khaki shorts and tank top. They whispered among themselves as she tentatively smiled at them. A moment later, they quieted, as a group of older men approached from the village. No doubt, the tribal elders.

The man in the lead immediately went to Javier,

embraced him, and clapped him on the back. When Javier realized she was watching his warm welcome, the engaging smile he had worn until then faded, and his full lips became a tight slash of disapproval. A muscle ticked along the fine, strong line of his jaw.

His continued resentment stung Jessica, although she hid it, pasting on her best smile as Javier formally introduced her to the man who had embraced him. "Doutora Morales. *Meu tio*, Antonio."

Javier's uncle was well into his sixties, with white hair, a bright smile, and an inquisitive gaze. He glanced from her to Javier, as if he sensed the undercurrents of dislike between.

"*Boa vinda*," he said, and took her outstretched hand, clasping it warmly between his work-roughened hands.

"I am sorry about your friend," he said carefully in English, surprising her. She had expected the tribe would speak only Portuguese, not English.

As if understanding her surprise, he added, "Javier's mother, my sister, married a Brazilian scientist from outside the tribe who brought many American friends to our home."

Jessica shot a quick look at Javier. His Brazilian father explained his larger height and build, as well as his caramel-colored skin, prominent facial bone structure, and dark hair color. At that moment, she realized her *mami* was probably right about her obsession with work. One of the most gorgeous men she had ever seen stood a few feet away, and she was looking at him as if he were a science project. She wondered if it bothered him that his mother had married an outsider.

Returning her gaze to the older man, Jessica lowered

her head deferentially to his uncle, who she had been told was the tribal shaman. "Thank you for having me here. It's nice to have someone make me feel welcome."

Her pointed comment was not lost on the shaman, whose gaze once again flitted between her and Javier before he introduced the five men behind him. She shook the hand of each elder and maintained a respectful posture until Antonio slipped his arm through hers and led her off the boat. He waved at his nephew over his shoulder.

"Bring her bags to the hut, Javier. She will need some rest so she can enjoy the feast tonight."

A small smile flickered across Jessica's face as she realized Javier must be scowling behind her. *Now whose turn is it to carry the bags?* she thought.

Antonio took her through the heart of the village, pointing out various landmarks and showing her a thatched hut near the edge of the jungle. She wondered as they approached if it had been Victor's hut.

"No, my dear. We have torn that hut down to release the spirits within," he said, as if reading her mind. He motioned to a bare area a few yards behind the hut.

At the door, he patted her hand. "Rest. The trip on the river can be tiring. We've planned a special feast for tonight before I take you into the rain forest tomorrow."

She hadn't expected him to take her into the jungle so soon.

"Is there a reason for the rush?" She had wanted to get the lay of the land first and also possibly speak to him about Victor's death before taking a trip to the plant's special habitat.

The smile on Antonio's face wavered a bit as he said,

"I worry that the loggers are getting too close to that area. It's best we not delay."

Without waiting for her reply, Antonio stepped away and disappeared back into the village. Javier, who was panting behind them as he lugged her bags, unceremoniously tossed her luggage at the foot of the hut's door.

"Do not stray on your own, especially into the jungle surrounding the village. It may not be safe," he warned her.

Defiantly raising her chin, she said, "I can take care of myself, remember?"

Javier eyed her up and down. The heat of desire flared in his gaze before he shook his head and laughed as he walked away, leaving her to stew.

The feast didn't begin until night had fallen.

Javier walked to Jessica's hut to escort her, frowning at the thought of another outsider's visit to the tribe. He knocked on the door, and she immediately answered.

She was still wearing a tank top in deference to the heat and humidity, but this one was feminine, black with a touch of black lace all around the neckline. The color accented the smooth creaminess of her skin, and the fabric clung to her, drawing his attention to her full breasts. As he admired her curves, he realized she had changed into a loose, gauzy skirt as well, which hung to mid-calf.

Her shoulder-length hair was pulled back into a fancy knot, although some slightly unruly wisps had escaped to feather around her forehead. The hairstyle exposed the fine features of her face and her hazel eyes. She peered at him intently.

"Are you ready?" he asked gruffly, and offered his arm.

Jessica hesitated. She had noted the attentive gleam in his gaze and tried to keep her own interest from roving up and down his nearly naked body. Still, it would be awkward to refuse, so she slipped her arm through his while he escorted her to the feast, trying to ignore his potent masculinity.

The tribe had built a large bonfire in the center of the village, and many people gathered around it, the men seated in smaller circles while the women served them food.

Javier led Jessica to the circle of tribal elders. As she approached, Antonio shifted to make space for her to sit with them. Javier squeezed in beside her.

Disconcerting, she thought, as they brushed shoulders in the tight circle. Javier had adopted the dress of his mother's tribe, even down to decorating his body with a series of small circles in a rosette pattern along his torso. A palm belt wrapped around the lean, ribbed muscles of his abdomen, and another rested just beneath his chest, almost grazing his dark copper nipples. He had no hair on his chest, much like the rest of the men present, but his short, dark hair was a shade lighter than that of the rest of the tribe, and his skin was noticeably paler, a rich color made more golden by the firelight.

Javier had forgone his jeans for a small loincloth, which barely covered his lean hips and exposed his sculpted midsection and long, thickly muscled legs. Legs that also brushed against hers as they sat beside each other. Goosebumps rose along her legs each time his thigh rubbed hers accidentally.

As she examined him from the corner of her eye, she

noted the palm band that encircled his forehead. It had a series of geometric designs, different from those the other men had adopted. Antonio leaned close to her and explained, "The patterns identify the clans within the tribe. Javier's is the jaguar, the strongest of all the animals within the jungle, much like my nephew."

Javier seemed embarrassed by his uncle's comment but said nothing as a woman handed him and Jessica bowls filled with some kind of fish stew. Jessica tried a sip and smiled. "It's delicious."

Antonio offered her a wooden cup containing a strong-smelling fruit punch. As he raised his cup in a toast, a man from another circle stood and began some kind of pantomime. Antonio explained, "The spirits we choose guide us. They open their arms to embrace us when we call upon them to help."

"Embrace you?"

Javier cautioned his uncle, "Tio. She cannot understand our ways so quickly." The condemnation in his tone implied she could never accept their ways.

Jessica took a bracing gulp of the drink. It immediately created a pleasant buzz of energy in her belly. Javier grabbed her wrist as she raised her cup for another sip. He warned her, "It's not just fruit punch. Be careful, or the alcohol and *guarana* will knock you on your ass."

He emphasized that statement by risking a quick appreciative glance downward to her posterior, but he quickly dropped her wrist and returned his attention to the men beside him.

"Really? I think I can handle the kick," she said, and took a healthy swig of the punch, earning a glare of annoyance from Javier.

The rest of the night passed pleasantly as the members of the tribe took turns dancing and acting out various stories. As they sang and danced before the fire, Antonio translated some of the stories for Jessica and explained the significance of the various tattoos and headbands. The food and punch continued to flow through the night, with the women bringing around yet more fish, in addition to plates with an assortment of root vegetables. Large platters of fresh fruits followed to end the meal.

Jessica was enjoying the night, even though Javier kept glaring at her. He seemed alternately puzzled and displeased by her presence there, and she sensed that it was because he wasn't sure of her reaction to the tribal customs. It seemed as if he was almost hoping for her disdain, so that he could justify his anger at having an outsider present for the feast. Despite that, she refused to let him ruin the night for her.

When one of the women pulled Jessica out of her seat, inviting her to join a group of women who were dancing closer to the bonfire, she went willingly, ignoring Javier's disbelieving look. By the time she had gamely handled the women's playful teasing as she struggled with their steps, it was late, but another cup of the *guarana* punch kept her awake and tuned into the activities all around. An hour later, however, people finally began to disperse and return to their huts.

Javier rose and held out his hand.

"I will walk you back," he said, but she shunned his offer.

He chuckled and waved dismissively. "By all means, go take care of yourself."

He walked away then, the flames from the fire

sweeping golden light over the strong muscles in his back and arms. She suddenly itched to touch his creamy *café con leche* skin. But she ignored the pull between her legs, a sure sign that maybe she *had* drunk too much punch.

Bidding good night to the elders, Jessica rose and strolled leisurely toward her hut. As she passed the first ring of structures, the night seemed to swallow her into the darkness. She paused, waiting for her eyes to adjust to the deep black, so different from the city at night with its unnatural lights.

A snap of a twig snagged her attention. She peered into the shadows but saw nothing as her eyes finally completed their adjustment. She took another step toward her hut, but before she could cry out someone grabbed her from behind and covered her mouth with his hand.

Years of martial arts training took over. Jessica stamped down hard on her attacker's foot, making him grunt and loosen his grip just enough that she could deliver a sharp elbow to his solar plexus.

He released his hold across her mouth. Jessica sucked in a breath, bent, and wrenched his arm, sending him up and over her to land with a dull thud.

A second later, something rushed past her, emitting a low growl as it did so. Javier appeared suddenly, seeming to rush out of nowhere.

Her attacker jumped to his feet and whipped something out of his pocket—a large knife. Its blade glinted brightly as the moonlight caught its edge.

The man jabbed at Javier with it, but he dodged the blade and somehow managed to strike out and land a blow on the man's face that rocked him backward.

As the man stumbled, the moonlight played over his features. He had a strong, stocky build, and his face and coloring were not that of the tribespeople. For a second, Jessica thought she had seen him before. *At the docks?* she wondered.

Javier advanced on the man again, but her attacker slashed the knife wildly through the air, driving Javier back. The man jabbed and lunged, his face filled with fear as Javier landed one blow and then another between wild swipes of the blade.

The man suddenly rushed forward but tripped on a loose vine. Javier couldn't react quickly enough to the change in the attacker's direction, and the two men went sprawling onto the ground in a heap.

Fearing that in such close quarters Javier might be injured by the knife, Jessica moved toward them. As her attacker's body became exposed for just a moment, she launched a kick at his side and sent him stumbling away from Javier. The knife went flying. Too far for the man to reach.

Seeing that the odds had suddenly turned, her attacker dashed off into the jungle, too quick for them to follow. Javier rose and stood beside her.

They were both breathing heavily from a combination of fear and exertion. As she faced Javier, Jessica realized he had one hand against his side. In the moonlight, the blood along his ribs seemed black against his skin.

"Damn," she cursed.

"I know you're too big and brave to ask for help, but I'm not. Do you think you could do something about this cut?"

CHAPTER 3

Jessica took hold of his hand and led him into her hut.

She flipped on a battery-powered lantern she had brought with her and quickly pulled a small first-aid kit from her luggage.

As she turned, Javier stepped closer to her, and her elbow brushed across his abs, reminding her of all his blatant masculinity.

"Sorry," she mumbled, but then laid a hand against the taut muscles at his waist to urge him toward the light so she could examine the wound.

The knife had caught him across a rib, preventing the blade from biting too deeply, but the long cut would need to be closed somehow. "This may hurt," she said, as she wet a piece of gauze with antiseptic.

"I think I can handle it," he replied, but he flinched, and his muscles tensed as she applied the gauze to his wound. He muttered a curse beneath his breath, even though her touch was gentle as she cleaned the area.

She told herself this was not the time to appreciate his amazing body as she worked, but it was nearly impossible to ignore so much lean muscle and creamy skin so enticingly close. She hurried as much as she could, using the butterfly bandages in her kit to close the gaping edges of the wound before taping a piece of gauze over the injury.

Lightly, she smoothed the tape around the edges of the gauze, trying to ignore his physical presence. Trying not to see how the reddish rosette patterns fo the *achiote* played across his skin and the palm bands hugged an impossibly lean waist and thick-muscled chest.

As she shot a glance up at him, she realized that he was as affected as she, despite their earlier enmity. His breath was ragged, but not with pain.

With desire.

He bent from his greater height until the edge of his jaw brushed the side of her forehead. His breath was warm against the sweat-damp skin at her temple.

She stroked her hand over the gauze covering the wound, but he laid his hand there and stilled the motion.

His hand was hot, his palm deliciously rough, and the pull came between her legs again as she imagined him touching her. Her nipples tightened in anticipation, and to battle that feeling, she asked, "Who was that man who attacked us?"

Javier stroked her hand lightly, slowly shifted his hand upward to caress her forearm. "One of Armando's goons."

Needing to touch him as he caressed her, she mimicked his action, laying her hand on the sculpted biceps of his arm. "Is the timber valuable enough—"

"To kill for? No. Armando has other reasons for hurting the tribe," he said, moving his hand up to cup the top of her arm, where he lightly caressed her shoulders with the pad of his thumb.

Her gaze locked with his, searching the strange gold-green gaze, which revealed nothing but desire.

"What kinds of reasons?" she asked, as she shifted her hand to his chest and traced the edge of the palm band encircling it. As she did, she fingered the hard nub of his nipple, dragging a ragged breath from him.

"Isn't it enough for you to know you need to watch out for yourself?" Even as he said it, he cradled her breast and tweaked her nipple through the thin cotton, rolling it gently between his thumb and forefinger. His actions caused a shudder to rip through her body.

"Well?" he challenged, as he snaked his hand upward, slipping beneath the edge of her tank top. He caressed her as he drew down both the shirt and her bra to reveal her breast to the warm evening air.

"Do you think you're owed this little look because you came to my rescue?" she asked, but she didn't stop him as he lowered his mouth to taste the nipple he had exposed. If anything, she held him closer, cradling the back of his head with her hand as she said, "Or do you think this is how to say thanks for my tending to you?"

He chuckled against her breast and gave her nipple an enticing lick with a cat-rough tongue before pulling away.

"You're quite different from what I expected," he said, nuzzling her nose with his lips before easing his mouth over hers. He tasted of the fruity *guarana* punch as she opened her mouth to his and licked his lips. They were soft and warm. He gave her a hint of a smile as she traced the edges of them with her tongue and then eased past the seam of his mouth to taste him fully.

The kiss went on and on as they sampled each other and eased close, passion rising until they were both breathing raggedly.

Jessica finally stepped back to break contact with him as she rearranged her clothing, suddenly embarrassed by the unexpected interlude and the force of her reaction. It had to be the alcohol and the *guarana*, she told herself, denying her attraction to him was based on anything else.

"So I'm not what you expected? Why?" she asked, crossing her arms before her as if to provide some defense against his still-hungry gaze.

"Because you've got more balls than most men I've met. Regardless, remember to be careful in the jungle tomorrow. Armando and his goons are getting bolder every day."

With that, he turned and walked out of the hut, leaving her to ponder just what had gone so wrong that she already had someone out to get her and why Javier had been in such a hurry to leave the room, just when things were starting to heat up.

She had come to the jungle for answers. To find out about the plant with the healing powers. To learn more about Victor's death.

After today's run-ins with Armando and his men, she was wondering if they had anything to do with her friend's death and vowed to find out.

The next morning, Javier's uncle was waiting for her in the center of the village, close to the remnants of the previous night's bonfire. Javier stood at his side, a rifle cradled in his arms, his face impassive. He did not reveal a scintilla of the passion present the night before or the slightest bit of injury from the knife would she'd dressed. It surprised her.

No one could heal that fast.

"Good morning," she said, earning a welcome from his uncle but only an annoyed grunt from Javier. It bothered her, but what had she expected? A good morning kiss?

Whatever had happened last night had probably been ill advised no matter how good it had felt.

With a curt nod in Javier's direction, she adjusted the straps on her knapsack, wanting the load to be balanced for their trip into the rain forest. It was just supposed to be a day trip, but she had decided to carry a small tent and sleeping bag in addition to other supplies, just in case. She had learned in her many adventures that you didn't take any chances.

Javier seemed to understand that, since he tossed her the rifle. "You should take this, assuming you know how to use it."

With practiced ease, she drew back the bolt, made sure the rifle was loaded, and slid the bolt back home, making the weapon ready to be fired. "Do you have any extra ammo?"

He reached for a small bag on the ground beside him and tossed it to her. "This should be more than enough."

She hadn't planned on arming herself, but after last night's incident, it seemed to make sense.

"Will you be joining us after all?" she asked. As far as she knew, his uncle would be her only guide.

"No, but I won't be far," he replied cryptically, and embraced his uncle, murmuring something to him in tones too low for her to understand.

He stalked off, leaving her and his uncle by the fire pit.

As she slung the ammo over her shoulder and the rifle under her arm, she looked at the tribal shaman, who was examining her intently.

"Are you sure you want to go ahead with this after last night? I am worried about Armando and his people. They may be close to where we are going."

She thought of Victor lying dead on the floor of the hut, his body maimed by the jungle cat, his skull crushed.

Hesitation filled her for a moment but was quickly replaced by the image of her sister's fever-ravaged face and the sounds of her struggling to breathe as the infection robbed her of life. *This plant could have saved her and it* will *save others*, Jessica thought.

"I'm sure," she repeated.

"Then I will take you there."

Antonio led her out into the jungle. He plunged into the underbrush but quickly found a path that had been trodden down by the passage of feet. He explained, "My people have been going to this place for many, many years to gather the plants and animals we use."

"The plant you showed Victor?" she asked as she plodded behind him, having to bend on occasion to avoid a branch or a dangling vine.

"Yes. Also a small tree frog and some leeches from one of the streams," he explained, but he became silent afterward, as if speaking somehow violated the spirits of the jungle, which swallowed them up the farther they got from the village.

At one point, Jessica sensed another presence and stopped. She listened to the noises around her. Something shifted nearby in the underbrush, and she whispered, "Antonio."

The shaman paused and picked up his head, as if scenting the wind. With a smile, he unerringly pointed toward the thick underbrush yards away.

She followed the direction of his arm and saw it then, just a flash of gold and brown amid the deep emerald foliage. Whipping the rifle around, she trained it on the blur she had seen, sighted the rifle as a massive gold-brown head came into view, thick pink tongue lolling from its mouth, sharp white fangs visible even at this distance.

"Do not worry, Jessica. It's a good spirit come to guide us," Antonio said, but she kept the rifle trained on the large jaguar.

The animal paused, eyeing them, and a low rumble came from its mouth. She tightened her finger on the trigger, but then, as she met the cat's intense eyes, she realized that there was no danger in the somehow familiar gaze.

Lowering the rifle, she accepted that maybe it *was* a good spirit sent to guide them, sent to protect them. Something about that gaze made her ask, "Tell me about Javier."

Antonio chuckled and shook his head. "What is there to say? He's a good boy. The light of our tribe."

The light, huh?

"If Javier is the light, what's Armando?"

Antonio stopped short and faced her silently. She

slipped her thumbs beneath the straps of her knapsack, fingering them before she added, "Javier thinks Armando wants to hurt the tribe. Why?"

With a shrug, Antonio turned and began to walk again. "Armando and Javier were always at odds as young boys, maybe because no matter what Armando did, he could never be as good as Javier."

"Because of that, he wants to destroy the tribe's lands?"

"There are other reasons," Antonio said as he plowed forward. She caught another blur of gold and dark brown nearby before it moved away from them.

As she walked, Jessica thought about the many reasons Armando would have a beef with Javier, and the most obvious one came to mind. "The fight is about a woman?"

Antonio gave a strangled chuckle. "Don't men always fight over women? But no, not a woman."

He stopped in his tracks and examined her carefully. "Why does this interest you so? I though perhaps that you and Javier—"

"Were at odds? We are . . . were. But after last night, it seems that I've become a part of their fight. That makes me want to know what's going on between them."

Especially if she and Javier were going to continue their rather enticing interlude.

With a nod, Antonio said, "Years ago, Armando's parents came down with an illness that one of our American visitors brought with him."

"One of your brother-in-law's friends?" she questioned, and Antonio confirmed it before he resumed their journey.

"But what about this plant you're taking me to?

Couldn't that have saved his parents?" she asked as she hurried after him, his steps surprisingly sure and spry for a man his age.

"Sometimes our medicines aren't enough."

Jessica understood. Sometimes man's medicines failed, and death won the battle.

They walked in silence until the rain forest canopy above them opened and gave way to blue skies and a large clearing.

She stepped into the open area, viewing the vegetation surrounding the spot and the shorter ferns and grasses blanketing the ground. Mixed among them, she recognized the broad, almost succulent leaves of the plant Victor had drawn in his field notebook. Victor had always been a wonderful artist, and he had quite accurately captured the plant that grew in thick abundance on the rain forest floor.

As Jessica bent to examine one of the plants, Antonio strode several yards away to one side of the clearing. He bent down and began gathering some of the plants. Jessica mimicked his movements, shifting to a spot on the far side of the clearing, where the plants were more plentiful. As she leaned over to gather more specimens, she sensed another presence.

Standing, Jessica peered into the thick plants and foliage a few yards away. The leaves shuddered, then parted, as an immense black cat stalked into the clearing—a black jaguar. But this was a very different animal from the golden jaguar spirit that had followed them earlier.

Jessica froze as she met the black jaguar's gaze, malevolent and dangerous. She somehow knew this was the cat that had killed Victor.

Now it was coming for her.

Barely ten feet separated her from the huge black cat.

She quickly searched the jungle around them. There was no sign of the golden jaguar she had seen earlier.

The distance between her and the black jaguar was too short for her to draw her rifle, sight, and fire, but she did so anyway, praying she could get off the shot before . . .

The large black cat sprang at her, jaws wide, claws outstretched to rip her to shreds.

She braced for impact.

CHAPTER 4

The killing strike never came, as a large golden body came out of nowhere and hurtled through the air, snaring the black cat in midflight.

The two cats collided, one black and one golden, and landed on the ground in a tumble of sharp claws and snarling complaint.

Jessica brought up the rifle, but the two animals were nearly inseparable, jaws clamped tightly on each other's body. Sharp claws tried to rip and tear as they rolled around on the ground, one seeking dominance over the other. Clods of grass and vegetation flew into the air from the fury of their struggles.

Antonio came to stand beside her. He laid a hand on her arm and urged her to lower the rifle. "The golden jaguar spirit is protecting us. You may hurt it if you fire."

She didn't relax her stance, following the fight as the two animals struggled before her. Her arms shook. Her hands were wet on the stock of the rifle as she watched the bloody combat. She couldn't lower the weapon, especially as it soon appeared that the golden jaguar might be waging a losing battle.

The black cat was so much bigger. Stronger. It had a tight hold on the golden jaguar, which began weakening before her eyes.

Gripping the rifle stock tightly, Jessica carefully tracked the two animals, and when the golden jaguar was forced to its hindquarters, it exposed the body of the bigger cat.

She fired, striking the black jaguar high up on its shoulder. With an odd, almost human scream, the animal stumbled back and released its hold on the golden cat. It turned its head toward her and growled.

She quickly worked the bolt on the rifle and fired again, missing this time as the bullet disappeared into the thick ground cover. The black jaguar whirled and ran away. She worked the bolt-action rifle once more and fired after the cat as it raced toward the underbrush, its gait awkward from the wound on its shoulder.

Then she trained the rifle on the golden jaguar that lingered in the clearing, badly mauled and struggling to remain on its feet. Its tongue lolled out of its mouth, and heavy rasping breaths shook its wounded sides. It slowly fell to the ground.

When the shaman walked fearlessly toward the jaguar, she dropped her weapon and cautiously followed her guide.

A large chunk of meat had been torn from high up on the animal's hindquarter. Deep furrows marred the beauty of its fur. The other cat's claws had raked viciously through muscle and down to pink-white bone.

The jaguar's muscles trembled and quivered from the pain, and its breathing was ragged.

As they approached, its green-eyed gaze, a strangely familiar gaze, swept over them before the cat's eyes rolled back in its head and a low growl of pain escaped the animal.

To her surprise, Antonio kneeled beside the jaguar and laid a hand on its side. She bent down beside him. The animal quieted as she crouched closer to the shaman. Then he whispered, "Release the spirit, Javier. Return to your human form."

Before her eyes, the cat's body shook, more violently than before. The gold and brown fur seemed to bleed away, fading from site until it was replaced by human skin, heavily bruised and scraped in spots. Next came the loud pop and crackle of sinew and bone. Before her eyes, the cat's skeleton shifted and moved, elongated and flattened from quadruped to biped.

She watched in a combination of shocked horror and scientific fascination as the broad face of the cat extended, and the muzzle became a nose. Sharply defined cheekbones emerged from the flatter planes of the cat's visage, and gold-green eyes—Javier's eyes—trained on her face as the transformation slowly completed.

Javier now lay on the jungle floor, bleeding profusely from a combination of bite and claw marks. Deep bruises marred large sections of his torso and arms. His muscles trembled beneath Antonio's hand as his uncle talked to him softly.

"Rest, Javier. We will care for you," he said, and looked up at her, asking for her assistance.

As confused and dazed as she was from what had

just happened, Javier had saved her life. She would help in any way she could.

"What can I do? I know first aid."

"Set up the tent. We'll have to spend the night until Javier is recovered. I'll make a mash to apply to the wounds," Antonio said.

Jessica quickly went to work, setting up the tent and laying out the sleeping bag within. She collected some deadfall, dry leaves, and branches she could use as tinder and fuel, because she wanted the materials handy when night fell so she could make some food, but also to keep away any animals that might decide to investigate their camp. She reloaded the rifle and kept it within close range.

Antonio helped Javier to his feet and then half carried him inside the tent. Javier lay down on the sleeping bag. When Antonio emerged from the tent, he motioned to the campfire she had prepared. "Why don't you start that? Javier will need to feed soon."

"Feed?" she wondered aloud. It sounded so animalistic. Not human.

But Javier wasn't human, only . . .

He wasn't an animal, either. At least, he wasn't one right now, as she snuck a peek through the opening of the tent and saw Javier's naked body. His magnificent naked human body, bruised, battered, and torn in so many spots that something inside her ached in sympathy.

Antonio laid a gentle hand on her arm. "Do not judge too quickly, Jessica."

She withdrew and concentrated on getting the fire going and heating some of the water from their canteens to make one of the freeze-dried stews she had packed into her knapsack. She lost track of time as she worked. Antonio returned with a small bunch of ripe bananas and some papayas. He placed them on the ground beside the fire. She realized night had started to fall around them.

Antonio sat beside her, and she grabbed one of the small bowls from her mess kit. She ladled some of the stew for the shaman. With a grateful nod, he accepted it, and she said, "Is there anything else we can do for Javier?"

"I made a mash from the plant and applied it to his wounds. That will help him heal more quickly," he said, and cradled the metal bowl in his hands.

She filled a second bowl and said, "I'll feed him—"

"Eat first. Let him rest for now."

She prepared a serving for herself and ate it mechanically, the stew tasteless as she considered the impossibility of what she had just seen. Javier's transformation was painful to behold on so many levels. Even now, the sickening sounds of bones and joints cracking and popping reverberated in her skull. She shuddered.

"I'm going to see how he's doing."

Without waiting for the shaman's reply, she refilled her bowl, grabbed some of the fruit, and slipped into the tent, easing over Javier's prone body. Someone had turned on the small battery-powered lantern she had brought, and it provided dim light, just enough to see Javier's wary gaze as she came in and kneeled beside him.

"How are you?" she asked. Her eyes swept up and down his body uneasily, noting the many injuries but also the splendor of his human form.

One hundred percent perfect male, she thought as she beheld him.

As a blush swept over her face, Javier grabbed the edge of the sleeping bag and covered himself as best he could, but it hid just half of his body and only some of his wounds. The smaller injuries had already knitted closed, thanks to the mash Antonio had worked into them.

"Hungry," Javier said, and motioned to the bowl she held in her hand. He was exhausted. She suspected that accepting his animal spirit and changing into the jaguar always took a great deal of energy from him. He needed to eat and rest to recharge.

She slipped one arm behind his back and helped him to sit up. He grimaced as he did so but bit back a groan of pain. He quickly ate the bowl of stew and polished off a few bananas and a papaya before lying back down. Jessica watched him guardedly, unsure what to expect. He finally said, "Ask away. I can tell you want to know."

Jessica leaned close and laid a hand on his shoulder, as if to convince herself of his humanity.

In a choked whisper, she said, "You're a human now, but before—"

"I called forth my spirit and became a jaguar."

She softly ran her fingers along the line of his collarbone, tracing a bruise there. Her gaze drifted over his body once again before locking with his. "The other cat—the black jaguar. Can I assume it was—"

"Armando," he jumped in.

"Was he the one who killed Victor?" she asked, her gaze roaming over his body as if she still didn't quite believe what she had seen earlier.

"I think he did, although I have no way of proving it."

Jessica moved her hand to his uninjured shoulder. The other one had a deep bite mark and bruising from the force of Armando's jaws. She winced and asked, "Does it hurt?"

"It's healing. If I call the spirit to return again—"

"The spirit? Were you bitten? Like a werewolf?" she asked.

"It can happen with a bite, but no. That wasn't how I became—"

"A were-jaguar."

He paused at her comment, considering how to answer. For his people, there was no such term, no stigma attached to the ability to take on an animal spirit. If anything, being chosen and accepting the spirit was something special. Beautiful. Respected.

As he glanced at Jessica, he saw confusion but, surprisingly, not revulsion. He didn't know why, but it gave him some hope that she might be different. Able to understand. So he explained how the people of his tribe summoned their animal guides and bonded with them. How they had a ritual for completing the union of man and beast.

"So you use this frog poison—"

"It creates a fever that prepares us for our journey," he clarified. "The fever burns away our fears and opens our senses to the jungle spirits."

"And you *chose* to have this happen?" she asked.

"My mother belonged to the jaguar clan. As her only son, it was my choice to follow in her footsteps or remain fully human as I was. As my father was."

A deep furrow marked the space between her brows

as Jessica concentrated. "Could your father have become like you? Would a bite—"

"As I said before, a bite may infuse you with the spirit, but if you are unwilling to embrace it, great misery can arise." He shot a wary look in her direction.

"And going from jaguar to man and back can help you heal?"

"The transformation causes all kinds of changes, and during those changes, some healing can occur."

She swept her gaze up and down his body once again, before motioning outside. "I should go help Antonio."

He laid a hand on her arm. "Antonio can take care of himself. He will warn us if danger approaches."

Jessica brought her hands to her thighs and rubbed the denim there in a nervous gesture as she considered his words.

"Is Antonio like you?"

He answered without hesitation. "Yes, although he has a different animal spirit."

She thought of the palm headbands she had seen the night before. Javier wore one for the jaguar clan, different from the one his uncle had worn. Different from that of the others in the tribe, which made her pause and ask, "Is everyone in the tribe—"

"Not all, but many," he said, and quickly motioned to the small bit of sleeping bag beside him. "Lie down. Get some rest."

As if I could get any rest at his side, she thought, but did as he asked, sensing that arguing would accomplish nothing. She lay down facing him, her head pillowed on her arm. In the dim light, Javier's skin seemed more golden, and in her mind's eye came the reminder of the lush golden fur with the dark, nearly black rosettes that had covered his body earlier.

The scientist in her continued to hold out that his transformation wasn't possible. To prove it to herself, she laid her hand on the deep, thick pectoral muscle of his chest. His skin was warm and smooth. Human. The nipple beneath her hand hardened with her touch. A human reaction.

"I'm not some science experiment, Jessica," he said, a muscle ticking along his jaw as he exerted control.

"I know, only . . ." She hesitated before she moved her hand to the biceps of his arm, where bright pink skin had replaced an earlier injury and a smaller bruise was already turning that yellowish color that hinted at healing. "Would you ever have told me what you are?"

"Would you have believed me?" he challenged. He reached up and smoothed a worry line from her brow. "Even now, you can't quite believe. Maybe you can't accept what I am."

"Don't judge me too quickly, Javier. But even if you had skipped the part about being a were-jaguar, why didn't you warn me about what was going on with Armando?"

He chuckled harshly and pulled his hand away. "Would it have changed your mind, Little Miss Save the World?"

She couldn't fail to miss the bitterness that laced the tones of his voice, and it occurred to her then. "Your parents died when Armando's did. When that illness—"

"It took several people from the tribe. My mother and Armando's parents. Armando blames my family and the tribe for his loss," he said with a sigh.

"Your father?" she pressed.

"Blamed himself for all the deaths. He died a few months later. Some might say of a broken heart." The harsh laugh that followed belied his belief in such romantic notions.

She shifted closer so she might reach him more easily. She laid her hand above his heart. A strong human beat greeted her palm, reminding her that whatever else he might be, he was also a man. A man who had on some level lied to her, and yet a man who intrigued her and who had saved her life.

"You should have told me," she repeated, although in her heart, she knew it wouldn't have changed anything. She still would have come to the jungle. Had to come. Because of Victor. Because of her sister. Because of Javier's mother and Armando's parents and so many others like them who could be saved with the right medicines.

She was pulling her hand away when he stayed the motion by laying his hand over hers. As their gazes met, she realized he needed that touch, and she needed it as well.

At dawn, Jessica woke flushed and warm, recalling the heat of his body when she had drifted closer to him sometime during the night. His contented rumble, like the purr of a well-satisfied cat, had finally lulled her to sleep, driving away the sounds and sights of the fight and his transformation.

She passed her hand over the spot where he had lain beside her. Still warm from his body.

He hasn't been gone long, she thought, and roused herself, knowing they couldn't linger in this clearing much longer. She had to collect her specimens and then head back to civilization for her presentation to the board.

She also knew it was time to leave because there was too much of a threat here. Armando could kill her, much as he had Victor. Javier could try to protect her, but for how long?

Armando was bigger and stronger, but Javier had heart. Courage. Things that couldn't be ignored in a fight. Things that called to her in a way that endangered her as well, for they touched her heart. That hadn't happened in a long time. Maybe never, she acknowledged.

Since her sister's death, Jessica had shut down her emotions, determined not to feel loss again. She convinced herself that she needed to find a way to help others avoid the kind of pain she had experienced. That driving need had kept her from developing any lasting relationships with the men in her life, even Victor.

Victor had come to understand that he was just a companion during their many trips together. That he could never touch the heart she had walled off from the world.

But what she was beginning to feel for Javier had opened a crack in that wall and made her feel vulnerable for the first time in years. She couldn't permit that. As soon as he was healed, she would demand that he guide her back to civilization. Her life was safer there, in so many ways.

When Jessica climbed out of the tent, she searched the clearing for Javier.

But he was gone.

Keen-eyed, Antonio noticed her interest and said,

"He needed to change back to finish the healing. He'll meet us at the village."

Knowing they would leave the clearing soon, Jessica collected a few dozen additional plant specimens and prepared for the trek back to the village.

Antonio had boiled some water, which he had mixed with some native berries and herbs, explaining that it would give her energy for the return trip.

As they finished packing, she glanced at Antonio and recalled Javier's words of the night before—that Antonio was like him.

She faced the old man, examining him carefully, and as he caught wind of her interest, he smiled.

"You wish to see what I am."

When she nodded, he said, "Watch, and follow me back to my people."

Antonio's transformation sped by in a blur, faster than Javier's. Where a moment before there had been copper-colored skin lined with age, there were now beautiful beige and brown feathers, as Antonio spread his arms out and they became wings. The snap and crackle of bone seemed less severe, lighter, like the hollow bones of a bird. Before her eyes, Antonio's flat, broad nose lengthened and hardened into the razor-sharp beak of a hawk.

A magnificent hawk, she thought. Antonio was regal and resplendent as he soared into the air above her, wings flapping and talons ready to pierce unsuspecting prey. With a quick spurt of power, he circled above her before moving forward into the rain forest canopy and along the trail they had taken the day before.

"Follow me," Antonio had said that day, and she did, while keeping one eye on him above her and the other on the trail. As she walked, Jessica got the sense that she wasn't alone, that in addition to Antonio sweeping the sky above her, Javier was also nearby, watching over them in his animal form. It brought Jessica a sense of comfort and contentment, but she quickly squelched the thought. Such emotions were too risky to the life she had built for herself—a nomadic life with no attachments.

Before reaching the village, Antonio swooped down from the skies and morphed back to his human form. The mind-boggling transformation reminded her that the authorities would never believe her if she told them about Victor's death and Armando's transformation into the black jaguar.

She was powerless. As powerless as she had been at her sister's bedside and it angered her.

Much as she had sworn to make a difference then, she would find a way to make a difference now. She just needed to decide how to do that without compromising the tribe or her standing in the scientific community. She doubted her colleagues would believe wild tales about people who could transform themselves into animals.

Since a long, hot shower always helped her think, Jessica decided to save her packing for later and take a break in the heat of the day to wash up, although the best she would get would be a bracing rainwater shower outside her hut.

CHAPTER 5

After undressing quickly, she stepped from her hut into the small alcove connecting it to the outdoor shower. She tossed her towel over the top of the wooden partition, but as she stood there naked, she caught sight of the jaguar nestled in the tree above.

Javier, she knew instinctively.

His powerful cat body was slung along the length of a thick branch, one paw dangling downward lazily. His gold-green gaze fixed on her body, causing an immediate and unwanted reaction.

Her nipples tightened, and a quick pulse beat between her legs.

She stepped into the stall and released the first quick blast of rainwater. It rushed down over her body, raising goosebumps with its slight chill and quickening her nipples into even tighter peaks.

Raising her hand, she touched one breast, strumming her thumb across the turgid tip. From above her, she heard a low, throaty rumble. As she looked up, she realized the jaguar had slunk closer on the branch for a better view.

She intended to give it to him, a payback of sorts for his voyeurism and his secrets. She wanted to punish him for the attraction that drew them together, even though she knew it would bring nothing but complications to both their lives.

With her free hand, she cupped her other breast. Slick, soapy skin slipped beneath her fingers. Her nipple had peaked from the chill of the water and was incredibly sensitive as she caressed herself, her gaze trained on the cat above her the whole time.

The jaguar inched ever forward, its balance more precarious the closer it got to the weaker end of the branch.

Between her legs, Jessica felt the thrum of need. She moved one hand down and eased it between her legs. As she found the nub hidden in the dark curls and played with it, a rough gasp escaped her.

At the sound, the jaguar grumbled in response and slinked just an inch closer—but an inch too far. The branch bent downward, unsettling the cat, who fell to the ground with a growl of complaint and a loud thud.

Jessica chuckled but then closed her eyes and tried to satisfy the need that had grown within her.

A second later, however, the door to the shower flew open. Javier stood there naked, erect, and hungry. All traces of the jaguar were gone as he closed the door behind him. His human body was still bruised in spots, but he seemed to be healing from most of his other injuries.

As her gaze met his, she knew what he wanted. She

could smell the animal need and musk of his arousal pouring off his skin.

She wouldn't deny him or herself. The physical attraction had been there from the start, and it was time to satisfy that need, no matter what the consequences.

Javier cupped her breast even as she moved her hand from between her legs. His shaft was wet, making his skin slick beneath the palm of her hand as she shifted it up and down the length of him.

A rough rumble came from his body as she stroked him, matching the sharp mewl of pleasure from her own throat as his strong fingers rotated her nipple into an ever tighter bud.

He stepped closer, and the tips of her breasts brushed the rock-hard wall of his chest. His skin was smooth and hot to the touch. Surprisingly so. With a little wiggle of her body, she rubbed her breasts against his chest, loving the feel of his skin and the hard muscle against the sensitive tips of her breasts.

Then she caressed his pectoral muscles with her free hand. She palmed the thick, well-defined muscles and swept her thumb across his dark brown nipple.

Another pleased kind of purr came from him, and she said, "This is crazy."

"Definitely *louco*," he said, and mimicked her actions, stroking the tight peak of her breast with his thumb, his caress sure and enticing.

Before he could say or do anything else, Jessica gave in to her desire. She bent her head and covered his nipple with her mouth. His skin was salty and firm beneath her lips. He groaned and cradled her head to him.

Somehow he managed to say, "Is this how you say thanks for saving your life?"

She chuckled and gently teethed the tight nub before meeting his gaze again. "I think we both know this is about more than thanks."

With a feral smile, Javier trailed his free hand down her body and between her legs. He unerringly found the center of her. She watched as he stroked her with his strong, capable hand and pressed his fingers against the swollen nub. Then he eased first one finger and then a second into her, drawing a rough moan out of her.

Tightening the grasp of her hand, she caressed his erection, stroking his length before running her hand over the head. As her knees weakened from his practiced caresses, she braced her other hand on his shoulder for support.

The pressure inside her built, and in her hand she could feel the growing strain and strength of his arousal, too. They were both breathing heavily, their bodies shaking, when he leaned forward and whispered, "I want to be inside you."

She wanted that, too, and as she braced both hands on his strong shoulders, he bent, slipped between her thighs, and positioned himself at her center. Slowly he entered her, his thickness and length stretching her to the point of both pleasure and pain. As he straightened to his full height, he cupped her buttocks and lifted her off the ground. She wrapped her legs around his waist, deepening his penetration.

The feel of him filling her dragged another rough gasp from her.

He stilled for a moment, as if to savor the wonder of their joining, but then he slowly flexed his hips, drawing in and out of her. His thrusts grew more determined as their passion rose.

Jessica's climax gathered at her core as he plunged deep inside her more roughly than before. She met his gaze, watching as he looked at her breasts swaying with the rhythm of his powerful thrusts.

She wanted his mouth on them and murmured her plea.

Javier held her tight with one arm, then reached up and released a torrent of water over their bodies, removing the last remnants of the soap. He quickly brought his mouth down and sucked on her breasts, teething and licking them both, until the tight knot of need within her exploded, releasing her climax through her body.

As she called out his name and cradled his head to her, Javier's muscles trembled beneath her hands. Jessica knew he could feel the pull and throb of her release deep within.

She kissed him gently and whispered, "Come with me, *querido*," and he did, his big body shuddering a moment before he let himself go inside her.

"*Meu amor*," he said, and took her mouth in a rough kiss, cupping her head to him until she was nearly breathless, his mouth moving on hers over and over, as if he wanted to eat her alive.

With their bodies still joined, he somehow managed to walk them back into her hut. At the edge of the bed, he bent and gently laid her down. She gazed up at him. His gold-green cat eyes blazed with desire.

"Javier," she whispered, half in question, but then she sensed the awakening of his erection again between her legs. She felt the thickness of him pressing deeper inside her and her own answering dampness surrounding him.

As he cradled her breasts, teasing the hard tips with his fingers, Javier roused her passion once more.

Jessica closed her eyes and gave herself over to the animal inside her. The one that wanted satisfaction no matter the consequences.

As yet another soul-shaking release built within her, she sensed that the price to be paid for such fulfillment would be costly.

It had to be the strength of his animal spirit that gave him such powers of recuperation.

Jessica barely had the power to roll onto her back, but Javier had gone outside to get some food and drink and returned. Now they lay cozily in bed, her back propped up against his chest as she sat between his legs. She fed him from the plate of fruits he had brought.

She broke off a piece of banana, and he leaned forward, biting it carefully from her hand. She took a piece for herself and ate it slowly. After, she sipped from a glass filled with fruit juice and handed it to him. As a little buzz awakened her, she realized it had *guarana* in it again but no alcohol.

Rich, ripe slices of mango were next, but as Javier accepted the last piece from her, he snared her hand and proceeded to lick the juices off her fingers, his tongue rough as he slowly sucked one finger and then another into his mouth.

"Javier," she protested, even as she was putting aside the food and turning to face him. Her legs straddled his thighs, and his erection—thick, long, and hard—pressed against the soft flatness of her belly.

He ignored her slight complaint, laid his hands on her waist, and gently urged her upward, so that he could lick the peaks of her breasts. As he did so, his erection slipped between her legs, and Jessica guided him to the center of her.

Slowly, she sank down, holding her breath as his thickness filled her. The pull of his mouth and the rough salve of his tongue awakened an almost animal need in her to take him.

She shifted her hips, and he wrapped his arms around her waist, helped her set a rhythm, dragging them slowly toward a climax.

Her gaze locked with his—those amazing gold-green eyes. Cat eyes, she now realized, and yet it brought no fear, nor did the low rumble and purr that came from him as they moved ever closer to satisfaction.

He thrust upward, dragging a ragged gasp from her, and the quickening surged through her body. Brushing aside the spill of her hair from the side of her face, he laid his cheek against hers and in low tones said, "Free yourself, Jess. Don't be afraid of the wildness inside you."

With his words, her release broke past the dam she had erected. She called out his name, and her body trembled in his arms.

Against his erection, the heat and wetness of her surrounded Javier. The tightening and rolling of muscle caressed him, urging him to join her.

It had been so long since he had allowed himself any pleasure. Since he had permitted the human side of him to seek release. To enjoy the pleasure of communion with a kindred spirit.

He realized it then, that he and Jessica shared a great deal in common. She was strong enough to handle all that he was.

The joy of that filled him, and he let go of his own restraint and embraced the climax that rushed over his body, bringing release.

They were lying face to face, still touching, hours later. They exchanged slow, languid caresses, but Jessica was beginning to feel disoriented. Disconnected from her everyday life. Distracted by a sense of . . . rightness.

This is so wrong, she thought. The comfort and sense of well-being she felt in his arms meant trouble because she knew their involvement could be nothing but a passing interlude. She couldn't let her fascination with Javier deter her from her promise to her sister or from seeking justice for Victor.

Javier immediately sensed her disquiet.

"What bothers you so? Armando?"

She chuckled harshly. Armando could kill her, but Javier was much more dangerous to her well-being. "No, not Armando. You."

"Why?" he asked, even as he cupped her breast and lazily stroked his thumb across the tip of it.

"Javier, *por favor*. Stop," she said, and he did as she asked, but he clearly wasn't done with the conversation.

"My people believe that while you may mate with many during your lifetime, only one is truly your soul mate."

Jessica looked away. If she believed in things like that, she might have grudgingly admitted that how she felt in his arms, by his side, could develop into something more. But there was no room in her life for a man, so she knew it would be simpler to push him away despite their incredible chemistry. She couldn't detour from what was important in her life for such uncertain feelings.

"I'm not sure this can ever be more. I have to be at a stockholders meeting at the start of next week. I have to go home, Javier. I've got obligations there."

He stiffened beside her, and as she looked up, she realized from the tight slash of his lips that he was angry.

"Home?" he questioned sharply. "I've seen your bio, Jessica. It seems to me there is nowhere you truly call home."

The moment shattered, she decided to retreat. Leaving the bed, she grabbed some clothes from a chair and slipped them on. Javier watched her dress, his angry gaze raking over her newly clothed body.

Even now, the thrum of desire called to her. Clenching her hands to keep from touching him again, she said, "I need to go back, because people need me and depend on me."

"Your company and its rich stockholders?"

"It's way more than that, and you know it. I have to try to figure out what to do about the plant. About Victor's murder."

"What will you tell the authorities? That a were-jaguar ate your friend?" His words were bitter and laced with disdain.

"I need to stop Armando," she said, as she grabbed her bags from the floor and tossed them on the bed beside him.

He vaulted from the bed and came to her side, fists clenched at his side. "Do you think it will be so easy to stop Armando?"

She shrugged. "There's got to be a way to get justice for Victor. Maybe if I can shut down the logging—"

"By showing them some special little plants? Do you think that will do it?"

Jessica didn't know how to answer him at first, but then she thought about Victor and her sister. About death that came before its rightful time. She knew then that she couldn't just let Armando continue with his revenge, because his actions wouldn't just hurt the tribe—they might hurt countless others who could possibly be helped by the plant.

"If flower power is all I have to fight with, then that's what I'll use. Seems to me the fang-to-fang fight hasn't accomplished much except getting Victor killed." With that, she grabbed some clothes and stuffed them into her bag.

Javier cupped her cheek and forced her to face him. "If I promise that Armando will receive his punishment—"

"Even if you did, I can't stay here."

Some of his anger faded, and with hands held out, almost pleading, he said, "Because of what I am?"

Jessica considered him. All that strength and beauty in front of her, basically asking to be hers. But Javier had been too right with his earlier statement about her not being able to call anywhere home.

Walking up to him, she cradled his cheek and said, "No, Javier. Because of me. I've chosen a path in my life—"

"A path to fame and glory."

Anger surged at his words and got the better of her. Jessica slapped him across the face, the impact so hard it left the imprint of her hand on his cheek. "You know *nothing* about what drives me!"

"Tell me it isn't what drives most of the outsiders

who come here. Tell me it isn't about greed or conquest—"

She cut him off with a brusque slash of her hand. "I lost my sister when she was only twenty. It was a weird infection the doctors couldn't control. She *died*, Javier, and I vowed I would spend my life making sure that nobody else would have to go through such pain and suffering again."

"So you run from place to place, searching for miracles?" he asked. His tone had changed. He tenderly caressed her cheek, his gentle touch making her feel guilty about slapping him.

"It's what I need to do. I can't let the same thing happen to someone else. I promised."

A resigned sigh slipped from his body. "Don't let the dead steal your life, Jessica."

"I have no other choice, Javier."

Tension crept into his features, and he pulled his hand away from her face. "You always have a choice, Jessica, but you've already made this one. It's best you go back to civilization now. The bullet you shot Armando with was silver and laced with silver nitrate. It should have weakened him enough that he might lie low today and give us time to get you out of here safely."

"But won't we be on the river at night?"

"Not for long. By then, we'll be close enough to town that it shouldn't be a problem. I'll let my *tio* know that you're leaving."

He quickly wrapped a towel around his waist and stalked out of her hut.

She watched him depart. With him gone, the room

felt empty. She wouldn't admit that a part of her felt empty as well.

But nothing could deter her from what she knew was right. From what she had to do.

Not even the words he had uttered during their argument.

Don't let the dead steal your life.

CHAPTER 6

It didn't take Jessica long to pack up the rest of her belongings, since she hadn't packed all that much to begin with. The things she took the most care with were the specimen plants she had collected earlier that morning. She had the necessary permits for removing them from the country and hoped that once she got the plants back to Jersey, she might be able to propagate more of them.

The tribe members gathered by the dock to wish her good-bye alongside the tribal elders. She smiled at all the people, shook hands with some, and heartily embraced Javier's uncle, the last person by the edge of the dock.

"Doutora Morales. Are you sure about what you're doing?" Antonio asked, concern etching deep grooves of worry into the lines of his face.

"There are things I must do at home, and I need to see what will be done about Armando," she said as she held his hand, cradling it warmly in hers.

Antonio shot a quick look at his nephew, who waited by the boat, arms folded across his chest. Javier looked angry but resolute. *He probably won't even miss me*, she decided.

"I'm sorry, Antonio, but it's best that I go now. Thank you for showing me the plant and for making me feel so welcome."

"You will come back to us," he said knowingly.

She embraced him again and then climbed onto the boat. As Javier jumped onboard, a number of men from the tribe surged forward to release the moorings. Then Javier gunned the engines, and the boat surged forward. He kept to the closest shore instead of cutting across the broad width of the river, and Jessica watched the underbrush and canopy for signs of anything unusual, but nothing caught her eye. An hour passed quietly, then another. Jessica began to grow tired of the silence.

She risked a glance at Javier, at the features that had become so familiar and dangerously enticing in too short a time.

"When we reach the city—"

His hands tightened on the wheel of the boat. "I'll make sure you're safe until you get on the plane."

Anger rose up swiftly. "I don't need you—"

"To keep you safe. *Eu sei, meu amor.*"

"Then why patronize me?" she accused.

"Because I thought you might want to spend some final time together. That it might help you decide whether you want to come back to this place," he said, and swept one arm outward to the majesty of all that surrounded them. "It could provide you with much that you seek."

In his words was the unspoken plea that he somehow might be part of what she sought. It moved her more than she wanted to admit. She couldn't quite remember why she was in such a hurry to return to New Jersey.

Rising, she stood before him and cradled the strong line of his jaw, brushed her thumb across the fullness of his lips.

The strong thrum of a powerful engine interrupted them.

Jessica moved from his side and to the back of the boat to investigate. A large speedboat was well behind them but gaining ground rapidly. It kicked up quite a wake, a testament to how swiftly it sped through the waters.

Too quickly, she realized, and as the boat drew nearer, she thought she detected a familiar face beside the man at the helm.

"Is that—"

"Armando," Javier said, and he reached for a pair of binoculars beside the steering wheel. He raised them and looked back at the boat. A muffled curse escaped him as he handed her the binoculars. He manipulated the engine controls, slowly increasing the speed of their boat.

Jessica peered through the binoculars. Armando stood beside the driver of the boat, looking relatively unscathed from his earlier encounter with Javier, although she thought she detected something bulky beneath the shirt he wore. *A bandage, maybe?* she wondered.

She shifted to Javier's side, but the tension in his body

confirmed to her what she had already suspected: they couldn't outrun the more powerful vessel. With each passing minute, the speedboat was gaining on them, making it possible for her to see that beside Armando were two other men armed with rifles. As the distance between the boats closed, one of the men picked up his weapon and opened fire.

The ping and crack of bullets striking the back of Javier's boat signaled that time was running out.

"Do you have a rifle?" Jessica asked, searching the confines of the boat for anything they could use as a weapon.

"Shotgun in the storage bin to your right, but that's only good at close range." As the bullets struck closer, tearing through the canopy over them, Javier looked back at the boat chasing them. "We can't afford that kind of close range."

A bullet whizzed by her head and slammed into the wood of the boat's cockpit. She crouched down behind the protective cover of the seat next to the captain's chair.

"What can we do?"

Javier crouched down as well, as more gunfire erupted. He pushed the engine ever faster, and the boat picked up a little speed, but with a shuddering complaint that said it couldn't go for long at such a pace. It was intended for leisurely travel, not flight.

Javier jerked his head toward the closest bank. "Just ahead, there's a tributary. It's shallower than the main river, but shortly past the entrance is a series of fairly wicked rapids."

"Will they be able to follow?" she asked, glancing

nervously at the larger speedboat as the gap between the two vessels narrowed with each passing second.

"No. The draft on their boat's too large, but even with our flat bottom, we might not might make it past the first few sets of rapids."

Even as he said it, he steered them toward the edge of the river, and when she peered past the bow of the boat, she could see that they were almost at the entrance to the offshoot he had mentioned.

"We don't have a choice," she said, and Javier nodded.

"Get ready to hang on."

With a lurch, he steered the boat into the narrower and shallower tributary.

Gunfire peppered the side of Javier's boat, but it stopped as they swiftly advanced into the rapidly moving waters of the side stream. The distance between the two boats widened considerably. As Jessica rose and looked back, she realized that the other boat had stopped at the mouth of the offshoot.

Armando was beside the captain, gesticulating roughly with those thick-muscled arms. He clearly wanted the other man to continue, but he wouldn't.

When she turned back around and stared ahead, she realized why.

The waters before them had turned into a roiling and churning mess, marked by large boulders and deep dips.

Javier cut their speed, but the boat still rushed forward, propelled by the current. When she met his gaze, he said, "Hold on, Jessica."

She wedged herself between the side of the boat and the chair. She looked for a life vest but couldn't see one, so she grabbed the rail along one wall and wrapped an arm around the chair as the nose of the boat dipped. They entered the turbulent waters.

Beside her, Javier braced himself but kept to the wheel and engine controls, trying to keep their course steady and safe.

The boat bucked and lurched violently, slamming her from side to side, but she kept her hands tight on the railing and the chair, fingers turning numb from the pressure she exerted to hang on.

Water crashed up and over the low sides of the boat, drenching them as they struggled against the violence of the current.

Javier fought the buck of the wheel, trying to steer the boat through the deepest and safest of the channels along the rapids. His arms strained as time and time again, the force of the waters nearly ripped the wheel from his hands.

Daring a glance at Jessica, he saw the determination in her gaze as she braced herself for yet another jolt.

And then it happened.

For just a second, the wheel eluded his grasp. The bow lurched without that second of control and grazed a large boulder to the right, flinging them violently to the left. The stern of the boat swung around sharply, catching them cross-current for a moment before they went sliding into the next rapid facing backward.

The bow of the boat swung up precariously, unseating both of them and sending them rolling to the back of the boat. The force of the current began to sink the boat.

The waters rose up over them.

Javier reached out for Jessica and managed to grab hold of her arm as the force of the current pulled them one way and the boat another.

He had a tenuous grip on her arm and tried to drag her toward him, even as the pull of the water threatened to suck them apart. He managed to push up to the surface for a moment so they could both breathe, but then he slammed into a boulder.

The strength of the impact knocked the breath from his body, but he never released his hold on her. With his were-strength, he might be able to survive the beating the rapids would inflict, but not Jessica. He had to protect her.

As the waters rolled them downward, he fought for a better grasp on Jessica, but when they flew over one cascade and he landed heavily against a jagged trio of rocks, the air was driven from his lungs, and Jessica was ripped from him by the strength of the current.

Javier managed to get upright in the roiling waters, clinging to the rocks long enough to see their boat, or what was left of it, being trashed against the various boulders and hidden rocks farther down the rapids. Jessica's head popped above the surface, and he watched as she slammed into a boulder and disappeared in the foamy water.

Javier dove toward her, pain lancing through his back as he tried to reach her. He tried to protect himself as time and time again, the current dashed him against the rocks, pummeling his body until all he could feel was the pain.

He tried not to think about how many times his body hit one of the boulders along the rapids. Instead, he concentrated on keeping to the least damaging course through the rocks and on finding Jessica in the midst of the watery turmoil.

When the waters finally deposited him in the calmer river beyond the rapids, Javier took a moment to collect himself, but then he immediately began his search.

Swimming to the shallower waters, he called out her name over and over, fighting desperation at the silence that answered him. He paddled back and forth, but saw no sign of her. He screamed out her name again one last time.

No answer came as Javier surged toward the river bank. He rushed and stumbled through the waters until he spied what was left of the boat, bobbing along on its side toward his edge of the bank. He crawled up onto the muddy bank for a better view.

Every movement brought agony from the assorted cuts and bruises caused by his wild ride. A deeper, knifelike pain in his side hinted at greater damage, but he forced it back, certain that a quick change into the jaguar would take care of his injuries.

Unlike Jessica, he thought. A different kind of agony created a sharp pain in the middle of his chest.

What was she wearing? he asked himself, and the answer came quickly.

A hot pink tank top.

He called out her name again and stepped back into the waters for a closer look. For a moment, he caught a glimpse of something just below the surface. He swam toward it. As he neared, the hot pink became a beacon.

Jessica floated facedown in the water. Totally motionless.

Fear gripped Javier's insides as he swam to her. He

rolled her onto her back and then pulled her to the bank, his side protesting the strain of carrying her with each stroke.

Once he had her on shore, Javier immediately began CPR, since she wasn't breathing. Long, agonizing moments passed as he applied pressure on her chest and gave her mouth-to-mouth.

Finally, her body twitched beneath his hands.

He turned her onto her side as she coughed up river water, but it was tinged with pink. A second round of coughing brought yet more blood.

Her breathing was shallow. A sickening gurgle followed each breath. He suspected a punctured lung. If the waters of the river hadn't drowned her, the blood seeping into her lung would.

Blood also trickled from one of her ears.

A concussion?

With gentle fingers, Javier probed the back of her skull and realized it was worse: a skull fracture.

He slipped his fingers over her wrist. A thready and almost nonexistent pulse beat against his fingers.

Cradling her in his arms, he allowed his animal spirit to sense her life force, but it only confirmed what he had already suspected.

Jessica is dying.

Cold rage and pain filled him. Guilt followed quickly.

This isn't right, he thought. She didn't deserve to die because of him. Because of Armando and his crazy vendetta.

Only one thing might possibly save her, but could he live with the aftermath of that choice?

With only a moment's consideration, Javier decided

that it would be easier to deal with her hatred than with her death.

Gently, he lowered her to the ground and stripped off her clothes. As he did so, he called forth his animal spirit, summoning the jaguar. Thick, lush fur sprouted, each strand piercing his human skin until it covered his entire form.

He dropped to his knees and roared out in pain as bone and muscle shifted, rearranging themselves until the jaguar emerged.

He bent his head and nuzzled the side of her face. He licked her cheek with his cat-rough tongue, but she didn't move. Didn't rouse. With a nudge of his massive head, he turned her head to the side, exposing the fragile line of her neck and shoulder.

He took her shoulder gently in his jaws, and as tenderly as he could, he bit down, urging his spirit to flow from his body to hers. The taste of her blood was rich against his fangs and mouth.

Beneath the gentle clasp of his jaws, he sensed her life spirit awakening as his bite called for her to respond.

Searing pain dragged Jessica from numbness to reality.

She moaned and tried to lift her hand, but she was too weak. She could feel the cold in her extremities and the heat pooling in the center of her, trying to preserve life.

She knew all the signs of imminent death.

But as the agony in her shoulder dragged her to full awareness, warmth began at that spot and raced outward to her extremities, driving away death.

In her brain came a rough rumble and the pull of

something elemental. A command to join with it. With him.

A shiver along her nerve endings grew into a rough shudder.

She opened her eyes and caught sight of the jaguar latched onto her shoulder a second before the animal gently released her.

She tried to speak, but nothing came out. In her head, she heard the rumble again and the insistent demand that she join the cat by her side.

As she turned onto her side, the urge to crawl pulled at her, and then something slammed into her, as powerful as a sledgehammer.

Breathing heavily, she fought a losing battle for control as her muscles trembled, ever more violently as each second passed. A snap, loud like a brittle branch, sounded in the quiet along the riverbank. Then there came another snap, accompanied by pain so strong she moaned, only it wasn't a human sound that escaped her.

Her low roar filled the air as the bones in her body shifted and muscles rearranged themselves. As the violence of her transformation slowly eased, she hesitantly rose to her feet. She struggled to remain on all fours, feeling better than before but still weak and disoriented.

The jaguar who had bitten her came to her side and, with a gentle nudge, urged her away from the water's edge and toward a small pad of moss and lush ferns beneath the canopy of the trees. She walked there drunkenly, aware of her condition and yet still in disbelief. She dropped onto the ground.

Scattered fragments of thought came to her. Recollections of Javier mentioning that the change could help heal wounds.

He bit me to save my life.

That thought brought no relief though, only confusion and anger. As she shut her cat's eyes, he settled himself close to her. His warmth drove away the chill of the river waters. His hesitant lick against her face seemed to beg for understanding.

But she didn't know if she could ever forgive him.

A low rumble came from him, and she thought it sounded like "I'm sorry."

But she lacked the strength to respond.

She gave herself up to unconsciousness, her body and heart drained by the day's events.

CHAPTER 7

Javier stayed by Jessica's side until the spirit left and her body morphed back to human. She was in better shape than when the transformation had begun but not completely healed. As he examined her naked body, the bruises snagged his attention—large angry smudges of deep purple along her ribs and back. He ran his hands over her and smiled when he realized that anything broken seemed back in the right place and on the way to healing.

She woke as he tended to her and said just one word. "Why?"

"Because I couldn't lose you," he admitted.

Her body was an assortment of aches and pains, but that didn't stop her from rising onto her elbows to face him. "You had no right to make that decision."

"You would have died."

Something primal awakened within her. Something feral had her lunging at him, swinging her fists at his head until he grabbed her wrists and pinned her to the soft bed of moss.

A warning growl erupted from him, and she quieted, the animal in her recognizing his dominance.

"You had no right," she repeated, a low rumble in her own voice as heat built deep in her center.

Beneath him, she quieted, and Javier sensed her confusion and acquiescence. "The warmth you feel is the animal spirit growing within you. Healing you. Rest."

She said nothing else and closed her eyes, but he lost any hope that he might have had about her returning to him. She could never forgive what he had done to her, even if it had been the only thing he could do to save her.

As the long hours passed, he collected what he could salvage from the boat. Some food and Jessica's bags. The shotgun loaded with regular pellets, which he replaced with the silver buckshot.

Returning to her side, he started a small fire, placed the gun within her reach, and removed some of her clothes from one of the bags. He draped them along some low-lying branches to dry.

He moved away from the makeshift campsite and went in search of deadfall so that he could heat some water for a quick meal. He was several yards away from her when he heard the nearby rustle of the underbrush, and the hackles on the back of his neck rose.

Armando stepped from the underbrush, alone and naked. A bright white bandage marked one shoulder, and Javier wondered if beneath the gauze his wound had already healed. If it had, he had seriously underestimated the strength of Armando's spirit.

"Time to die, Javier," the other man said, a broad grin visible even in the dim light of dusk.

Javier had no doubt he meant it. Their feud had been brewing for a long time. Maybe even since before the deaths of their parents. As much as he hated the thought, Javier knew that the death of one of them was the only way there would ever be peace.

"Let's have at it, then," Javier called out, and he dropped to all fours. He summoned the jaguar and let it consume him body and soul.

Armando did the same, and with a surge, they bounded toward each other, intent on a fight to the death.

Javier engaged Armando head-on, nearly up on his hind legs as they pawed at each other. Claws slashed and struck, catching an arm here and a side there as they flew at each other time and time again. Javier danced away like a prize fighter, knowing that Armando's greater size and strength would kill him if he got the upper hand.

Armando, mad with anger and blood lust, kept on coming at Javier until the attacks were wild and unthinking.

Javier knew the moment would come soon when Armando would tire and drop his guard.

At last, Armando exposed one shoulder. Javier erupted past his poor defense and sank his fangs deep into the thick muscle of Armando's shoulder.

The black jaguar howled and clawed at him in protest, raking his claws deep into Javier's sides and back. But Javier didn't release his hold on the other cat. Pooling all his strength, he fought Armando to the ground, ignoring the pain as the other cat continued to tear into him.

He held on. He tossed his head and felt muscle and bone crunch beneath his massive jaws. He began to weaken from the loss of blood from his injuries, but he sensed Armando weakening also as blood poured from the deep wound in his shoulder.

Javier relaxed his hold for just a moment, and Armando took advantage, reversing their positions until Javier was on the ground.

With a twist of his massive head, Javier ripped out a large chunk of Armando's flesh. Blood spurted viciously from the wound, splattering across his body as Armando fell back, grievously injured.

Javier had gotten an artery. That much was obvious as the blood continued to spurt unimpeded, bright red against the vibrant green of the moss along the river bank.

He moved away from Armando, waiting to see what would happen, trying to recover for a final attack, because he sensed that if Armando knew he was dying, he would try to take Javier with him.

As Javier expected, Armando rushed him one last time.

Heat swept across her body. Strange telltale heat reminding her she was something other than human now. Whatever that something else was smelled the blood, heard the snarled challenges laced with pain.

Jessica opened her eyes and turned toward the sound. Armando and Javier, locked in battle some distance away along the riverbank. To the death, if the amount of blood across the ground and the two cats was any indication.

Inside her, something twisted and warmed. The

hairs on her arm began to thicken and lengthen, fur emerging to replace skin, but she fought it back, drove it deep inside as she sat up and her gaze settled on the shotgun Javier had left beside her.

She grabbed the gun and rose, her stance precarious as pain lanced through her ribs and a wave of weakness assaulted her. Much as she had driven back the jaguar struggling to emerge, she fought her injuries and moved toward the two animals.

She was furious with Javier, but she couldn't let him die.

Picking up the shotgun, she trained it on Armando, waiting for an opening.

It came more quickly than she expected, as Javier pushed the other cat away and Armando flew backward, blood coating his glistening black fur. Before the cat could move toward Javier again, she opened fire, catching Armando full in the chest.

The black jaguar stumbled backward, then righted himself and turned to charge at her.

She fired again.

This time, Armando fell to the ground, the gaping holes torn into him by the shotgun blasts crimson against his ebony fur.

Jessica dropped the shotgun and wrapped her arms tight around her waist, as if that would help her keep a handle on herself.

A moment later, Javier was at her side. A human Javier, bearing the wounds of his fight with Armando. He wrapped his arms around her and whispered against her ear, "You did him a favor. He was as good as dead."

She shot him a confused look, and he explained. "I

had torn open his brachial artery before you fired. He would have bled to death shortly."

His words should have brought some measure of comfort, but they didn't. Maybe because she had wanted Armando dead. For Victor. For what she had become on his account.

As she gazed at Armando's body, lifeless near the edge of the riverbank, she asked, "Will he stay like that? Like a cat?"

Javier stroked her arm, trying to calm her. "The silver pellets in the shotgun will prevent any transformation."

"Even in death?"

"Even in death," he confirmed.

With a nod, she said, "Then it's over. Get me the hell out of here."

CHAPTER 8

Four months later,
New Brunswick, New Jersey

Jessica braced her arms on the metal railing of her balcony, staring down at the slow-moving river before her. The Raritan moved sluggishly through town and toward the Atlantic. Across the way, people were still in the park, even though it was almost dusk. Along the nearest riverbank, a crew team was pulling up to the boathouse dock, while another team walked the scull in for storage.

So much activity.

Too much.

It seemed as if a lifetime had passed since she and Javier had buried Armando's body by the riverbank, thought it had really only been a few months.

Her anger had been too great then. She was furious at Armando for killing Victor and, in essence, destroying her. She hated Javier for biting her and for stirring up a mix of emotions she couldn't seem to escape.

She hadn't spoken a word to him during the entire trek back to the mouth of the tributary, where a passing boat had picked them up and returned them to the tribal reservation. She hadn't said a word to him for the three days his uncle had tended to her wounds and explained what she now was: a were-jaguar like Javier.

The shaman had urged her to embrace her spirit by undergoing the tribal ritual for bonding with it, but she had refused, needing time and distance to think about all that had happened before making such a life-changing decision.

Despite denying Antonio's request, the scientist in her had listened carefully when he described the ritual, storing away as many facts as she could, while the woman within had carefully contained her emotions, schooled the anger she felt at the violation of her body—her body, which felt foreign to her each time she transformed.

But you would be dead right now, the little voice in her head had whispered to her over and over during the last few months.

Dead and unable to help anyone, and yet . . .

She felt unable to help herself. Try as she might to ignore it, something animal lingered within her. Something that had driven her more often than she cared to admit into long treks deep into the mountains, where she would pitch a tent and, after night rose, release the animal spirit within her and savor the darkness.

In her jaguar form, she had even given chase to a deer early one morning before realizing that she had to return to her tent and let the human reassume control.

She was surprised that the ability to change could be dominated and contained, although the process itself still elicited intense pain during each side of the transformation. Even with that pain, the call of the jaguar was too great to resist at times.

If she was honest with herself, so was the pull of what she had experienced in Javier's arms. In her quest to help others, Jessica had forgotten that sometimes you had to put yourself first.

In the months since she had last seen him, a sense of restlessness had sprung up inside her. Even the joy of propagating more plants and isolating the active ingredient from them had been diminished. With the active ingredient now in her pharmaceutical company's pipeline for additional testing, her everyday work had almost become boring.

Something was lacking. Something vital.

Go to him, the voice whispered, and it was echoed by another voice—masculine but with an animal's rumble: *Come to me.*

As she gazed down at the city below, she knew she would.

The anticipation within her—born of both human and animal desire—said there was still too much left unresolved in the Amazon.

She would return and try to put things right, find a way to balance her old human existence with the new realities of her life as a were-jaguar.

Javier's words came back to her. *This place could provide you with much that you seek.*

The Amazon held a wealth of possible new medicines, with so many species and areas left to be discovered. She might be able to keep her promise to her sister and continue her career—not to mention find balance in her personal life—by turning her attention to the Amazon's undiscovered bounty.

Jessica hoped that in the process of balancing all those things, she could somehow find a way to share her life with Javier.

She had been unable to reach Javier by phone. His private cell number went immediately to voicemail, and after leaving a dozen unreturned messages, she stopped calling.

The man who had answered Javier's office number told her he worked for Javier's tour company but that he didn't know when his boss would be in town again. Apparently, Javier had been spending quite a bit of time at the reservation during the last few months.

She had arranged for the man to take her upriver, but not to the reservation. Apparently, he was forbidden from traveling there. "The boss's instructions," he explained apologetically.

She masked her anger and disappointment as she arrived at the dock and was greeted solely by Javier's employee. *Javier must still hate me for leaving him,* she thought. The hope she'd had about sharing her life with him seemed to be quickly slipping away.

The man brought her upriver in a brand-new boat. "The boss's brand-new boat," he explained.

The hours on the water were long, and she was unable to enjoy the many sights the way she had during her first trip. The closer they got to the reservation, however, the more the spirit within her stirred, eager to be loose.

When they were near, she motioned to the man to beach the boat and grabbed her small knapsack. She had packed light, thinking there was little she would need once she reached the tribe.

If I get there, she thought as she slipped over the side of the boat and sloshed through the shallow waters until she was along the bank. She signaled the boat-man that she was fine, and rather reluctantly, he pulled away, seemingly torn between displeasing his boss and leaving her alone in the wild.

She carefully eased through the underbrush until she was well within the embrace of the rain forest canopy. Once there, she undressed and tucked her clothes into her knapsack. Dropping onto all fours, she closed her eyes and inhaled deeply, taking the scents of the jungle deep within her.

She embraced the wild that had been calling to her for months.

Heat built within her, searing her, firing along her nerve endings as the transformation began.

A low rumble started as her skin warmed, and golden fur, spotted with nearly black rosettes, replaced the skin. An ache began in the center of her forehead, spreading across her face as it broadened into the flat planes of the cat. The pop and snap of bone and muscle swiftly followed, until the change was complete and the jaguar emerged.

Jessica inhaled, searching for the scent of something familiar, listening for the sound of humanity. From far away, she detected what she sought.

Grabbing the strap of the knapsack in her mouth, she loped ahead, her paws digging into the soft ground, kicking up divots as she picked up speed in her haste to be back at the reservation.

The scents grew stronger. The smells of cooking and humanity. The sounds of activity coming from the village.

She raced into a clearing, eager to arrive, and from above her came a loud, raucous screech. Thudding to an awkward stop, she looked upward.

A large hawk rode the air currents above her, circling around and around before it swooped down to land before her.

In a blink, feathers became skin, and Antonio stood before her, his golden gaze inquisitive as it settled on her.

"Jessica?"

She growled her answer, and Antonio smiled, held out his hand to her.

It was impossible to refuse the pull of his humanity. She summoned that part of her, morphing back to her human form.

Antonio smiled and said, "Welcome home, Jessica."

She wasn't quite sure she could call it home, but there was a sense of connection here that she had missed while she was in New Jersey.

"I'm glad that I'm welcome, Antonio," she said, and reached for her knapsack.

He turned and looked away as she dressed, but then he slipped his arm through hers and guided her the last few yards to the village.

As they walked down the main trail, villagers came out of their huts, and by the time they reached the center, a happy group of tribespeople greeted her, welcoming her return.

But as she searched the crowd, she realized Javier was not among them. She shouldn't have wondered at his absence, given his failure to return her phone calls and his instructions to his employees. Somehow, though, she had hoped he would be at the reservation.

Antonio walked her to the hut she had first inhabited so many months earlier. He must have sensed her disquiet. "You are sorry he is not here?"

She wasn't sure *sorry* was the word. "Worried. He is well, isn't he? Recovered from the fight with Armando?"

Antonio nodded and shot her a glance from the corner of his eye. "He is physically well."

Carefully chosen words intended to deliver a carefully chosen message, she realized. As she stepped into the hut and tossed her bag onto the bed, Antonio came to stand beside her. He clasped his hands before him and asked, "Why have you returned, Jessica?"

"I feel the animal inside me. It's unhappy," she admitted.

"You speak of it as if it wasn't a part of you, but it is," he said, and motioned for her to sit.

She took a spot next to her bag and, with a shrug, said, "Will I ever feel that way?"

"That is up to you to decide. You can battle the spirit Javier gifted you with—"

"Some gift," she mumbled under her breath, but Antonio plowed forward, undissuaded.

"Or you can ask it to accept you."

Accept me? Isn't it supposed to be the other way around? she thought.

After her hesitation, he asked, "Do you wish to do the ritual?"

She searched his peaceful face. It was the face of a man clearly in tune with himself and all around him. She wondered if Javier had found peace with her gone.

Antonio must have sensed her question, since he said, "He has been at war with himself since you left."

At war with himself?

Maybe in the same way she had been tearing herself apart as she struggled to discover what she wanted. What would end the restlessness of her soul?

"Will the ritual bring peace?"

A glimmer of a smile crept into his features. "It will bring enlightenment. It is up to you to decide what to do with that knowledge."

EPILOGUE

Jessica stood naked before the bonfire, arms outstretched as Antonio anointed her body with the ointment made from a native tree frog. Antonio had warned her that the frog's excretions would bring pain and certainly fever but that it was necessary for her to experience pain as she surrendered herself to the jungle and the spirits within its embrace.

Javier's words came back to her.

The fever burns away our fears and opens our senses to the jungle spirits.

After Antonio finished the anointing, he grabbed a bowl with the red *achiote* and painted her body with that dye, creating a pattern of rosettes like those she had seen on Javier the night of the feast. Like the dark rosettes on his golden jaguar skin. The gentle touch of the brush on her skin awakened the animal essence within her.

In soft tones, Antonio began chanting a prayer, and the group joined in unison, the cadence of their voices soft and lulling her to a peaceful state as her body began to tingle and then burn in those spots where Antonio had dabbed the ointment and the *achiote*.

As she met his gaze, he nodded and said, "Go now into the jungle. Meet your spirit, and allow it within you."

She looked around the group, and their faces blurred in her vision, but not so much that she couldn't realize that Javier was still not there.

Pain came in the center of her chest, but she tamped it down and turned, racing into the underbrush. She was determined to face the demand of the animal within and put her world to right.

She dashed past the huts and into the underbrush, which lashed at her body as she streaked by, deeper and deeper into the rain forest. The evening air was damp but welcome against the growing heat of her skin. A chill sweat joined the moistness of the night as she raced onward, until her breath rasped in her lungs and her legs collapsed beneath her.

She lay on the jungle floor, the ferns and plants lush on the skin of her back. The light of the moon burned her sensitized eyes. Everything around her seemed brighter and more vibrant. Her head spun as her senses drank in the musky aroma of another animal nearby.

Her head flopped to one side, and she glimpsed the distinctive markings of a jaguar then, gold and brown against the lush green leaves of the underbrush, until the animal slipped closer.

Javier, she somehow knew. *Javier.* His name raced in her brain and heart, but she remained immobile on the jungle floor, her body refusing to cooperate. Her skin burned with fever from the frog's poison painted on her body by the shaman.

• • •

Her scent had been carried to him on the night breeze as the jaguar loped through the rain forest.

Jessica.

How many months had he prowled the jungle, trying to outrun what he had done? Trying to forget her so that he might find peace?

Now she was here, he realized, and he followed her scent into a moonlit clearing.

She was sprawled on the ground, the pale skin of her naked body bathed in moonlight.

He approached slowly. Muscles loose and head down, to dispel any fear she might have, but he sensed that fear was not what she was feeling.

The heat of her anger and lust touched him from even a few feet away. He dropped to the ground until his belly rubbed against the soft ferns of the jungle floor.

Tentatively, he shuffled forward on his paws, as afraid of driving her away as he was at seeing her, at having her near again.

A surge of heat swept through Jessica, coalescing in her center as Javier's jaguar form finally reached her side. With a loud snuffle, he nuzzled her cheek with a low, repentant growl.

The ball of heat exploded in her, and the animal erupted from within, her body straining and groaning with the change. A howl erupted from her, and suddenly she was on him, her claws lashing out at the jaguar, who embraced her within his paws and rolled with her.

The snarls and moans of their semibattle filled the

night, as they thrashed together along the jungle floor until another change came upon them, and little by little their animal spirits receded, leaving their human forms behind.

Their bodies lay plastered against each other in the thick underbrush of the jungle.

Jessica looked up at him. At the face she both hated and needed. "I wasn't sure I could come back here."

"And now?" he asked, the tones of his voice low and with an animal rumble that created a sympathetic pull between her legs.

"I'm not sure I can leave again without . . ."

"Without what?

"Without you," she said. A part of her had seemed empty without him, without the forces of the jungle that had summoned her that night.

"And I'm not sure I can stay here without you. I've missed you more than I can say," he admitted.

She reached up and cupped his cheek. "I've missed you as well."

A tight smile came to his lips. "I'm sorry about doubting your intent when you first came here, and I'm sorry that I bit you, only . . ." He wound his hand through her hair and cradled the back of her head closer, as if afraid she would run from him again. "I'd bite you again if it meant saving your life. Even knowing you'd hate me afterward."

She rested her forehead against his. "I don't hate you, Javier, but I was confused. I still am confused."

"We will find a way, Jessica. We will build a life together somehow. Share time in each other's world." He cupped her cheek and ran his thumb across the skin there.

CRAZY FOR THE CAT

"You'd go to Jersey with me?" she asked with surprise.

"If I have to," he replied, but a teasing lilt filled his tone.

"I want to share my life with you. Explore what it is that I am now," she whispered.

He bent his head and nuzzled his nose against hers. "I will help you with that, *meu amor*."

She reached up, covered his hand with hers, and urged it downward to cover her breast. "Then love me, Javier."

A shudder worked through his body, touching her heart. His body, so big and strong, was moved by her words. By her plea, which she repeated again, more urgently. "*Amame*, Javier."

He kissed her, his mouth moving against hers urgently, his tongue slipping in to taste her mouth as he parted her legs and eased inside. The width and length of him filled her completely, and he rested within her, content just to linger for a moment.

She brought her legs up and cradled his thighs, shifting her hips and increasing his penetration. He groaned, the sound loud and vibrating against her lips as he continued to kiss her.

Shifting her face, she dropped a kiss against his cheek and urged his head down to her breast, where his rough tongue circled the tip and made her body tremble.

When he sucked the tip into his mouth, she held his head to her and arched her back, the pleasure growing intensely.

She reached down and cupped his balls, exerted gentle pressure, and he groaned once again.

"This is crazy, isn't it?" she asked, not that an answer was necessary, as his body jumped against her and he swelled inside her.

He reciprocated by trailing his hand down her body to where their bodies joined. As he shifted, drawing in and out of her, he parted the curls at the juncture of her legs and found the swollen nub. He applied gentle pressure, rotating his thumb against her clitoris, slick and wet from the caress of his body.

She came, her cry sharp in the night, followed by his harsh shout and the explosion of his body in hers.

They settled back onto the jungle floor, the ferns and underbrush alive against their still-joined bodies. They caressed each other, allowed passion to rise over and over again through the course of the night, until the first fingers of dawn crept into the night sky.

Javier moved from her then but maintained a firm grasp on her waist with one big hand. "Come with me."

Something in his touch communicated his intent. She called to her spirit to join him, and she released her hold on the animal within. She quickly morphed into a jaguar alongside Javier as he underwent his own transformation.

With one huge leap, he bounded into the jungle in the direction of the village, and she followed.

Together they would find a way. She would continue her quest to honor the promise she had made to her sister. Only now she would no longer be alone.

She was crazy for the cat and wouldn't deny it a second longer.

DISCOVER DESIRE AFTER DARK

WITH THESE BESTSELLING PARANORMAL ROMANCES FROM POCKET BOOKS!

PRIMAL DESIRES SUSAN SIZEMORE

Only one woman can satisfy this Vampire Prime's
every hunger...

THIRTY NIGHTS WITH A HIGHLAND HUSBAND MELISSA MAYHUE

Transported back in time, a modern-day woman falls in love
with a Highlander descended from the faerie folk—who can
only be hers for thirty nights.

IN DARKNESS REBORN ALEXIS MORGAN

Will an immortal warrior stay true to his people—or
risk everything for the woman he loves?

SOMETHING WICKED CATHERINE MULVANY

Wicked desires lead to insatiable passions—passions
no vampire can deny.

THE LURE OF THE WOLF JENNIFER ST. GILES

Be lured by a seductive shape-shifter whose dark allure
is impossible to resist...
